Praise for Steve Weddle's *Country Hardball*

"Downright dazzling."

"This debut collection of twenty tal poor folks in contemporary rural Arkansas. Dark, noirish, and worth a look."

—*Kirkus Reviews*

"Ex-con Roy Alison would like to go straight, but he can't seem to make up for past mistakes . . . Weddle's debut novel is a suspenseful series of interrelated stories . . . of people facing nothing but bad options, though Roy eventually manages to make something good come from his situation."

—*Publishers Weekly*

"These skillfully wrought interconnected stories form a debut novel that is relentless in describing the lives of people who are captives not only of their environment but also of their own histories."

—*Booklist*

"Shiny bits of story weave in and out of this novel in stories, painting a lush portrait of economic and social hardship in a rural southern town."

—*LitReactor*

THE COUNTY LINE

OTHER TITLES BY STEVE WEDDLE

Country Hardball

THE COUNTY LINE

A NOVEL

STEVE WEDDLE

LAKE UNION PUBLISHING

This is a work of fiction. Names, characters, organizations, places, events, and incidents are either products of the author's imagination or are used fictitiously.

Published by Lake Union Publishing, Seattle

www.apub.com

ISBN-13: 9781662515262 (paperback)
ISBN-13: 9781662515255 (digital)

Cover design by Kathleen Lynch/Black Kat Design
Cover image: © Christy Berry / ArcAngel; © Rouzes, © nopow, © Jt Botka, © vaitekune / Getty; © etraveler / Shutterstock

Printed in the United States of America

For Em & Jack

1

In the summer of 1933, a little north of the Louisiana line, not too far into Arkansas, Cottonmouth Tomlin stepped from Miss Phoebe's pie shop into the afternoon sun and, not for the first time since his return, felt lost in his hometown.

Across Jefferson Avenue on the courthouse lawn, the Thurman twins were chasing a brown-and-white dog that must have belonged to someone. Three years since he'd left the county for New Orleans and then Honduras, and Cottonmouth once again looked up and down the street to see what had changed. The harness store Old Man Coggin ran was still in business, though with all the cars rolling up and down the roads now, who knew how long that would last? Morgan Sullivan's drugstore, where he'd gone as a little boy with his mother for her medicine, before she had taken off, had the same shelved items, best he could figure, still in the window. He scratched the back of his neck. Or maybe it didn't. Maybe he'd never paid that much attention, but everything felt the same, a small room in someone else's house, where the air just settled.

The Thurman twins, three years older and a half foot taller than he remembered them, had chased the dog along the edge of Jefferson Avenue now—the dog dashed into the street, crossing the muddy ruts as a dark Buick coupe came down the road, the driver's gaze everywhere but the dog. Cottonmouth took three steps into the street, into the car's path; raised his hand; and said "Hold on" as the car stopped a few feet from the bewildered dog. One Thurman boy was scrunched up near the dog with his eyes closed; the other stood on the edge of the street, eyes wide.

A second later, dog and twins were off again, through the alley between Miss Phoebe's and whatever was next door. Had he been asked, Cottonmouth would have guessed it had been a lawyer's office when he'd said goodbye to the town a few years back. But the only question anyone was asking him was what in the sam hill he was doing standing in the road like a goddamn moron.

Cottonmouth looked at the man who had posed this question, the driver of the car, a fellow he didn't recognize. Cottonmouth eased to the driver's side of the car, took a couple of steps toward the man, reached behind himself for the knife in his belt. For a moment they looked at each other, the man maybe just on his way to take some bread to his invalid mother in Taylor, and Cottonmouth a moment away from puncturing the man beneath the ribs.

"Friend," Cottonmouth said, "you don't seem a big-enough fellow to talk to me like that."

The man looked back to the road in front of him, drove on.

Cottonmouth shook his head, told himself the number of morons in the county had likely increased the last few years, and then stepped back onto the sidewalk to head to an afternoon poker game at Moon's store, a group he had been assured at his uncle's funeral two weeks back had carried on in his absence and would welcome taking his money as soon as he felt up to it.

~

A few minutes later, Cottonmouth Tomlin was sitting in the back of Moon's Grocery, the air clouded by cigar smoke and shelf dust; shifting cards in a losing hand; wondering which of the men at the table would last more than a month in a Honduran jungle, these men who hadn't set foot out of the county their entire lives unless one of their sisters married some hayseed the next county over.

"You in or out?" Monkey Pribble asked Cottonmouth. "Ain't got all night. I got places to be next Thursday."

"You ain't got no place to be next Thursday," one of them said.

Cottonmouth tossed his cards into the middle of the table, squawked back his chair. He figured not one of them would last a week, much less a month.

It was good to be home, he told himself. He kept telling himself that, hoping it would stick. Soon enough, he'd have whatever control he wanted, settle back into the county, put what he'd learned while away to good use. But for the moment, as he sat there with a busted flush, the cards weren't in his favor.

"Giving up so easy?" Bill Moon asked.

Cottonmouth smiled, said a fella had to know when he was beat.

Another man—a bald man whose mouth was too big for his face, a mouth with more teeth than seemed mathematically possible, his nose a little sawed-down tree stump at the top edge of an avalanching cavern—said maybe cut the man a break, what with his uncle just passing away and all.

Monkey Pribble said yeah, they were all real sorry about it. Beurie Tomlin was a good man. A good man.

Everyone nodded along. He sure was a good man.

"Left you that camp he was running for outlaws—ain't that right?" Pribble said, and everyone winced. Being a Pribble, he wasn't given to subtleties in social situations, but folks usually let him slide because, being a Pribble, he'd end up shot in the back soon enough. Or lying in a ditch with his neck broken from a horse fall. Or blown up in a shed trying to find a cheaper way to make corn liquor. It'd be something. It always was with that lot.

Cottonmouth said that was right; his uncle had left him the camp, such as it was, a scattering of cabins and an impassable road. A couple of guests. Some stories of how things used to be.

The bald man with the overfilled mouth said he remembered spending time down there, years back, when Cottonmouth's father and uncle had run it as a hunting lodge.

Bill Moon said those were good days, simpler times.

Cottonmouth said they were.

Monkey Pribble said those days were sure better than they had now.

Bill Moon said, "Goddamn Roosevelt."

Goddamn Roosevelt, they all agreed.

"So you still getting them fellows down there?" the man with the mouth asked. "What did your uncle Beurie say—he was in the 'hospitality business'?"

"Doing fine," Cottonmouth lied. No sense involving this lot in anything serious.

After Moon forearmed his winnings toward himself, Pribble asked Cottonmouth if he wanted to be dealt out. He said he was in. "Deal me in," he said. "Can't make any money sitting out."

As the cards were going around, Pribble said it was good to see Cottonmouth back. "Sorry for your uncle's passing. Still, we weren't sure you were going to make it back, all the warring in Mexico. Read about it in the papers."

"Honduras," Cottonmouth corrected.

"Thought it was Mexico," Moon said.

"So did I," the man with the mouth said.

Cottonmouth looked at the cards he'd just been dealt. "It wasn't."

"Never did hear what you were fighting for," Moon said.

"Just my pay, same as everybody."

They all nodded.

"Heard you'd joined the army," Pribble said.

"Worked with them," Cottonmouth said.

"So you bring all that pay you were working for back to the county?" Moon asked, always interested in spending money, investing money.

"Wasn't that much pay. Not for the ones doing the fighting," Cottonmouth said. "This what you hens been doing while I was gone? Gossiping instead of playing cards?"

They all nodded, said that seemed to be it, sure.

Moon said he'd read somewhere that there was money to be made down there. Moon was always reading about businessmen, about men spinning hay into gold. *Life* magazine story last year, he said. Man called Sam Zebra or some such.

"Zemurray," Cottonmouth said. "Sam Zemurray. That was him. They called him the Banana Man, seeing as how that was his business. Clearing land and growing bananas. Amazing man. Russian. Had this big house in New Orleans. Corinthian columns. Only know that because he told me over and over. Could buy this county and every county that touches it, I figure. Worked for him in New Orleans, until he sent me down to Honduras, work there. Man owned land from New Orleans to Florida. Owned half of Central America. Hell, guess he still does."

Moon said he'd read the man made a fortune down there.

"Seemed that way. Got these huge curtains on his wall, in that New Orleans castle of his. Tapestries. King Arthur, hanging all over the walls there. Like one of those museums you see in a picture book, just rooms of furniture and rugs and tapestries. Not to keep the cold out either. Just tapestries. Just hanging there, man needing something to spend his money on, I guess." Cottonmouth shook his head back and forth.

"Seems like that much down there," Monkey Pribble said, "ought to be enough for everybody."

"You'd think so," Cottonmouth said.

Bill Moon said the Russian sounded like a smart man. Said it had to be hard work running that company, said people didn't realize what it took, making a success of yourself like that.

They passed cards around, bid, threw in coins.

Cottonmouth kept on. "Sure. That's the one man in charge. The rest of you spend the day eating, pissing, fighting, drinking. Get through the day." Quick memories of mud, bugs, and fistfights. "Get through the next day. Man like this Russian, he's got the whole year planned. The next ten years."

Bill Moon said a successful man was always working a dozen steps ahead, said it was like chess. Said it didn't come easy.

They nodded. Like chess, a couple of them said, none of them having played chess. Monkey Pribble shuffled the cards in his hand, peeked again at the card he'd slipped under his thigh.

"The man in charge," Moon said, "he's the one takes all the risks. He can't spend his night drinking with the boys. He invests what it takes. The workers, they can come and go. Don't much matter. They're free. Not the man in charge. He's done give up his freedom. He's the one what worries in the middle of the night about how everything is running. All the cogs. See, the workers, they're the cogs in the wheel." Moon had set his cards face down now and was waving his hands as if he were showing off the inside of a shining miracle. Moon owned a business and thought it gave him the right to explain things. "The spokes in the machine. And there's a thousand cogs in a hundred wheels, and he has to watch them all. The cogs just see the other cogs, you see. What's right there. Immediate. He has to see the whole machine. You break—he has to find another cog. He breaks—well, he can't break, you see? Everything has to work together. That's what's important to the machine."

"And what's important to the cog?" the man with the big mouth asked.

"Who gives a good goddamn about the cog?" Pribble asked, laughing.

"The cog," Cottonmouth said as he reached across, pulled the jack of clubs from under Pribble's leg, laid down three jacks and a pair of sevens.

2

Three men in a sedan eased their way through Oklahoma, south of the Neosho River, then east across the Arkansas line, avoiding any of the bigger towns. Easy did it.

"You sure about this?" Beans said, pulling off the road just north of Hazelton onto the drive to a park that hadn't been used much since the townsfolk had burned down a Hooverville there the year before.

Everett Logan said he was sure as Beans slowed, pulled up under an oak tree, the thin Arkansas road dust following behind them, passing through the car as they stopped.

"You don't want me to drive?" Jimmy the Hook said from the back seat. "Beans, you ever driven a Fast Four?"

"I'm getting the hang of it," the smaller man said. "I've driven a Dodge before."

"Have you now?" Jimmy said.

Beans said he had.

"I was driving Dodge Brothers cars back when the Dodge brothers were alive," Jimmy said, kicking the seat in front of him.

Everett said, "Hey, now. No need for that." He opened his door, stepped out to the park. He opened the back door on his side, said to Jimmy, "Hand me that box of sandwiches."

Everett carried the box to a broken table under some shade, set it down.

Jimmy leaned onto his good arm, fumbled himself from the back seat as Beans stood by to help.

Everett yelled from across the way, "Jimmy, if only the Dodge brothers could see you now."

Jimmy grunted. "Ah, go shit in your hat."

Beans offered an arm to help Jimmy get his balance, but Jimmy waved him off, walked to the table, Beans shutting the doors behind him.

Jimmy settled next to the table, Everett on the other side, Beans between them.

Everett reached into the box, pulled out a sandwich, peeled back the wax paper, sniffed. "Phew. Jimmy, this one's yours."

Jimmy folded back the wrapping, took a bite from the corner of the sandwich. "Act like you never had a peanut butter–mayonnaise sandwich," he said, wiping his bottom lip with the back of his good hand, then licking his hand.

"Tomato and eggs," Everett said, pulling out another sandwich. "That must be you." Beans took the sandwich.

"Which leaves the bacon and egg for me," Everett said, setting his sandwich in front of him, then opening a big paper sack of peanuts for them to share. He opened a ginger ale for Jimmy, an orange soda each for him and Beans.

After each man had downed a few bites, Jimmy said this had better be easy money after whatever town that was in Oklahoma.

"Vinita," Everett said.

Jimmy asked was that right, and Everett said it was.

Beans asked how was the arm, and Jimmy said the arm was getting better; he wasn't so sure about the hand. He raised his arm best he could, looked at the bandages on the hand, where the bullet had gone through. "Don't figure Branch Rickey is asking me to pitch for the Gashouse Gang anytime soon, but it's better than it was."

Everett said that was all you could hope for.

The men looked around, looked toward town.

"Never been to Hazelton before," Jimmy said.

"Don't get too attached," Everett said. "We're in and out and on our way to the bayou."

Beans said he liked that idea, said they could use a good turn. Said they were due.

Jimmy took another bite. "Still ain't told me what you thought of the Sawyer job."

Everett took a drink, swallowed, wiped his mouth. "'Good for them,' I said."

"So you think it's something we could do?"

Everett said that wasn't what he'd said. "I said, 'Good for them.' Didn't say it would be good for us."

Beans asked if that was the kidnapping or the blackmailing one.

"Kidnapping," Jimmy said. "Edward Sawyer. The bank president. Father owns the brewery. Stuck him in a fishing cabin in Illinois for a week. Made a hundred grand."

Beans tried to whistle, a piece of egg shooting from his mouth.

"Good for them," Everett said. "For us, it's banks and not bankers, at least for now."

Jimmy asked didn't he want to talk about it.

Everett said he'd done all the talking about down-the-road jobs he was going to do. "Let's talk about this bank job here. After this, we can worry about the next job. Then we can talk about the Sawyer job. Now we just focus on doing good here."

"We do good here," Jimmy said. "I want to go a full year without ever having to eat a sandwich again."

Beans asked what was he planning to eat instead.

"Steak. And I don't mean one of those Swiss steaks. I mean one of them with the French name, chateau something or other."

"Chateau something?" Beans asked.

"*Chateau* means 'house' in French," Everett said.

"I don't speak French," Jimmy said.

Everett took another bite. "I gathered as much."

"Chateau," Jimmy tried. "Something with a *b*. Chateau . . . what's a French word starts with a *b*?"

"Baguette? Bon appétit?" Beans asked.

"Brioche?" Everett tried.

Jimmy snapped his fingers, a slop of peanut butter in the corner of his mouth. "Brioche. Chateaubrioche. They cook the meat between two other pieces of meat. And then they throw the other two pieces away."

"Sounds expensive," Beans said.

"It is. This broad I used to see, she worked at a place in New York. All these fancy dishes. Can't get that around here. How about you two?"

"She was all right," Everett said, taking a swig of orange soda. "Bit of a sloppy kisser."

Jimmy looked for something to throw, but Beans said, "Steak would be good. Wouldn't mind a piece of chocolate pie."

Everett said they could get that about anywhere. "That's nothing to dream about."

"But it's what I want," Beans said.

"It's gotta be something you can't get," Everett said. "Otherwise what's the point of dreaming?"

Jimmy finished off his ginger ale, said they were talking about things to wish for, for when they were rich.

"Fine," Beans said. "I'll take the whole pie."

"This place on the bayou we're heading after the bank job," Everett said. "Place in town has really good pies."

Beans said good.

"But first," Everett said, "we have to live through this job. Not counting the Brownings, what have we got, Jimmy? Start with the pistols. I don't want to go in blasting the place up. The pistols?"

"Four pistols, seven bullets."

Beans finished his sandwich. "Seven is a lucky number."

Everett raised his soda bottle in a toast. "That it is, Beans. That it is."

~

Everett boxed up their trash, walked to the car, looked across the open field in the distance, put the box in the back.

Once, people had gathered here for festivals and carnivals, he figured, before Hoover, before Black Tuesday, back when he was just a boy watching middle-aged men write about Alexander the Great on a chalkboard at the end of a room. Quiz answers from the correspondence course he was now enrolled in floated through his brain as he looked at the empty field. Macedon. Pella. Aristotle.

"You giving up your job already?" Jimmy was talking to Beans, who'd slid into the back seat.

"What are you doing?" Everett asked him.

"Oh," Beans said, sliding out of the back, easing behind the wheel. "Forgot I was driving today."

"Don't think I don't want my job back when I'm fit."

"Just keeping your seat warm."

"You sure you're all right with this?" Everett asked Beans.

"I'm fine. We head into town, pass the hotel, the railroad tracks, park just down from the bank. Bakery was there last time you were here. Maybe it is—maybe it isn't. Either way, I park just down from the bank. You and Jimmy inside. I count two minutes, tops. The two of you head out with the money, Jimmy coming up behind. You in the front. You two get in the car, and we're gone."

"What if the road is blocked? What if there's shooting?"

Beans said the name of the main road. Then he said the name of the alternate road, then the alternate to the alternate. "All we have to do is make it back to the switch car, which should be where we left it before lunch. Did I miss anything?"

Everett said no, he didn't miss anything. "Just make sure you've got room for pie tomorrow."

"The whole thing," Beans said.

"The whole thing."

~

Beans looked around as he drove into town, clouds covering the sun, a smooth glaze coming off the sedans and buildings. "Nice day. Pretty name for a town," he said. "Hazelton. Has a nice sound."

"Some railroad man named it after his daughter," Everett said.

Beans shrugged. "Still a pretty name."

3

A few doors down from Bill Moon's store, Sheriff Monroe McCollum was sitting in a barber's chair.

When the time had come years back, McCollum had been among the first Arkansans to volunteer when President Wilson had pulled the country into the war. He had killed about the right number of soldiers in France and more than he'd needed to during an agitated month in Italy, had been sent back a little early and settled into his family's Columbia County home with a handful of stories and four medals no one much cared about.

He'd been sheriff for a little while now, shorter tenure than some, longer than most, and had begun to get used to the idea of being sheriff.

Old Man Searcy finished brushing him off as the sheriff stepped down from the barber's chair, asked how he liked the shave. Searcy had seen better days, when he'd been able to see those days better, but the sheriff wasn't one to complain about the patchwork job left under one side of his jawline. "Just fine, just fine," he told the fog-eyed man, then asked about that aftershave on the back shelf. When the older man turned to fetch it, the sheriff reached for the straightedge and snicked away what Searcy had missed.

"There now," the barber said, coming back and handing McCollum the bottle. The sheriff said he appreciated it, paid, overtipped, then walked through the front door and onto Washington, looking left to the courthouse, then across the square to the Culver Hotel. He put on his hat just in time to tip it to Mrs. W. A. Hicks and Miss Levina Lankford, two Union County ladies who spent their money across the line here in town rather than El Dorado due to an unfortunate misunderstanding between W. A. Hicks himself and Camden Tucker in 1922 or 1923, the details of which no one recalled, save that there seemed to have been a dead horse by the name of Jasper involved.

"Afternoon, ladies," he said as the two women nodded, smiled, kept on their way.

He walked along the narrow sidewalk in front of the stores to his right, courthouse to his left—what the old-timers called "the new courthouse" just to remind folks that they remembered the old courthouse, though Mr. Hall had built this one nearly thirty years back.

The sheriff crossed the road to the Culver Hotel. He entered, nodded to the barman, climbed the stairs to the owners' suite.

~

"Have you dealt with the Hutcheson boy?" Henrietta Rudd asked, still seated as when the sheriff had knocked and been admitted. Before the appointment with the sheriff, Henrietta and her sister, Abigail, had been talking about nothing in particular.

The sheriff said he had, indeed, dealt with the Hutcheson boy.

"Get anything extra off him?"

The sheriff pulled nearly fifty dollars out of his coat pocket, laid it on the table for her, but didn't mention the pistol or the watch or the eighty-seven or so dollars in silver he'd left back at his own house.

Henrietta asked was that all, and the sheriff said it was.

Abigail was in the back of the room watching her sister work the sheriff.

Henrietta pursed her lips, said she'd thought the boy had been doing better than that, and the sheriff said you never can tell with people. Henrietta said ain't that God's honest truth.

Henrietta lit a White Owl, took a few quick puffs, propped her feet up on the coffee table next to the cash the sheriff had laid out, gave him another chance to be honest with her. "You sure that's all of it?" she asked, waited. After a few seconds, the sheriff said, "Yes," and she said, "Sure, all right," waved her hand. "Now tell me about Claude."

"Umbach?"

"Unless you know a Claude other than Claude Madison Umbach I should be interested in. This one is trying to set up a little den of iniquity down in Emerson. There another Claude doing something worse than that, or is it all right with you if we talk about him?"

"I leaned on him, like you said. Let him know you could help him. Suggested as to how that was help he didn't want to pass up on. Said how things had gone so poorly for the Shewmake fellow up the road in Brister." The sheriff was settling back down now that the scare with the money was over, not sure yet whether he'd won or lost that round. But he knew what she was after, knew she liked to think she was the one planning, the one who could see things. He knew if he could convince her that he had the vision as well, this could work itself into a nice partnership. "So now if you wanted to go in and talk to him about payoffs and securing the peace and . . ."

Henrietta ashed her cigar near a saucer on the coffee table. "Sheriff, it is highly unlikely I need you to tell me what my next step should be. You just have to put one foot in front of the other as instructed. We'll worry about the entire dance, if that's all right with you, Sheriff."

He nodded, said it was.

She asked had he spoken with Cottonmouth Tomlin.

"Not since the funeral," he said. "I can if you want."

She nodded. "If that's what I want, I will let you know. I think it's important I welcome him back myself, his family being members of the community for so long."

The sheriff nodded.

"And there being the matter of the money his uncle owed us."

~

After the sheriff had gone, Abigail Rudd stuttered across the room to the liquor cart, poured a few fingers of gin—more of a fist, really—into a highball glass. She took a large-bladed knife from the tray, tested its edge against the fleshy tip of her index finger, and then quartered a lime. She wiped the damp, glossy bits of translucent lime from the steel, dragged the flat of the blade along the back of her hand, flipped the blade, and repeated the motion, leaving glistening specks of fruit along her hand, which she lifted to her face to sniff in the acrid sting. The limes had come from somewhere down south—through New Orleans, she figured, setting the blade down.

"Your sheriff is stealing from us," she said.

"Our sheriff," Henrietta said. "Ours. We chose him together, mind. And you have to allow them their little victories now and again; otherwise you'll never know what they're really after."

Abigail took two of the lime quarters, squeezed them into her ginned glass, added an afterthought of club soda, said, "Oh."

"Let the little men stretch their necks out for what they really want. Let them think they can reach their hopes."

Abigail swirled the glass, took a swig, and wiped her mouth on her lime-dotted hand. "What's that line you like? From that poet?"

"'A man's reach should exceed his grasp, or what's a heaven for?'" she said. "Something like that."

Abigail asked for the name of the poem.

"No idea," Henrietta said. "All I ever cared about was that one line."

"And what will you do when he reaches for more?"

Henrietta shrugged, smiled. "Sever skull from spine, of course."

Abigail laughed. "Sounds fun. Now let's have another drink," she said, looking at her freshly emptied glass.

4

Everett walked the manager to the back of the bank, told him to open the safe.

This is too easy, Everett thought. *Finally things are going our way.*

As the white-haired bank manager reached to pull the safe door open, Everett saw him smile and lean back, just as a shuffling sound came from inside the safe.

At the front of the bank, Jimmy the Hook waved the empty shotgun in a slow arc through the room, easing around the four men lying face down on the floor. "Be over soon," he said. "You'll have a good story to tell your wives when you get home. Just make sure you end up home tonight and not at the undertaker's. They bury heroes around here, you know," he said, going on and on about how everyone should stay calm, and they did.

A few doors down from the bank, Beans stood next to the car in front of the bakery, wondering how quickly he could get in and out with a piece of chocolate pie. Did they have them sliced and on the counter, just waiting? He listened for shots from the bank, yelling, but didn't hear anything.

"Hey, buddy," a man coming out of the bakery said. "You can't park here." He motioned to the car.

"Say, how much is a piece of pie in there?" Beans asked.

"A what?"

"Pie. A piece of pie."

"I don't know. A nickel?" The man pointed to the car again. "You're going to get in big trouble you don't move that car."

Beans turned around to look at their car, as if it could have changed in the last minute. When he turned back, the man was gone. Or maybe he was still there, but Beans was looking through the bakery window for a nickel slice of pie.

The man inside the bank safe made a move toward Everett, but Everett kicked the man in his dick, shoved him back, slammed the safe door closed before he knew what was happening. A shot went off inside the safe, muffled but still loud, followed by a high-pitched squeal. Everett collected himself, saw the banker's hand had been caught in the safe—the banker was trying to pull his arm back, it being wedged in there good now. When Everett had been seven or eight, he'd come upon some older boys torturing a calico cat, and the sound the banker made reminded him of that, of the sounds those boys had made when he was done with them.

Everett looked around, saw Jimmy putting the butt of the shotgun into the temple of a man who'd decided now was a good time to make his move. "Let's git. Let's git," Everett said as he and Jimmy left the bank with only the guns they'd come in with.

Beans was standing near the car but not near enough. Back turned, he hadn't heard the commotion.

"Let's go, let's go," Everett said, heading to the car.

Beans heard them, turned with half a slice of pie in his hand, half in his mouth. He looked at the pie in his hand, did his best calculations relative to the amount he'd spent on the pie and the amount of room he still had in his mouth, decided against making the attempt, and set the rest of the slice on the ground beside him as he moved to the car.

The people who'd been inside the bank a minute back—the quiet, behaved people—were now running out onto the street, boldly screaming, "They're robbing the bank! They're robbing the bank!" which, while being highly unusual in Everett's experience, was, he thought, demonstrably false.

Two men in overalls and caps came running toward the car, until Everett raised his gun and fired a shot at their feet, which slowed them down. Another man, young, weighing maybe a buck twenty, white dress shirt with the sleeves rolled up, came rushing at Everett as he got into the car. Everett was yelling at Beans without even meaning to, and Beans took off down the road, heading any way that was away, the name of every road he'd ever heard having fallen clear out of his head.

~

Jefferson Faubus was tending to his goats when he heard the racket from a couple of blocks away. He'd spent the week reading about various bank robberies and kidnappings. In one of his detective magazines he had been reading that morning, *True Detective* or *Actual Detective* or *Dynamic Detective*—he couldn't remember which—there'd been a bank robbery and hostage story that Inspector Joe McDougall had ended when he'd shot out the tires of the gangsters' sedan. Jefferson Faubus turned to get his rifle from the house, the rifle good mostly for killing any varmint that got on his bad side. Then he remembered he'd given the gun to the Elam boy in town to hold for collateral a few days back. He looked around the yard at the goats and the fallen fence posts. The car was coming up the road to his left and would have to turn at the edge of his land, make its way back past him on the other side. He grabbed the first thing he could find and ran to the fence line by the road.

As they turned the corner, the sedan caught itself in ruts, veered to the edge of the road. As Beans was righting the car, he made another turn, nearly overcorrecting himself right into a fence but settling down as the guns and Jimmy in the back seat fell to the floorboard.

Jimmy was yelling to slow down, while Everett was in the passenger seat, hanging out the window and firing behind them, yelling go go go.

Beans saw Jefferson Faubus at the edge of the road, just this side of the broken fence. The man squatted, then uncurled himself, his arms extending, an unwieldy tree stump flying through the air at the car. Beans swerved, the tree stump landing, bouncing, rolling, catching the corner of the car, the car veering into the fence, *ka-thump*, *ka-thump*, then through the small field, the unplanted rows, up and down, a gin-soaked drunkard spinning around, falling downstairs, *ka-thump*, *ka-thump*, *ka-thump*.

The first bump had sent Everett's pistol flying from his hand. The next thud had sent his head into the ceiling of the car. After that it was all punches to the head, the shoulder, the elbow—a glancing blow to the temple, then a solid cross to the jaw. At one point, Everett saw Jimmy fly by from one side of the car to the other, the two meeting each other midway as they flew back to their respective sides. Everett, frozen in space, caught a boot to the forehead, somehow went face first into the floorboard, then suddenly found himself sitting upright pretty as you please, eyes blinking like in that uncertain moment when you're just waking up in someone else's house.

A thud, and Everett watched as something flew past the car. He wiped water and mud from his face but pulled away his palm to find hair and blood. He patted himself, patted himself more, before realizing. "Goddamn it, Beans. You just ran over a goat."

5

After a break, the men in the back of Moon's store moved the money around, shifted their cards, set them face down as Cottonmouth came back to the table.

Cottonmouth shifted a pair of deuces to one end, wound up with a third, pulled the pot to him when it was done.

A couple of hands later, Cottonmouth watched as Monkey Pribble opened strong.

"You seem pretty confident," the bald man said, and Pribble just grinned and nodded along.

Bill Moon and the bald man were chattering on about the often-injured Travis Jackson, the kid born and raised about ten miles from where they were sitting.

"I'm just telling you I expect the boy's knee to be better this year," the bald man said.

Moon shook his head, shifted his cards. "Played just fifty games last season because of that knee. And the mumps. The flu. Appendix. He's had a rough go of it. Five'll get you ten he won't get fifty hits this year."

The bald man said he'd take that as Cottonmouth saw Monkey Pribble look at the new card he'd just gotten, Pribble's cheeks going slack, shoulders dropping.

Moon and the bald man were rattling on about the Giants' lefty, guy called Hubbell, who'd been stringing together some good games.

Pribble raised, sliding more money in, trying to bluff his way through it.

"Good thing we're playing small stakes," Moon joked when the hand was over and Pribble was sitting at a blank part of the table where his money had been.

"That was quite a night, gentlemen," the bald man said, standing to leave. "Thanks for the show."

"You cleaned me out," Pribble said to Cottonmouth. "Come back to town and cleaned me out. Have I got a tell? You counting cards?"

"What are you going on about?" Cottonmouth said, moving the coins and paper money around on the table, counting how much was there, whether it would be enough to do any good.

"How'd you beat me?" Pribble asked.

"Pretty easily, I thought," Cottonmouth said. "You overplayed your hand."

"Overplayed?"

"Down in Honduras—you all were asking about Honduras, and to tell you the truth, I didn't learn too much down there. Sure not enough to do me much good, don't figure. But I learned I don't care much for papaya, and I learned how to tell when someone is overplaying their hand, which comes in pretty handy these days."

"Well, I'll be John Brown," Pribble said, shaking his head and collecting his hat as they were all making their way to the front door.

Moon unlocked the front door so they could leave, told them good night, asked Cottonmouth to hold back for a minute, said he had something to discuss.

~

"Never really answered me," Moon said. "Business good down there at the old camp?"

Cottonmouth nodded, said it was doing fine.

Moon saw him look off as he said it. "I know things get tough, specially these days, Roosevelt and all. How you set for food, supplies? You know I got the McMahen boy delivering for me now. Can set up a schedule so as you don't even have to worry about it, you see? Every Tuesday or Friday or however you want it. You're about, what, twenty miles from here? Won't be a problem. You just send him back with a list or stop by when you're in town. We can take care of the money in whatever works for you, you see? Hoping things pick up for you and you'll need more than just the occasional bottle of whiskey."

Cottonmouth said he was hoping much the same.

Moon reached for a tube of Listerine. "Modern dentifrice, Cottonmouth. That's what they're selling here. Twenty-five cents a pop. And here," he said, picking up a tube of Pepsodent, "here's another one. These things are coming in by the box and leaving one at a time. Cottonmouth, I tell you—the world is going to hell, and people are still worried about their teeth. Man in here last week wants to set up a corner of the store to sell pumps and sinks, get houses outfitted with all the modern conveniences, he says. The Hoovervilles and West Dallas and all that you hear about, you see—that's on the outs. I'm not saying Roosevelt is the savior. I'm not saying there is a savior, Cottonmouth, but I'm telling you people are buying things, and they'll always be buying things. The worse it's getting out there, the more people want to stay comfortable in their homes. I got cases of food in the back that'll be gone by Tuesday."

"That sounds like you're doing just fine, Bill."

"Well, that's just it. It's fine, but it's nothing worthwhile, you see? I'm selling toothpaste a tube at a time. Ain't nobody ever got rich doing that. The Banana Man you were talking about. He didn't get that way from selling one banana at a time, did he? I tell you he didn't."

"Not sure what you're getting at," Cottonmouth said.

"I'm looking for investors, Cottonmouth. A while back, your uncle came in asking if I wanted to invest in that camp of his, and I couldn't. Didn't have the money to lay my hands on. I look back over the years, you know? If I'd done this. If I'd done that. There are people who did those things. They made a little money; then they had to find money to make a little more."

"Still not sure I entirely get what you're talking to me about here."

"I get enough money in here, I can buy more product and I can move more product. I got a man in El Dorado, set up a little after the oil took off, but he's feeling it now—let me tell you. And I got a sister down in Shreveport too. Cotton and oil money, just for the taking. But it takes money to make money. And I know you got people you know, people with access to cash, you see. There ain't but so much you can do with that kind of cash, especially cash that's been recently, shall we say, liberated? Can't buy gold—at least not on the level, you can't. Had to take some payments last few years in livestock, IOUs, gold coins, gold certificates, jewelry, and such, folks not having the cash. And now Roosevelt wants to take the gold. And cash or gold or what have you, you don't want to put it in a bank, I hear, as those aren't as safe as they once were."

"So I hear."

"What I was thinking, you see, is that I get enough to make some larger purchases; then we work on a distribution line. You know people coming and going. Maybe we can work something out—drivers, vehicles, something to work for both of us? I don't have all the details worked out."

"You just figure you need some more cogs?"

"Yes," he said, then stumbled over that a bit, remembering what Cottonmouth had said about cogs. "No, I mean, it takes people to put together a plan. People who have a head for this. And then it takes the people to buy this. The manufacturer and the consumer, if you understand."

"And which are you?"

"Well, I'm the man in the middle. The man connecting the two ends, you see?"

Cottonmouth said he saw it just fine.

Moon said the way the Banana Man made money was taking a chance. "You think he made all that money by sitting around while everyone else acted? No. He got an idea, weighed the options, then went to work. If you want that, you have to take the chances. That's why a man like that wins. He'd rather take the chance than watch everything go right past him. I been working out things with my lawyer. You know him, Gus Webster?"

"I don't," Cottonmouth said.

"He's been helping me get things set up."

"Still not sure what any of this has to do with me."

"Your uncle used to have a good bit of money coming through there. I don't know how things are looking now," he said.

Cottonmouth cut him off. "Not great. Figure some changes can be made. Picked up a few things here and there, maybe put some of that to use."

Moon said that was a good point.

"I been back just a couple weeks, and all I know is things at the camp aren't going as well as they used to, and my uncle had fallen behind in his payments."

"To the bank?" Moon asked.

"The Rudd sisters," Cottonmouth said and watched the air leave Bill Moon's body, saw the man shrink in on himself.

Moon nodded. "Yeah. Well, you might want to take care of that."

Cottonmouth said he planned to. “Had enough trouble down in Honduras with that lot. Trying to settle in here now. Not interested in starting any fights with the locals.”

Moon laughed, said Cottonmouth was a local.

“Used to be,” Cottonmouth said. “Either way, not looking to have to fight with anyone.”

“Maybe,” Moon said. “But there’s no profit in peace.”

6

In a cottage in a motor court between Hazelton and the Tomlin camp, Everett Logan stood at the curtains, parted them slightly, waiting.

He could feel trouble coming through the early-June air, the way you might sense overnight rain in a once-snapped finger.

He pulled the curtains a little more, squinted through the dusk, past the Buick they'd appropriated a few miles south of Hazelton, their goat-and-tree-stump-afflicted sedan no longer much use. He looked past the cars perched next to the other cottages in the tourist court. He hadn't counted when they had been outside, too occupied with keeping Jimmy the Hook's arm attached to his body, the smash and slam following the bank job making things worse for him on that count. He reckoned now there were a dozen cottages, half of them filled with families, white-shirted men and long-skirted women, standing around and talking about nothing much, he figured. He looked to see if any of them were considering him, but he was too far away from anyone to tell.

Everett watched the end of the row of cabins, where a middle-aged man with his shirtsleeves rolled up tossed a baseball back and forth with a boy. Closer, a few men standing outside a cabin looked to be talking, likely about Roosevelt, Everett figured. In office just three months and already stirring up so much. Couldn't own gold now. Everyone was talking about Roosevelt. People wondering if they could bring back

Hoover. Those men talking about nothing much at all, he figured. The bigger the matter men like that were talking about, the less it mattered. When they started talking about what was going on closer to them, started thinking about what was happening closer to them, that was when they could do something, when they could impact what was close to them. Until then, their talk didn't matter.

Up in Missouri, where they'd stayed so long last month it had seemed like a vacation, the tourist camps had closed garages, three restaurants nearby, and a pawnshop across the park behind them. Here, they had none of those things, not even a radio. And they had to park next to the cottage in the open, had to rely on the man at the station for what passed as food, and didn't have any hope for selling or buying from a pawnshop. Up in Missouri, there'd been a hockshop across the Kansas line in Frontenac that now held a wristwatch that he'd been talked into parting with, a move he'd woken up each morning since regretting. The man behind the counter had called it a Cartier Santos, but Everett knew it only as a watch like his grandfather had worn. Everett had taken it off a displeased Wichita banker about six months back and had worn it every day since. Until they'd run out of money. Until the week nothing had gone right. There were weeks like that sometimes. Months. He knew. No reason to panic, he'd said. Still, Jimmy the Hook and Beans had decided to pawn what they had, and after all, it wasn't really Everett's grandfather's watch, just one exactly like it, down to the scratch on the back.

Everett shut the curtain as Jimmy's moans got louder.

"I think he'll be fine," Everett said as he turned to Beans, who was holding a shirt against Jimmy the Hook's bleeding arm.

"Keeping his blood on the inside now," Beans said, slowly pulling back the shirt, wadded, red, and damp.

"I'll make sure it stays that way," Everett said. "You take some of the cash and go across the street and see do they have anything that looks like food."

Beans stood, went to the bag he'd carried into the cottage, stared at the loose change in the bag—the change they'd taken from the register at the Texaco outside Dripping Springs. He reached in, pulled out a handful of change, let it fall through his fingers, jinglejangling back into the bag. He took some nickels, some dimes.

Everett looked past the curtains again, leaning forward and squinting, as if the two or three inches he was leaning would make a difference. "Still clear." Everett stepped back from the curtains, settled them as tight as he could against the windowsill, looked at the palm of his hand.

"Will you look at that? Look at that dust," he said, holding his dirty hand up for his partners to see. "They need to take better care of this place."

Jimmy the Hook said maybe Everett should write a letter to the manager. "Seeing as how you're doing all that college now. Impress him with your big words, make him think we're important goons. Maybe he'll put us up in the presidential suite. Of course, I don't think we have that many nickels or dimes."

"We're doing fine," Everett said. "We'll get 'em next time."

"I thought the bank was the next time," Jimmy said.

"Didn't work out that way, did it?"

"No," Jimmy said. "Or the last time. But next time, that's our time. Right?"

Christ, Everett thought. "Can you give it a rest? We're doing the best we can."

Under his breath, Jimmy said that was what worried him.

Beans jangled the coins in his pocket, reached into the bag, pulled out a cap, settled it on his head.

Jimmy laughed, the tension broken. "You can't wear the cap we took off that kid."

"Took nothing. I paid him fair and square."

Everett threw his hands up. "We were robbing the place, Beans."

"We weren't robbing *him*, by god."

After Beans had gone, Everett took his bone-handle barlow knife from his pocket, wiped it on his pant leg.

"You sure that's clean?" Jimmy asked.

"Cleaner than your arm right now."

Everett set the knife on the edge of the sink, took a cup, poured some water over Jimmy's shoulder. He used the tip of the knife to poke away at the little flaps of skin until he felt resistance, the shotgun pellet he was searching for.

Jimmy the Hook said "Goddamn" as Everett dug underneath one of the pellets, popping it loose from the shoulder meat, the pebble clattering into the sink, then rolling around the drain until it disappeared into the darkness beneath them.

"I think that's the only one," Jimmy said. "I'm good now."

"Oh, hold still, you baby."

Jimmy started to pull back his arm, said he was fine, all better.

"Just give me your arm."

And so Jimmy did, and Everett fished out two more pellets, said, "See. That wasn't so bad."

Jimmy rubbed his arm. "Says you."

A knock at the door.

Everett and Jimmy looked at each other, then around the bathroom for a gun, a weapon of some kind. Everett wiped the knife on a towel, then slid the blade into his pocket.

Everett handed Jimmy the towel, said "The law won't knock when they come," and shut the door behind him as he walked into the main room to answer the door.

Beans, hands full of chicken and beer, was standing at the door with the owner behind him, looking at Everett and past Everett and through Everett into the cottage room.

"The owner is behind me," Beans whispered, loud enough that it wasn't a whisper.

The owner tipped his hat. "Evening. Offered to help him carry your dinner, but he wouldn't have it."

Everett stepped aside to let Beans into the cottage, then closed the door and stepped outside, asked, "Something you needed?"

"Just making sure you boys were all right," the owner said. "And I had to come over to get the license plate number off your car."

"That so? Didn't you get it when we checked in?"

"Plumb forgot, we were so busy."

Everett gave thought to dragging the owner into the room and settling things quietly. He considered. He waited.

"Right. So if I can just get that number, I'll be back on my way."

Everett said it wasn't a problem, stepped from the cottage, walked the owner to the car. They had just enough light to make out the license plate, the man penciling the number onto a notepad.

The owner thanked Everett, apologized for the trouble, turned to walk away, but stopped next to the car.

Everett asked was there a problem. The man shook his head, stuttering out "No, not at all, no" before he turned to walk back to the office. Everett walked to where the man had been standing next to the car, looked into the back seat and saw a shotgun and two rifles they'd neglected to bring into the cottage with them.

He looked across the parking lot, the drive, the road, saw the man walking into the office, arms flustering about.

He reckoned they had maybe ten minutes to get out. He was wrong.

7

Cottonmouth Tomlin walked through the restaurant doors, which Miss Phoebe locked behind him. He took his seat at the table, asked for a cup of coffee and a piece of pie.

After a few minutes of silence, Henrietta Rudd said, "Well, we appreciate your stopping by on such short notice. We just wanted to follow up on what you and the sheriff had discussed, see how things were going down at the camp, pass on our condolences about your uncle."

He said he didn't have any complaints.

"Because there's a lot of money tied up in that camp," she said.

He said he knew that. Christ, he knew. He could see her smugness. Could smell it. "Years too," he said. "Family. Working for it."

"Your family running the hunting lodge," she said. "You know, my own father—our own father," she corrected, looking at Abigail sitting nearby with a drink on the table and a book in her lap. "Our own father was never sure that would succeed. Never much of a hunter, really. Didn't see profit there. The hunting lodge was one thing, charging bankers to shoot our deer. But then that changed, didn't it? Your mother leaving with that man with the wagon. What was it?" she asked, pausing, knowing the answer. "Rawleigh Remedies, wasn't it?" she asked, knowing it was. "Yes, and then your father chasing off after her." She shook her head. "You people sure are keen on running away from here. You sure coming back here was the right call?"

"Didn't see any other option," he said.

"No. You wouldn't have, I don't suppose. Still, your uncle did stay. Had a good run, until he didn't. Times being what they are. I suppose it seemed a good idea, opening it up for poker playing and a camp for outlaws, which was not ideal, not for us, but if the outlawing is done out there outside the county, that's one thing. It can be good business, bringing their money to our county and providing it to us so we're not just handing each other our own money. Smart business. But we don't want anything unsavory—you understand?"

"Nothing unsavory," Cottonmouth told her. *Keep it simple,* he told himself. *This is just talk.* If she wanted to make a move, she'd have made it. Like with the Becketts' farm in the summer of '26. This wasn't like that. Not yet. And it didn't have to be. *Relax. Say words. Let them fall into line, fall from your mouth. She's just trying to show she's in charge, which is fine.*

"Drinking and cards, you figure that's the downfall of our country, now?" he asked. "All that's going on in this country, Roosevelt taking control, banks closing down, giant monkeys climbing to the top of New York buildings—you figure card playing is about to doom us all?" Cottonmouth flicked a bug's shell from the table.

"Nothing against playing cards," she said. "I like the idea of the old families of this county running the business of this county. I believe I've been clear on that. Makes me feel like there's an order to things."

He said that sounded fine to him.

"But when there's trouble or agreements being broken or threats of disorder, well, that makes me sad, Cottonmouth. And I don't like to be sad." She looked off, then back again. "It tires me."

Cottonmouth looked up from the table. The woman's eyes, sharp, clear. Black glass marble on a white field, no blood threads at the edges. He looked over to Abigail, still deep in her reading, then turned back to Henrietta. "I get the feeling you didn't ask me here to talk about playing cards."

"I was told you'd gotten smarter during your absence, and I can tell now that's the case. I was told you were very clever now, and here we are. You see, we like to support the local businesses like your uncle built up, like you're handling now. After all, that's what is going to save this country from the likes of the Roosevelts and the Carnegies and the other Yankees trying to take us over again. Local. Community. And, like I said, if outsiders want to come for a quiet, peaceful stay, whether it's playing cards at your camp or coming into town and visiting the Culver for drinks and dancing, well, we'll be glad to take their money, won't we? They can leave their money and move along."

He said that was the idea.

"But we don't want their trouble," she said. "Outsiders come in; we let them cause problems for the people what built this town, this county—well, might as well be living in Chicago or Kansas City. You know the Carringtons over in the Taylor area?"

He said he recognized the name.

"Horace takes a trip to Texarkana last month to see a man about a Chevrolet Confederate. Found what was left of him on the edge of Rusty Creek, minus the six hundred dollars he'd had on him for the sedan."

Cottonmouth said that was a shame.

"Happens all the time, head to the city. No order. People coming and going, no respect for the way things ought to be. We don't want that here—I think you'll agree."

He did.

"We have to preserve what we've got here. What our families built. Your family. My family. Most of them coming across from Georgia near a hundred years back now, you know."

He nodded.

"They didn't come all this way to have to fend off outsiders coming in to shoot, stab, and rob us all. Lose control of this county, might as well hand it over to the Pribbles and Stoneciphers."

He said she seemed to be driving toward something.

"Family, Mr. Tomlin. I know a body up in the Lamartine area, has the safest, best liquor around. Bourbon. Gin. Times being what they are, you can't always trust outside liquor, you know. That can cause all sorts of bodily injury. And we wouldn't want anyone getting seriously hurt, would we?"

Cottonmouth knew the answer to that. "That's your cousin up in Lamartine?"

"As a matter of fact, it is. Nothing but blood what holds us together. Family is important. You know that."

"Some families more than others, I reckon?"

"That's the way it goes, isn't it? But that's not the point. Point is you've been buying your drink from an outsider, which breaks an agreement we had with your uncle."

"Been getting liquor wherever I could get the best deal," he said.

"Best deal for you," she said. "At the moment. Not the best deal for the county, for the families here. And, if I'm being honest, likely not the best deal for you in the long run. Not the safest deal for you," she said under a raised eyebrow.

"Last whiskey I got came from Moon's store, and he gets his from Captain Warnock. And his family's got as much claim here as any of us."

"Oh, I beg your pardon." She raised her hands, pretending to give up. "When I heard Mr. Moon was getting his whiskey from Captain Warnock in Garland, I didn't know they'd moved Garland out of Lafayette County. Or has the Red River shifted that much?"

Cottonmouth said Warnock was in Garland and Garland was still in Lafayette County. "Lafayette County is our neighbor. And Captain Warnock is as good a man as any. Everyone knows him."

"Now, Cottonmouth. I can't help that, what everyone knows. That don't carry a lick of weight. Not one drop. What we have going on here is booze from Lafayette County encroaching on our own people. I can't vouch for that, now. For all I know, they could be mixing the gin with sharecropper piss and Alabama spit. We can't have that. Can't have people from other counties, people from Little Rock and Washington, can't have all those people over us, taking from us. Changing everything our families have built up, everything they poured their own blood into."

Cottonmouth said OK.

"When your uncle came to us asking for help, that was part of the agreement. Part of supporting the families in the county."

"Your family?"

"We're all family. Your family's story is all over this county. I know that. In the dirt and on top of it. Your family's got blood runs all through this county, no matter ain't much left of them. Hellfire, your granddaddy and my uncles fought together to keep the Yankees from taking everything. But you know well as I do you ain't been around for a lot of this, what's gone on past few years with Governor Parnell nearly being the ruination of all Arkansas and now Roosevelt taking whatever we've got left. How we got to keep fighting for this land, for our families. See, we've been fighting off encroachers since we got here, all of us, while you were off doing whatever that was in the jungle down there."

"Serving my country."

She shook her head. "Country ain't never done a damn thing for me, Cottonmouth. I'm talking about family. Community. I'm talking about all of us, together. And you may not like it, but family still includes even them kin we don't speak with much anymore. I'm talking about the people what raised you up, fed you, healed you. Made sure you got to church on Sundays. Made sure you got to school the rest of the days. Brought food to you and your dad when your mama left. Then to you and your uncle after your father left. Stood vigil and cooked soups a dozen times over when any y'all were sick. Country ever do that? Country ever show up at your house after the wind took it down, and country ever built it back up again, likely as not better than before? Country ever do that? I'm talking about holding together, holding on to what we got left. We have to make sure we're all supporting each other."

"A big happy family in the county—everybody else be damned?"

"Everybody's already damned, Cottonmouth. That's the whole point of staying together. Now, I've talked to the good people up in Lamartine, and they tell me they've got this little welcome-back deal they're offering you. First hundred you buy, you get twenty free."

"Doesn't sound like something I can pass up."

"No, not at all. Set those twenty aside, you and me are square."

"I start buying my liquor from your cousin, then give some to you? Then you can sell it back to me."

"Sounds like the best deal you're gonna get today, don't it?"

"Don't it just?"

"We clear?" Henrietta Rudd asked, sliding back from the table, her sister slipping a bookmark between pages, draining her glass as she stood. "I'd rather not have any more trouble from this. Or anything else. A nice, quiet life. Enjoy everything our county has to offer. I want trouble, I'll visit Hot Springs. Clear?"

Cottonmouth traced his back teeth with his tongue, the inside of his bottom lip, the cracked tooth, twisted his neck to popping. A slowing he'd learned a few years back, a continent away, when he'd been a world away from a quiet life. "Don't imagine there'll be much trouble."

"That's good. Good to have you back, settled in."

"Right."

"Good to find a place you belong; isn't that right?" she said, standing to go, not really asking. "Good to know your place in the world."

He nodded as she and her sister were leaving, said, "Must be a goddamn comfort."

8

Everett Logan walked back into the cottage, found Beans and Jimmy sitting at the little coffee table, eating chicken and drinking beer. Everett said to wrap it up, fellows—said to get while the getting was good.

Beans took a napkin, wrapped up a chicken leg, dropped it into his left coat pocket and a can of beer into his right, stood up and dusted off his hands.

As Jimmy the Hook was standing, right hand holding his bandaged left arm, Everett reached for a chicken wing, quickly chewed off the strips of meat, dropped the bone back onto the table.

"Thought we were going to take a night to lick our wounds, regroup," Jimmy said. "Count up the money we don't have."

"Not working out that way," Everett said. "Had a little trouble with the owner. Expect company."

Beans asked how far was it to the camp, if that was still where they were going.

Everett pulled a pistol from his pocket, made sure it was loaded. Reached for a rifle. "Like I said this morning, should be able to get down there in a few hours from here, Lord willing and the creek don't rise. Maybe should have gone straight there, but I thought we deserved a night to recover. Didn't expect . . . well, guess you don't expect a surprise, do you?"

Jimmy piped up, said not to worry about it. "We're patched up, got some chicken in us. And now we're on to that camp. You never been there, right, Beans?"

Beans said he hadn't. "Could use a little rest and relaxation." He rubbed his side where he'd been stabbed too recently, felt the warmth of the scar still there. Looked up to see Everett and the bandaged Jimmy, then said, "Guess we all could."

"It's an old hunting cabin," Jimmy said. "Can still do some fishing there, you want."

Beans said he'd never been fishing.

"We get there," Everett said, "first thing we'll do is go fishing."

"What kind of fish they got there?" Beans asked.

Jimmy breech-loaded his shotgun, slid extra shells into his coat pocket. "The worm-eating kind. You ready?"

Beans said he was. Jimmy looked at Everett, who nodded.

They gathered what they had, double-checked the money bags, and were walking to the door when they heard the other cars pulling up.

Everett walked to the window, eased back the curtains again, saw two cars sideways in front of the cottage between them and the road, another car closer to theirs, blocking their way to the road.

Everett looked to the back wall, a corner of his mind hoping that he'd overlooked a back door to the cottage when they'd checked in that morning.

He hadn't.

Everett asked if they could knock a hole in the back and sneak out. Jimmy grunted. Beans, earnest, not getting the joke, looked closely at the wall, scratched the back of his head, and said, "I can try whacking through the soft spots if you want. Don't know how long it'll take, but I can try."

Everett could hear someone through the window, someone hollering commands to them, but couldn't make out what was being said. He looked to Jimmy, who grunted again, this time adding a shrug.

Everett walked past the door, stood behind the wall, reached back and turned the knob, the door falling open a little. "You mind repeating that?" he yelled through the opening.

"We know who you are. You fellas are in a world of hurt," came the bellowing from outside.

The three men inside the cottage looked at one another. Beans said, "I thought they were supposed to bargain with us. You know, hands up and no one gets hurt. You can still get out of this alive. It's not too late—that sort of thing."

After Jimmy grunted in agreement, Everett said, "Guess we've just gotten used to dealing with a more agreeable sort of law in Missouri than down here."

"Oklahoma too," Beans said. "Remember? What was that town? The one with the two poodles by the bank."

"Earlsboro," Everett and Jimmy said as the bellowing started up again outside the cottage.

"You fellas have exactly one minute, starting now," the man outside said.

In the cottage, Beans held a shotgun to his chest, walked across to the window. "How many you figure out there?"

Everett said maybe a dozen. He pointed out the front of the cabin, then to the right corner, saying "Two cars, one car" as he did.

Everett looked from the corner of the window, leaned back against a wall. "Car lights all over out there, but I counted a half dozen coppers, and I swear they brought that banker with them."

"From Hazelton?" Jimmy asked, and Everett wondered why Jimmy would ask such a dumb question but let it go.

"Yeah."

Beans asked why they'd brought the banker, and Jimmy blurted out that it was probably to identify their bodies.

Then the bellowing outside told them their time was up.

Everett turned to Jimmy. "If I'm being honest, that felt more like forty seconds."

The first shot came from Everett's left, popped some stonework around the doorjamb. Everett fired back with the shotgun, said "Let's go, let's go," and they did.

The men outside had their sedans turned sideways, were hiding behind them and firing at the cottage, the two windows in front gone in the first volleys. The only lights in the darkness were coming from the cottage and from the sedans, whose lights were aimed sideways into the woods. When all three men had cleared the backlight from the cottage, the lawmen realized their mistake, started yelling at one another to move cars.

"Get the lights on them damned bank-robbin' bastards," one of them said.

Everett helped Beans get the bags into the back of the car, then pulled a blanket from the floorboard and grabbed the Browning Automatic, loaded a mag, and was firing into the sedans as they were turning their lights on the cottage. The cops began trying to swing the light around to the outlaws' car until Everett shattered their headlamps and pierced the flanks of their cars.

The three men fell into the car as Jimmy drove, one-armed, into the side of the cottage, into the rear of one of the cars, over a scrambling deputy.

The car hit something, then slowed as Jimmy fought with the gears, with the steering.

Everett leaned out the car to see what they'd hit, then saw his chance. He jumped from the back of the car, grabbed the cowering white-haired bank manager from the ground, and threw him into the back seat, then closed the door behind them. He yelled, "Drive! Drive!" and suddenly they were off, onto the road and south, headed for the Tomlin camp in southern Arkansas and what they thought was safety.

9

South of town, in what passed for bayou in that part of Arkansas, Cottonmouth was sitting in a chair, penciling numbers into a notebook, about to go back in for another beer when Othel Walker came out, spit a thread of something thin over the rail, into the evening darkness. He sat down, a chair of pine and bent nails between them.

Cottonmouth settled back in.

"All cleaned up," Othel said, nodding toward the kitchen. "Be good we could get some decent meat in here."

Cottonmouth said he knew it would. "Need to get some funding in first."

Othel said he understood. "Been a couple things I been wanting to try. Saw them in a book over in Texarkana last weekend."

Cottonmouth said that sounded all right to him.

"Goose piquant," Othel said.

Cottonmouth said he didn't know the word.

"Means 'spicy,' I think," Othel said. "Marinate the goose in vinegar and garlic, cayenne pepper. Peppercorns. Then you add in some onions and roast it."

"My uncle ever have goose here?"

Othel said he couldn't recall but figured not.

Cottonmouth asked what they had left, said he'd seen some macaroni, some oatmeal.

"Tomatoes, corn. Got some hot dogs. Some bread. Cans of this and that. Can make a dozen different kinds of soup."

"Can't feed too many people on corn soup for long," Cottonmouth said.

"Hillstrom's leaving tomorrow," Othel said.

Cottonmouth asked who that left.

"Hyer and Drunk Eddie. And I think they're leaving too. Got a job up around Hot Springs to grab a banker, I hear."

"All three out at once, huh?"

"Don't worry. They're paid up," Othel said. "Left a little something extra. Seem to be doing well, those guys."

Cottonmouth said he wasn't worried, and Othel let the lie go.

"Heard Frank Nash was up in Hot Springs," Othel said. "They say he just got married."

"Again? Lord," Cottonmouth said, little facts from when he was last in the area coming in here and there. "Well, maybe he'll settle down around there."

Othel said he didn't know about that, said there always seemed to be something going on somewhere.

"Guess there's been a lot going on since I was gone."

"Good of you to come back," Othel said, looking out at the night around the cabins. "Keep things going along. Do him proud."

"You'd tell me if my uncle had any money buried around here, right?" Cottonmouth asked.

"Wouldn't stay buried for long. Not with this bunch."

Cottonmouth said that sounded right.

"Speaking of money, heard Charlie hit the bank in Lewisville," Othel said in Cottonmouth's direction.

"Frazier?"

Othel said that was him.

"You know he got much?"

"Not as much as he used to, I figure."

Cottonmouth nodded.

Both men waited awhile, dogs barking, howling in the distance, the deep growls and sharp, quick yaps. Night coming along slowly. Cottonmouth tried to figure how far away were the barks, like counting between the lightning and the thunder. He closed his eyes, tried to picture the cypress trees rising, the spaces between, the dogs in the distance, but kept seeing a river from another continent, a village jagged with flames, the crackle, the crashing collapse of roof beams, the caving in while soldiers watched from a distance. He stood, walked to the edge of the porch to look out at the woods, the swamp of Dorcheat Bayou that protected the camp, the only road now basically impassable. Cypress trees dangling snapped arms of Spanish moss.

Still the same trees as when he'd left. Still the same trees as when his father had left. When his mother had left. When he and his father had hunted here. When they'd brought the deer meat back and he and his father and his mother had sat down to dinner—they had scolded him about something he'd done wrong at school that day. At least the trees hadn't changed.

His mother had gone off. His father had taken off after. And now his uncle was dead and gone.

Cottonmouth knew he could ask Othel for suggestions, his uncle having trusted the man enough while Cottonmouth was gone. But something about that felt like giving up. Something about saying out loud that he was worried he couldn't handle this, that his uncle had made a mistake leaving him the camp. *I've gone off myself,* Cottonmouth thought. *And here I've come back. Down to New Orleans, on to Honduras. Traveled the world. I'm the Tomlin what's come back. And for what? To curl up now? To beg for help?*

There was a man in Honduras when he'd gotten there, a man they called LC. He'd been questioning some of the locals, and a soldier had asked which of the two men they'd captured to question first. LC had said the name of one of the men, and the soldier had nodded, left. LC had asked Cottonmouth why he was shaking his head, and Cottonmouth had said he didn't understand how LC had chosen.

"Which man didn't matter," he said. "What mattered was that the soldier thinks I know what I'm doing. They have to think the man in charge has the answers."

Dorcheat Bayou lay out around him now, and Cottonmouth knew he couldn't talk to Othel about it, about the money. He knew if he so much as blinked, Charlie Frazier or Frank Nash or damn near any one of them would gut him as soon as look at him.

Besides, just because his uncle trusted this man didn't mean he had enough reason to.

He dragged his palm along the flat of the railing, pressing jagged nailheads into his hand to test the dead skin, the scarring, see how deep he could get into his flesh before he felt anything.

"Charlie heading here?" Cottonmouth asked. Then, with a grudge, he added, "Or the Campbell place?"

"Hadn't heard. Could head up to Doc Gramm's ranch too. Hear he added on up there."

"Thought that place had burned down," Cottonmouth said.

"That was a couple years back. Built it up again. Don't know any of those places are doing any better than we are."

"Well, Charlie oughta lay low somewhere." Cottonmouth sat back down, kept his eyes on the tree line.

"You know how he is."

Cottonmouth nodded. "Yeah." He knew how they all were, how they'd been before he'd left, his uncle just starting to make a go of the camp.

"Word is he's taking some shots in Ray Hamilton's backyard soon as he knows how long Ray's liable to be locked up."

"Which one's Ray?" Cottonmouth asked.

"You met him when you and your uncle went to Lawton to pick up that stove. Short guy. Oklahoma. Mean streak."

"Mean streak don't narrow it down much." Cottonmouth set his empty bottle on the windowsill behind him, plank wood, weather splintered, a gap widening with each day of rain, each afternoon of sun.

"Guess it don't," Othel said. "Still, you're serious about saving this place here, you'll need to watch yourself. Easy enough to wake up dead."

Cottonmouth didn't disagree with that, listened to birds squawk back and forth at each other, birds he should have known the names of, having spent his first couple of decades right within a few dozen miles of those woods, never leaving at all until he was leaving for good, he thought.

Othel leaned forward to look for the moon.

"Wasn't my uncle saving this place all along? What I understood from all those papers last week, signing probably twice as many papers as I read, best I figure, all what could be loaned against the camp has done been loaned."

"Near as I know," Othel said. "That was your uncle's business. I know he had to make some decisions while you were gone, keep this place afloat. Deal with folks he'd rather not have dealt with. Times being what they are. But what's done is done, and now we can work on digging ourselves out."

Ourselves, Cottonmouth heard. *We.* Othel had taken to considering himself some kind of owner here, part or otherwise. Cottonmouth gave a thought to setting down some understanding of who owned the camp and who cooked the stew but figured he needed Othel. Or needed someone to do the things Othel did. The cooking. The help with the camp. The bringing people through the swamp to the camp. The knowledge of how things were taken care of when his uncle ran the place. He needed things done. Back just a couple of weeks now, he couldn't run off the only person his uncle had trusted.

Othel said maybe get some more card games going, asked Cottonmouth how the card games were down in Mexico.

Just then, Drunk Eddie walked through the cabin doorway and onto the porch, said good evening to them both. "Making my evening visit to the Roosevelt Room, you fellows don't mind," he said, then whiskey-swayed around the corner to the outhouse, copy of the local paper in his hand.

When he'd gotten out of earshot, Cottonmouth said it was Honduras, said he'd had good nights in Trujillo, sure. "Place called the Curtain. Had some bad nights in, well, all the other places."

"Make any money?"

"None that I still have," Cottonmouth said. "Saw money being made. Saw a whole jungle turned into a money factory." He looked around him. "Someone smarter than me could do that here, say."

"Your uncle and I did the best could be done," Othel said. "Guarantee you that."

"I know. I know."

"Not a man around could have done better than we done, with what little came through here lately."

"Don't doubt that," Cottonmouth said. "Now I'm here, maybe we try something different."

"Lot changed since you were here," Othel said. "Lot of change you ain't even seen yet."

"Reckon I've changed too," Cottonmouth said.

The dogs started up again, a little closer this time.

"Dogs going after something tonight?" Cottonmouth asked.

"Sometimes dogs just got to bark."

A year or so back, Uncle Beurie had brought up a truckload of Catahoula curs after he'd heard stories about the Campbells' camp down toward Shreveport. Dogs that could bring down razorbacks were good dogs to have, he figured. Let them run across the acres here at night, protect the camp, dipping in and out of the water, the brackish banks of the bayou. What Dorcheat Bayou didn't swallow, the dogs would take care of. And what the dogs couldn't—well, there were other ways to handle those problems. Always had been. The ways Cottonmouth had gotten used to. The ways he'd come back to Arkansas to avoid.

Cottonmouth said maybe they'd cornered a goose or two. "You can finally fix up that fancy recipe you want. About time to try something new."

10

On the edge of the bayou that separated the Tomlin camp from the rest of the world, Othel Walker settled the johnboat against the bank, by a cypress. Now on solid ground, he led Cottonmouth toward the house that served as a way station for the camp and had been in the Walker family since just after the War for Southern Independence.

Othel's son came out to meet them about halfway, and Cottonmouth asked how many.

"Three," the teenager said. "Well, four."

Cottonmouth asked had he seen them before.

"Recognized one of them, maybe a second. Third's new to me."

Cottonmouth asked about the fourth, and the boy said he couldn't get a good look.

They'd talked their way closer to the house.

Cottonmouth asked was there anything he should know about the men from when they'd stayed before.

"Far as I can recall, never caused no trouble. Paid up just fine."

Cottonmouth said he guessed that was all you could ask, then stopped. "What do you mean you didn't get a good look at the fourth?"

The back door opened, and Cottonmouth looked up to see a pistol barrel in his face. He was more a rifle guy than a pistol guy but could tell he was looking down a Colt M1911. Single action. Magazine fed with .45s, though from this range just the one should do it.

Cottonmouth asked did the man holding the gun mind aiming it somewhere else.

Everett Logan kept the gun pointed at Cottonmouth but looked to Othel's boy, then to Othel. "This ain't Beurie."

"I told you that would take some explaining," Othel's son said.

Everett said now was as good a time as any to get on with the explaining.

"Good lord," Cottonmouth mumbled. "Uncle Beurie's dead. Left me in charge. Which means when I ask you to aim that pistol somewhere else, I'd appreciate it if you aimed that pistol somewhere else."

Everett looked to Othel.

"What are you looking to him for?" Cottonmouth asked, pistol still at his forehead.

"I know him and the boy. I don't know you."

"Christ on a cracker," Cottonmouth said, pushing the pistol out of his face and walking past Everett. "Who else we got in here?" He looked around the living room to see Beans and Jimmy sitting on a couch, either side of a man in a dress shirt, dress pants, and dress shoes, with a burlap sack over his head.

Cottonmouth turned back to the open door. Everett had lowered his pistol but kept it by his side.

"Costume party I didn't get invited to?" Cottonmouth asked.

"Picked up a friend on the way here," Everett said, walking into the room to stand between Cottonmouth and the other men.

"Drove a long way to make it here," Beans said. Then slowly and clearly so the kidnapped banker could hear him, he said, "To this house just outside Atlanta, Texas."

Cottonmouth raised an eyebrow and turned to Everett, the man who seemed to be in charge, or at least the man who had the pistol out, which usually amounted to the same thing.

Everett shrugged, nodded, which Cottonmouth took to mean "just go with it."

Cottonmouth turned to Othel, asked him and the boy to stay inside while Cottonmouth and Everett stepped outside to talk.

When they were standing in the mud-packed yard, Cottonmouth asked Everett what was going on.

"What's going on is we came down here expecting to find Beurie Tomlin to welcome us. Instead the boy there is cagey, says he's not sure we're welcome on account of the guest we brought, says he'll have to see. We ask after Beurie, and he says it'll be explained. Then you show up on the back step of this safe house, and I'm not sure anymore what's going on or who you are, other than you said you're Beurie Tomlin's kin."

Cottonmouth took some comfort in noticing the pistol was back in the man's belt. "You seem to be of a mind to be upset, to think you got that coming. But I'm the one gets a gun pulled on him."

"Just being careful."

"Pulling a gun on me is the opposite of careful," Cottonmouth said but added he could appreciate careful. "Trouble is you three showing up with the man in the burlap bag."

"Might take some explaining."

"Nothing else on my dance card," Cottonmouth said, waving his hands.

Everett asked could they get settled first. "Been a long couple days," he said, then paused. "Weeks. Years."

Cottonmouth said he knew what that was like.

Everett said they had been counting on Beurie's being there, said how he'd always been there, how they'd been there for each other the past few years.

Cottonmouth said, "Well, he ain't here." Asked was there anywhere else they could settle for the night.

Everett said there wasn't, unless they could stay in the house overnight.

"Figure that's even worse. Too much in the open," Cottonmouth said.

"Well, we don't want to get nabbed driving away from here," Everett said, which caused Cottonmouth to close his eyes, take a deep breath.

"Speaking of 'too much out in the open,'" he said, nodded for Everett to follow him back into the house. Cottonmouth shut the door behind them, looked around the room at the other men.

Everett leaned toward Cottonmouth, saying how they could pay a little extra.

"It ain't about that," Cottonmouth said, though the extra money did sound good. "I'm back here just a few weeks, and I'm not about to put all that at risk for men I don't know wanting to bring trouble."

Jimmy the Hook said they could just shoot the man and be done with it—the bank man then started shaking, trying to stand up until Jimmy elbowed him back down. Jimmy patted the man on the shoulder, said he was just kidding, said, "Can't you take a joke?" Then he nodded to the other men, winked, mimed shooting the man in the head.

Othel said to hang on a second, walked to Cottonmouth and Everett. "Excuse me," he said to Everett, then pulled Cottonmouth to the side so he could speak quietly with him. "Just thinking here, but you know Hillstrom?"

"The one staying at my camp a few hundred yards that way? I haven't forgotten him this quick."

"That's him. Word is he was the one kidnapped that businessman down in Monroe few months back."

"I know you're not suggesting we get into the kidnap business, not after you putting the fear of God into me about the Rudds."

"No, no," Othel said, looking back at the men with the banker. "But he can help these fellas figure out what to do. And if there's a little extra money in it for not much extra work, what's wrong with that?"

"So you're suggesting we get across the water, sit down, and work on a plan you're coming up with yourself?"

Othel said that wasn't what he was thinking at all. Said it was worth talking to Hillstrom about. "He may know how to deal with this quietly. Use his experience. There's men just across the water who have done just this sort of thing."

Something wasn't sitting right with Cottonmouth, but he didn't know what it was. Then he knew. "I need you or Hillstrom to start running things, I'll let you know."

Othel said that wasn't what he was getting at.

"I'll ferry us all across," Cottonmouth said, "if you'll just run the car into town. I can take it from here." He could tell Othel didn't like the idea of taking the car into town, doing the job the boy usually did. And he figured Othel wasn't too keen on his coming back to the county, stepping in where maybe Othel wanted someone else. Maybe Othel wanted things handled differently with the camp. This was all gnawing at the back of his head, a little voice telling him Othel wasn't happy with anything changing. The voice in the front of his head was telling him they'd all starve to death if he didn't change things around here. That was clear. But he had to keep the peace until he could figure out what to do. Cottonmouth asked if Othel could handle getting the car to town.

"Won't be a problem."

Cottonmouth turned his back, led the visitors toward the johnboat and the camp, settled the bagged man on the floor of the boat, worked his way across the bayou to camp.

Othel turned and walked the other way.

11

In town, Othel Walker nodded to the barman of the Culver Hotel.

"Evening, Earl," he said, easing up to the bar.

The youngest Withers boy, now a ripe fifty, nodded back. "Evening."

Othel asked was Fannie in, did Earl know, and Earl did know, so he nodded to Fannie herself, leaning up against the old upright—mostly upright—player piano along the wall, the piano standing now through luck and mulishness, and most townsfolk not even noticing something so broken, leaving the piano itself under no rush to fall to pieces just yet, each dent and gap, each scraggled piece of Cuban mahogany and Brazilian rosewood now some sort of taunt to the scientific, not to mention aesthetic, arguments of the universe.

Othel asked Fannie could she move from where she was leaning or would the piano miss her, and she said, "Let's find out." So they went upstairs to room 203, where they'd gone each Tuesday night for the past few months, Othel having been able to pick up a little extra money here and there lately.

Iva Lacewell, known semiprofessionally as Fannie, closed the door behind them and led Othel to the chair by the window. She'd learned to keep her dance card clear for these nights. She asked Othel if he'd like a drink, though she knew well enough he would like a drink, and so he said he would. She asked was whiskey fine, and he said it would get the job done. She pulled the stopper from a bottle on the dresser, dragged her finger along the inside of a tumbler to clear some of the dirt, and eased a long pour into the glass.

She walked the glass to the chair where he was sitting, and when she got close enough, he eased his right index finger along the outside of her left leg, covered now in a layer of skirt and slip, and she said, "Not so fast; give it time now," and handed him his drink.

She stood back a step as he drank, asked had he made any new friends, did he have any new stories to tell.

He said he'd met some men, thought they'd been in some trouble. "But ain't we all been in some trouble lately?" he asked, and she said that was right, that was sure right, what he'd said there, and she got up from sitting on the edge of the bed, slipped from her shoes, poured him another drink, sat back down on the edge of the bed, lifting her skirts up just a little bit—then, when he noticed, just a little bit more.

"Long as you stay clear of any trouble," she said. "Wouldn't want to have to visit you in jail."

He said not to worry about that. "This job, it's good steady work now. Never figured I'd be a chef, but ain't the world full of surprises?"

She said it was, a little surprised that Othel considered himself a chef, when she knew full well he spent his time at the Tomlin camp pouring drinks, sweeping floors, mending and tending the shitter, and sometimes cutting up vegetables for the stew. But only a little surprised, as she also knew he considered himself a skilled lover. But everybody had to have their eyes gauzed when they looked at themselves—otherwise you saw yourself as you were, you couldn't keep moving, she knew. She spent most of her time telling herself she was making it all right, after all. Telling herself she was doing what she had to do, just having to get through another rough patch to find some sort of eventual comfort. So if he wanted to call himself a chef when he scooped crap and cut potatoes, what did she care? He didn't call her a liar when she said she was happy.

"Not sure they're going to make it much longer down there at the camp," he said, "but they're doing their best, and at least I'm getting paid for now."

She said that was all you could hope for, and he said, "Well, do you want to get started?" And so they did.

~

Othel, who had taken to singing "Amazing Grace" when rutting in town, was working on his second time through the hymn, just starting the part about the flesh and heart failing when everything started falling apart.

"When flesh and heart shall fail," he sang, sliding loose from Fannie, his knee slipping on and off the back of her sweat-shined calf, before working his front parts to her back part again, finding his place. "And mortal life shall cease," he droned on, pounding away on the beat, easing up when it felt right. "I shall possess, within the veil." The iambic retreat and return, a hammering of footsteps outside, the creak and give of the bed frame, the whole of the world in perfect metrical harmony, sweat finding a path through his eyebrows and into his eyes, his hands wiping away, his body losing its balance, finding balance, finding rhythm, a resonance rarely duplicated, Othel reaching a life of joy and peace, when through the door a crowd suddenly came, as did he.

He turned back, dripping, to the door, pulled an often-stained pillow to his weeping crotch, got halfway through "What's the meaning of this?" when he noticed the Rudd sisters and Sheriff Monroe McCollum walking through the doorway.

"No, no," Henrietta said as Abigail walked to the dresser on the other side of the room and the sheriff shut the door behind them.

"Don't get up. We won't be staying long." Abigail set down the whiskey bottle she'd picked up, shrugged, walked back toward the door.

Fannie stepped from the bed, pulled her drawers back on, said, "He ain't even paid me yet."

Henrietta said not to worry. "This one's on me," she said, and Fannie said, "Well, thank you, ma'am," and finished dressing as Henrietta took a few steps toward Othel, who was sitting motionless on the edge of the bed behind the dampening pillow.

"Miss Rudd," he managed, nodding. "Sheriff. Miss Rudd."

"Othel," Henrietta said, "we heard that you were in town and just wanted to stop by to remind you of our arrangement."

He said he hadn't forgotten.

"Because it seems to me that our agreement—now correct me if I'm wrong—that our agreement called on you to stop by and pass along information whenever you were in town."

"I was on my way," he said, starting to stand, until Henrietta placed the end of her walking stick into the hollow atop his collarbone, and he sat back down.

Fannie asked could she go, and the sheriff opened the door for her.

When she'd gone, Henrietta said, "Sister, it appears we will be staying a little longer than I'd thought. Might as well have that drink now."

Othel looked to the sheriff, then to Abigail, back to Henrietta, and quickly to the floor.

Henrietta removed her gloves. "See, when you tell me you were on your way and I find you here otherwise engaged—well, you can understand my concern."

Othel said, "Yes, ma'am."

She nodded. "I dislike being lied to, you understand."

"Yes, ma'am."

"I dislike it more than I dislike violence," she said, tapping the metal knob of her walking stick against his right knee.

"Yes, ma'am."

Then she smiled and leaned closer to his ear. "I'm just playing with you," she said, and he seemed to loosen. She leaned across to his other ear. "I don't really dislike violence at all."

Othel's face shifted as Henrietta stepped back and said, "Monroe."

The sheriff took a deep breath, then stepped toward the softening man.

12

Cottonmouth Tomlin walked along the side of a disused cabin, the one farthest away, placed his hand on splintering wood. He looked across the swamped mud to the two cabins he and his uncle had gotten into shape years back—the long one with the cardplayers scheming and the other one with the banker tied up. And here he was working on the third cabin, as if bringing one more building back would solve the trouble—a couple of cabins for sleeping, one for eating, and one for storing things his uncle never could get rid of. He looked around him—the outhouses on the edges near the tree line, the paths through the dirt, stands still set up for the last animals that had been gutted and stripped years back, a refuge for hunters then, not the hunted.

The firepits, surrounded by leftover chunks of log benches, stacks of logs collapsing on themselves, stump logs for tables. A week back, the DeLurio men had headed out, leaving him and Othel there by themselves for a bit. They'd taken their banjo, thank god, and left behind enough payment to set up for whoever was coming next. Turned out it was the Blackstone boys, who had come in for a night, then raced off again. He hadn't been back long, and already he'd seen so many men stop by and go out again. *Ought to stay awhile,* he thought. Or maybe the money was better if they didn't stick around, if they just spent a night and moved on, like he used to do.

If he'd stuck around here, like his uncle had wanted, he would have known the DeLurio men, would have known Schuyler Blackstone and his men, would have known Everett and Beans and Jimmy the Hook. Now the DeLurio men rolled in, or the Blackstone boys stayed a night or two, settled up, and moved on. From hunting camp to way station, Cottonmouth simply the station attendant. A clerk. A bellhop. There had to be something more. He'd seen an empire carved out of the Honduran jungle by a Russian in New Orleans. He'd seen it himself. He looked around the camp to what had been carved out here, took a breath.

The one called Hyer walked across the mud to where Cottonmouth was replacing some rotting wood at the base of the cabin wall.

"Appreciate the hospitality," Hyer said, handing Cottonmouth some money. "Figured that's what we still owed you."

Cottonmouth pocketed the money. "You boys heading out now?"

Hyer said he was, looked a little uncertainly at Cottonmouth, then the pocket with the money. "Usually hand that money to Othel. He counts it, makes sure it's all there."

Cottonmouth asked was it all there.

Hyer said it was.

"Then what do I need to count it for?"

"Wasn't sure you trusted me," Hyer said.

"There a reason I shouldn't?" Cottonmouth squinted, the sun coming up a little more just now, stabbing light through the pine needles, the taller cypress.

"No, no. Course not." He looked back to the main cabin. "Ask you a question?"

Cottonmouth said sure.

"Fellas what came in here last night. Saw a couple of them at breakfast. Talked to them a little about a guest they brought."

"Yeah. Bit of a surprise to me."

"Just didn't know," Hyer started again, "if things had changed. Hillstrom, he does work like that. And there's another man down toward Shreveport. Looks like good business is all. Didn't know if this was that kind of place. Times being what they are."

Cottonmouth said nothing had changed, said whatever people did out there was their business. He asked how long Hyer had been coming to the camp.

"Couple years now, I guess. Came here first with my brother-in-law."

Cottonmouth asked was he liking it all right, if he'd had a good stay.

"Good enough," Hyer said.

Cottonmouth said he was glad to hear that, asked were they ready to get ferried across.

"I'll go round the fellas up," he said and headed back to get Hillstrom and Drunk Eddie.

~

After Hyer had gone, Cottonmouth looked around again at the camp, knew it could be much more, could be a meeting place for John Dillinger's gang or Creepy Karpis. He knew "good enough" left room for improvement. Bonnie and Clyde had been just down the road near Waldo not that long ago, after all. Get the word around. Some coded mention in *Black Mask* magazine. Why not right here, on this ground? After all, his uncle had had that in mind a few years back, taking over the hunting camp to make it into this. And for what? To set it up as nothing more than a way station? A poor man's Culver Hotel? And what would be wrong with that? No reason you had to aim for the Biltmore. Cottonmouth wiped his forehead with his sleeve, the June sunlight finding its way through the oak and pine and cypress around him. But who cared about the Biltmore? Why not the Culver Hotel? A steady barman. Card tables. Good beds. Modern toilets and kitchen. Not a thing wrong with just settling in.

Get some names here, he thought. *Word of mouth.* Hadn't Edna Murray, the Kissing Bandit herself, stayed here with Volney Davis just last year, his uncle had written him? Pictures of the famous could line the walls of the big house. When he had been in Tegucigalpa, hadn't there been a sign saying that Froylán Turcios had slept there? And one for O. Henry? Or was that New Orleans? And when his uncle had taken him to Muskogee a few years back, didn't one of the banks have a sign saying it had been robbed by Matthew Kimes and Ray Terrill? Let it be known that this was the place—not just a safe place, not just a refuge, but a place you could come and plan, a place you could come and gamble. A place that had a history of that, had standing.

The gambling clubs and poker rooms he'd enjoyed down in New Orleans did well taking a cut, didn't they? He nodded to himself, just thinking of it, sizing up the amount of land he'd need. Over on the far side, there was that fickle makeshift path his uncle had gotten the Rambler stuck in years back trying to roll into the hunting camp in style, impress old Colonel Gwynn from Texarkana, Uncle Beurie and Cottonmouth's father thinking Texarkana politicians were the high-class clientele to attract. Much of the Rambler was still there, he knew, if he'd bother to check under the overgrowth for the rusted chassis and flake-dry tires. His uncle had said, "Well, every idea's a good one until you try it," and maybe that was the first time he'd said that. It wasn't the last.

Cottonmouth walked inside the farthest cabin now, looked at what it would take to bring it back. If he'd been here the past few years, he could have already brought it back, could have helped bring all this back. But if he'd stayed, he'd be just as clueless as the men at Moon's store he'd wiped out—well, wiped out what little they had at the poker table.

Instead of staying, he had drifted down to New Orleans after the Rohrbacher killing in Camden that hadn't been his fault, had found safety with Silver Dollar Sam's family, until that had gone south, and Cottonmouth had gone too. South to Honduras, until he'd come back. If he'd stayed there, toughed it out working for Zemurray's men, he could have had his own place by now, or at least a piece of one. Though he'd done some things there, made choices he'd just as soon get away from. But so had so many of the men down there. You just did what you had to do. Maybe he would have lasted down there. Maybe not.

If he hadn't come back for the camp, he'd likely have been back soon enough. Or run somewhere else, he knew. If he'd fought through the troubles he'd come up against the past dozen years instead of running from them, maybe he'd be the one planning jobs. But running to Camden. Then New Orleans. Then Honduras. And now back here, back home. He'd left New Orleans for Honduras with a change of clothes and hope in the future. He'd come back with just a change of clothes. Better clothes, it was true, but not by much.

He could move on now, sure. Sell whatever stake he had left in the land here or let the lenders take it back, then leave well enough alone. Head out to Texas. Head back to somewhere else he'd been. He could always move on. There was nothing holding a soul back what wanted to go, what needed to go on. To move.

Sure, maybe he could have ended up with a piece of something in Honduras or wound up being a part of something in New Orleans. But what good was a life made up of pieces and parts? Men like Banana Man Sam Zemurray, they weren't just part of something bigger. Zemurray was the something bigger.

If Cottonmouth did stay here, working to make this camp the something bigger, first thing he'd have to do was get rid of that banker. That morning he'd tried to impress on Everett and those men the danger they were bringing in, and maybe it had made an impression. They'd said they'd grabbed the man on the spur of the moment, and that seemed likely.

Or he could just take off again. Let Othel deal with it.

Silver Dollar Sam down in New Orleans was soon to be home from a couple of years locked up. Maybe someone would give him another chance. He told himself he'd been good at moving guns from one place to another, hadn't he? Had it in his sights to make good money one day at it? And another Sam in New Orleans, Sam Zemurray, running Honduras from that castle in New Orleans until, Cottonmouth had read somewhere, selling off and retiring, digging in even deeper back home with a plantation. He had worked for them and maybe could again. Or maybe people could work for him now. Maybe if he were set up with something to start with, he thought. Why them and not Cottonmouth? Because they'd dug in, he knew. Because they'd made it work where they were, instead of running at the first sign of trouble. Cogs turning in the machine. Instead of letting themselves get pushed from one place to another, a cracked oak leaf on a wind someone else was blowing.

He drew his hand along the doorframe. The hinge on the cabin door had gone, rusted tight, then shaken loose. Once hard to seal shut, now swinging loose, unfitting. Broken but repairable. Screws dangling loose. Grooves, once a solid descent into a frame, now rotting away as each screw hole fell in on itself, collapsed into damp fragments, the frame consuming itself by shards, slight pieces separating, decaying, falling farther away into dust, each groove nicked apart into crumbles. Finding the weak points and building from strength. He would have to focus, he knew, to make this work.

Get rid of that banker now. Cottonmouth had come out here to cool off after losing his temper in there with those men, arguing about the banker. They'd said they hadn't been thinking, and that much was clear.

He sleeved loose the sweat-caked dirt from his brow, walked to the edge of the cut yard, footsteps silent on the packed mud, pissed against the base of an oak. He walked back to the cabin, took the hinges from the frame, laid the door on its side against the outside wall. The wood in the frame had been splintering, perhaps for years, each hinge covering the damage. He reached down to the box at his feet, moved the claw hammer, the razor, the box of nails. Eased fingertips beneath to the rough sheet, pulled loose the sandpaper. He brushed his thumb against the jagged inside of the upper part of the frame, flicked a splinter until it loosed, picked it free.

There was a line from Sunday school he'd been thinking about. Miss Mattie's class. She'd talked about hiding your talent away—talent being money. It was coming back to him, the way things did when there was a parallel, a reminder of something that tied the now to the then. Connected. His uncle gone now. In the Bible story, a man had gone away and left each of his three servants with a talent. One had wasted it, one had invested it, and one had hidden it away so he wouldn't lose it. You were supposed to do something with it, Cottonmouth remembered. That was the lesson. Don't hide it away for safety's sake. You have to use your talent, to take your chances. And when the man came back, he scolded the one who had buried his talent in the yard.

He looked back to the main cabin, to where the johnboat was pulled up onto the land. One of the men was standing there, waiting for the other two.

Cottonmouth worked the sandpaper back and forth, first in stutters against the grain, roughing the wood, working loose what he could, then smooth with the grain until he'd worked solid a spot, an evenness. He knelt, touched the damage, and then worked another smoothness into the frame.

This, he could manage. This door. This bit here. And this being the test. His uncle leaving him this camp, to see what he'd do with his talent. Any moron could keep things the same, he figured. Would Silver Dollar Sam or Sam Zemurray in New Orleans just let things stand, hope to keep everything the same? Give a man five dollars to go to the horse track or a card game, and if he comes back with five dollars, well, what good is he? You could have put the money under a rock and had the same result. Maybe the answer was taking a chance. Finding your chance and taking it.

If they were cheating so openly at the Culver Hotel and in the back room at Moon's store, then maybe this place was to be the home of honest play. Like he had been saying to the one called Hyer earlier, if you wanted to live outside the law, you had to be honest about it. They'd cheat you as sure as look at you, but you had to look out for yourself. That was all you can count on, after all. That was what his mother had taught him, what his father had taught him. *Goodbye, Mom. Goodbye, Dad. Don't worry about me. I'll be fine on my own.*

He packed up the toolbox, looked back at the door to the cabin. *That'll do. One day soon, we'll have people in this cabin. We'll have people in a new cabin. Maybe we'll get that old road back open so we don't have to float people in. I'll take care of all this,* he thought. *Word will spread. Soon enough, we'll have new, important faces here, and we'll be making some money. You couldn't get Colonel Gwynn and his cronies here, but I'll do you even better than that.*

He got everything together as the three men gathered near the johnboat, and he walked back toward the main cabin. He watched as Othel walked from the edge of the woods to help load the men onto the johnboat.

Well, I'll be damned, Cottonmouth thought. *He must have snuck in while I wasn't looking.* He watched as one of the men shifted, and Cottonmouth could see the bagged banker being loaded onto the boat, Hillstrom, Hyer, and Drunk Eddie close to him. *Well, I'll be double-dog damned. They're taking the banker with them. Problem solved.* Cottonmouth walked a little faster to the main cabin, ready to find out who he owed a drink to.

13

"So you just let him go?" Cottonmouth asked, walking into the main cabin, where Jimmy and Everett were cleaning their guns, Beans napping in the corner.

Everett explained they'd come to a financial arrangement. Made more sense.

Cottonmouth said that sounded like a smart move.

"We brought him here, and like I said, we weren't thinking," Everett said. "We said we'd see him on his way. Made a little money out of it."

Cottonmouth asked was that right.

"Not as much as if we'd held him here, set up the ransom, the exchange. Now Hyer and Hillstrom have to take care of all that."

"And where's he holding him?"

"Didn't ask for too many particulars," Everett said. "Wasn't much of my business after he paid for the banker."

Cottonmouth asked did the man know what he was doing.

"He was kind enough to walk me through how he'd handled a man from Monroe earlier this year," Everett said.

Jimmy laughed. "See? Talk to the man for ten minutes, and you learn more than a year of reading them college textbooks."

Cottonmouth sat down at a table next to theirs. "So he took the banker you snatched, paid you for the snatching, and he's going to ransom the man off, back up in Hazelton?"

"That seemed to be his plan," Everett said. "We got something like a finder's fee. And it turns out he knows of a fishing cabin in the woods around Umpire. That's as specific as he got, which is fine by me." Everett set a Colt on the table, picked up a brush, worked clean the barrel. "So it really doesn't have to be banks. Or filling stations."

Cottonmouth said of course not, said there were plenty of ways to make money outside of banks, but kidnapping was bringing trouble where it didn't need to be. "Do a job out there," he said, nodding toward the woods, "and bring the money in. Just leave the job itself out there, not tied up and gagged in a cabin here, even just overnight. Johnny Law comes walking in here, we're just a bunch of nuns at church."

"Remember the Denver Mint job?" Everett asked him.

Cottonmouth squinted, said maybe, then asked when was that.

"Decade back," Everett said.

Beans had been stirring the past few minutes, all the talk waking him, and said, "King Tut." Everyone looked his way. "Remember? Right around the time that British guy found King Tut. Pyramids. Egypt."

They all said OK.

"Remember?" Beans asked again. "Man named Carter. Was in all the papers. Then the Denver thing was in all the papers."

They all nodded. Something was always in the papers. Grave robbing. Bank robbing.

"So ten years back," Cottonmouth said, trying to get them back to the point. "Denver Mint."

Jimmy was remembering now too. "Two hundred thousand they got away with. All five-dollar bills, wasn't it? Left half of someone's face behind was all. Wasn't that Bailey?"

"Harvey Bailey, yeah," Everett said. "Never got him for that one. Got him for something, can't remember."

"Funny you bring up the Denver job," Jimmy said. "Bailey broke out on Thursday or Friday. Dallas. He's up in Tulsa now. Maybe Joplin. You should spend more time reading the newspapers and less time with those textbooks of yours."

Everett lifted the pistol, moved it around, inspecting. "Who broke him out?"

"Paper said it was three unidentified individuals. Figure it was Stumpy and those boys. The twins from Frontenac."

"Next time you see something like that in the papers, you let me know?"

"What for?" Jimmy asked. "Thought you were leaving all this soon as you could. You and your business degree. Thought you were getting out soon as you could."

Everett set down the pistol he'd been cleaning, sighed. "This again?"

Jimmy kept his eyes on the little boxes he was filling with bullets, though they were all filled by now.

Beans looked back and forth from Jimmy to Everett. Maybe Everett was close to changing his mind. Sure, the bank robbing had gotten tougher, but maybe they could do something else, something where Everett didn't leave.

Cottonmouth broke in. "Denver Mint. You were saying about the Denver Mint." He was hoping to get them off this kidnapping idea, back to hitting banks and filling stations and, sure, federal mints. Why not? Had to be one around here, he figured. Little Rock. Dallas.

Everett said to hold on for a minute. "Forget the mint for a minute. That might be a good business, come to think of it—breaking people like Harvey out. Get busted after a bank robbery, figure there's still some money around the cops haven't picked up."

Jimmy shook his head. "I don't know about getting that close to a prison these days. I'm not that interested in seeing Eastham again, if it's all the same to you."

Everett said he had a point there. Sure did. Said to forget it, then.

"And they never did find all the money from Denver, you know," Jimmy said.

"Right," Everett said, picking the Denver Mint idea back up. "That's the point I was getting at. Doesn't have to be banks. Could be anywhere there's money."

Christ, Cottonmouth thought. *These men. Can't hold one idea to the next.* The Banana Man. That was what Cottonmouth remembered about him. Focus. If he had an idea, he worked through it. Of course, he was just one man. How could Cottonmouth get these men to give up the idea of kidnapping, of bringing trouble to his camp? How could they get more money? Meaning how could he end up with more money? What would the Banana Man do with the camp?

Jimmy was nodding at what Everett had said about anywhere there was money. "The banks get their money from the mints, or some of it. And then what do they do with it? Think about it. Follow the money. It leaves that bank, and they give a hunk of it to Smithland Lumber Company or US Steel or whoever has to pay their workers."

Everett saw where he was going but wasn't having it. "Hit a payroll office? Taking people's pay? Never liked that."

"Why not? Fewer guns. It's just people waiting to get paid."

Cottonmouth jumped in. "I see what Everett's saying. Man works all week cutting the heads off chickens and comes in at the end of the week to get paid, and you want to take that from him?"

Jimmy nodded to them. "Oh, that's a good point."

Everett stood, slid the pistol into his coat pocket. "You take from a bank, the bank has more money. You hit a place on payday, people don't get paid."

"You think Rockefeller can't find more money to pay the boys at Standard Oil?" Jimmy asked, following Everett to the card table.

"Of course he can. Which is why you go right to him."

Cottonmouth found himself nodding along, took a seat at the card table, making a third.

Jimmy dragged the back of his thumb across his bottom lip, gave it some thought. "No chance I'm picking the pocket of John D. Rockefeller."

"Wasn't suggesting that," Everett said, pulling a pack of cards from another coat pocket.

Everett worked the cards as Beans stood, stretched, sat down to join them.

Jimmy asked what was he saying, then. Asked was there some secret in his college textbooks he wanted to share with the rest of the class.

Everett said there was no secret, dealt cards to the four of them.

"You planning one last big score before you go straight with all that book learning?" Jimmy asked.

Everett chuckled, said he'd seen enough of the "one last job" men get shot to hell or burned alive. "That's not a story I want any part in," he said. "And the book learning, well, that's slow going. We have to eat now, don't we? Like you said, you can learn more from talking to someone sometimes. And banks aren't what they used to be is all I was saying a minute ago. Options. We need options. And sure, maybe some of that is in the books I've been reading. Diversify. What with goddamn Roosevelt taking away all our gold. Look around you here. Men wake up with an oil well in their backyard; next thing you know, they own the county."

Jimmy said wasn't that the next county over.

"Union County," Beans said, helping.

Cottonmouth said that was right, said he was here to see it. Union County. El Dorado. "Took the town from five thousand people to twenty-five thousand overnight. Two dozen trains a day. People, money, in and out. Next county over." Cottonmouth shook his head. "Always the next county over."

"Well," Everett said, "Roosevelt can take their gold, but they're still pulling oil out of the ground."

Jimmy said he wasn't interested in digging an oil well. Or drilling. Whatever they did.

"Neither am I," Everett said. "But you heard what Alabama Bobby was saying last week when we were in Kansas? What he was saying about the bank up in Saint Louis. Where they gave all the tellers .22 pistols and said to shoot any bank robber in the face."

Beans agreed that getting shot in the face didn't sound appealing.

Jimmy turned to Cottonmouth. "You know Lucky Lefty Malone?"

Cottonmouth said he didn't. They really couldn't stick to one idea, could they? One plan?

"Works out of Frontenac, up in Kansas."

Cottonmouth said he knew a Lou Malone from there, few years back, asked were they related.

"No, that's him. Was robbing a bank in Oklahoma. McAlester, I think. Teller shot him through his right hand. Took a couple fingers right off. Black Francis was with him, put the fingers in his pocket. Didn't matter. Good as gone. Got seventy-three dollars out of the bank and lost his right hand. Now they call him Lucky Lefty instead of Lou."

Cottonmouth asked why they called him Lucky.

"Because he's left handed," Jimmy said.

Cottonmouth nodded. "Well, he is now."

"Just shows we have to do something," Everett said. "I don't want to get shot in the face or the hand, if I can help it, and I don't want to run over any more goats."

"Banks. Gold. Oil," Jimmy said. "Has to be something for the taking."

"We'll find it," Everett said. "We have to."

14

After they'd cleaned up the breakfast and the men had gone back to their own cabins, Cottonmouth Tomlin led Othel Walker through to one of the storage cabins.

"You sure you ought to be walking around?" Cottonmouth asked, nodding toward Othel's new limp.

"Just a little drunken brawl," Othel lied. "Sore knee and some bruised ribs." He didn't mention the wrist the sheriff had put a little too much pressure on. Truth was he should have come to the Rudd sisters as soon as he'd gotten into town, but there hadn't been much to tell, other than there wasn't much to tell them. But he'd sure told the sheriff everything he'd wanted to hear and a few things he hadn't. And what now? He'd never thought the nephew would come back from South America or wherever it had been. And maybe he should have gone straight to the sisters when he'd gone to town instead of going to see Fannie. But now they knew. And maybe they thought they couldn't trust him, either, what with the not going right to them. Why hadn't he? That was what he'd like to know. He should have, and maybe they would have said Cottonmouth had broken the peace. Could he trust them to keep their word? They kept hinting that he himself would do a good job running the camp. But now the nephew was here. And sure, when Cottonmouth's uncle Beurie had been running things, Othel might have given the Rudd sisters some answers to questions they had been asking. But never anything that could put Beurie and the camp in real trouble. In the back of his mind, Othel had just been hoping someday the Rudd sisters or Beurie or someone would see how he deserved to take over the camp. But maybe that time had gone. Maybe he should tell Cottonmouth right now, say how the Rudds were waiting for him to slip up, to use it to get him locked up or run out of town for good. But Othel knew they probably could have already done that had they wanted to, could have found some reason to keep Cottonmouth from taking what was his by family, what should have been Othel's by . . . by what? By hard work? Loyalty to Cottonmouth's uncle? Or loyalty to the Rudds? What had any of that gotten him? A house on the edge of the swamp to hold bank robbers and thieves until it was time to ferry them through the cypress trees and hanging moss to this godforsaken spit of land? A wife living with her mother over in Texarkana, likely seeing that man from Bradley she couldn't stay away from. And here he was, working here for the nephew of a good man, the nephew who'd come back with ideas about how things should be done. Lord save them all from big ideas.

"Don't go getting yourself killed," Cottonmouth said, wondering if maybe Othel had gone off looking for trouble, being upset with Cottonmouth bossing him around.

Othel said he'd try his best.

Cottonmouth said to hope their best was good enough. "We've got, I don't know, a couple months' worth of money. That seem right?"

Othel said things would turn around. "Rains always come."

"Can't count on that," Cottonmouth said. "Not with Roosevelt up there and all the gold being taken away and all the banks shutting down."

"Never saw much gold to begin with—not around here," Othel said.

"Lot less than there used to be."

"Maybe Roosevelt just wants us tied to the paper money, government money."

"Well, that's what we need now," Cottonmouth said. "And there oughta be plenty of paper money moving through here," he said, looking out toward the woods. "From Texarkana. Shreveport. Dallas. City money."

Othel said something would come along. "Maybe folks don't know we're still open for business, with your uncle gone. Maybe we need to do a better job getting the word out."

Cottonmouth said he wasn't worried about words, said no one ever made a good living from words. "Might be time to think about something a little closer to home. Reckon we're making it too hard on ourselves, not taking what's close and available to us. Low-hanging fruit."

"Not a good idea," Othel said. "The law will be all over us. That's what your uncle was worried about. Something close to home like that could shut this place down."

"We don't get any money through here, won't be anything left to shut down."

Othel said changing the way things were done just wasn't an option, said Cottonmouth's uncle would never have allowed that. "Rules you have to follow you want to live outside the law. That's what your uncle used to say." Othel rubbed his bad knee with his good hand.

"Well, he ain't here, is he?" Cottonmouth opened the door to the storage cabin. "This here is what I wanted to show you," he said, moving some boxes of empty bottles, pulling the blanket off some other boxes. He nodded to the boxes that had been covered with a blanket, a couple of spaces that were clear of dust, where boxes had been. "What can you tell me about this? My uncle in the middle of something?"

"We moved some merchandise through here few months back, gave the place a little money, coupled with what he could borrow from town."

Cottonmouth asked what used to be there, pointing to the empty spots.

"Crates of Brownings, couple Lewis guns, some Colts. Maybe some others. Your uncle came across them from a fellow doing work at Barksdale Field, down at Shreveport."

"Might make sense to restock the supply? Work with the men I knew in New Orleans. We've got the room here. The big cabin, the three smaller ones for sleeping. The couple for storing things." He looked out the window.

Othel ran his tongue around the teeth he had left. "Putting a storehouse of guns in the middle of this place?"

Cottonmouth nodded slowly. "Not sure about having the Charlie Fraziers and Alvin Karpises of the world walking around that kind of inventory, now that I'm thinking of it."

Othel said he was pretty sure there were easier ways to make money. "Your uncle ended up not getting as much for the guns as he'd hoped."

"Maybe we end up able to make more money for the guns than we can off a man who just held up a filling station."

Othel said he might want to check with the sheriff, see was that allowed.

"That what my uncle would have done?"

Othel didn't have an answer.

"So Uncle Beurie got rid of the guns, but what's left in those far crates?"

"Far crates?" Othel asked, then turned to look and nodded. "You remember Billy the Boxman out of Shongaloo?"

Cottonmouth said he didn't.

"The Nesbits' boy moved down there. Married a woman out of Haynesville. Face like a Boston terrier lost a fight with a gravel road. Billy's their oldest."

Cottonmouth said all right.

"Asked could your uncle get him some boom sticks. That's what he called it. Boom sticks. Kid's a goddamn comedian." Othel laughed just a little bit, then rubbed his sore ribs. "Said he needed them for cracking open a couple safes that had come into his possession. Anyway, your uncle and I get him some explosives off a railroad man, had to take more than we needed because it was all-or-nothing kind of thing, but next thing you know, kid gets himself in a heap of trouble around Denton, Texas, lands himself in Eastham for God knows how long, and we're sitting on enough dynamite to take out half the county and no way to collect."

Cottonmouth nodded. They left the cabin, locking the door behind them. "That just proves what I've been saying," Cottonmouth said. "Find ways to get more money out of these guys. Guess we raise the rates."

"Your uncle tried that a while back. Didn't go well. Got Campbell's place down the road a piece. The Gramm place too."

"Competition," Cottonmouth said.

Othel nodded. Competition.

"I'm no banker, but either we get more money from each person, or we get more people. From what you've been telling me since I got here, we're getting fewer and fewer people than used to come through here."

"Your uncle just wanted a solid place," Othel said.

Cottonmouth stopped, set his jaw, and turned. "I appreciate your taking care of things with my uncle and making sure to tell me what he thought and what he wanted. I'm here now, and now I appreciate your help with things. But whatever my uncle did or didn't want, there are things that can get done. There's opportunity. Dumber men than me have made more with less. We've just got to reach out and grab it."

Othel nodded. "Your uncle just didn't want to do anything that would bring the Rudds or the sheriff down on us is all."

"Speaking of that," Cottonmouth said, "weren't you supposed to be meeting with the sheriff at Miss Phoebe's today?"

Othel said he was about to head over there when he and Cottonmouth were done.

Cottonmouth said he'd take care of that from now on. "I'll start to take care of more things. You just make sure the stewpot is full."

15

Cottonmouth looked at the other diners in the restaurant, at the tables he'd sat at, propped up in a chair, as a boy, with his mother and father. *What was it now?* he wondered. *Couple decades back?* Must have been. He'd eat platesful of rice with sugar and butter, meal after meal, his mom and dad holding hands across the table. But that had been a long time ago.

The sheriff told Miss Phoebe he'd have a piece of pie.

She read from the board at the other end of the restaurant. "Rhubarb. Lemon. Chocolate. What'll you have?"

"Let's start with the lemon," the sheriff said.

"Start? You started with the rhubarb not two hours ago. I think you mean 'continue with the lemon,'" she said, then asked Cottonmouth what he wanted.

"I'm sure it's all good. I'll start with whatever you need to get rid of."

She walked off, brought them some coffee, walked off again.

"Like I was saying," the sheriff said, "I know you did army work down there, but you know I was in the war too."

"Different war," Cottonmouth told him. "I was in Honduras. Little battles. No war."

"Well, I got to see France. In the springtime. Bombs in the air and corpses on the ground." He shook his head. "Got hit in the face one time near a town called Sedan, like the car. Me and a couple boys from Liverpool—that's in England—we were walking up and down some canal. All of a sudden this tree limb hits me in the face. I mean, I thought it was a tree limb. Look down—it's a leg. Pants. Boot. A leg. Then we hear this explosion, and next thing I know, I'm in a hospital bed in a room with three dozen other soldiers. You ever see any combat like that?"

"Can't say I've seen anything like that."

The sheriff took a sip of his coffee. "Well, at least I get to say I saw France in the springtime."

Miss Phoebe slid their plates in front of them, walked on to another table, making it a point to show that she was most certainly not eavesdropping at all. No, sir.

The sheriff said to Cottonmouth how he was sorry about Cottonmouth's uncle, always liked the man, got along fine, county needed more good men like that, and so on.

Cottonmouth said he appreciated that, said the world did need more men like his uncle.

After what seemed to the sheriff like a reasonable pause for respecting the dead, he said that Othel usually met him, said he hoped everything was all right.

"Now that you mention it," Cottonmouth said, "he did seem a little sore when I saw him."

"Nothing serious, I hope."

"Didn't seem to be. Said he ran into a little trouble in town."

"That so?" the sheriff asked, wondering if Othel had told Cottonmouth anything.

Cottonmouth shrugged, slurped his coffee. "Bound to happen. Times being what they are. Besides, figure it's best that I meet with you instead, seeing as how it's my family's place."

"So you're back and now the proud owner of the camp for wayward boys?"

Cottonmouth said it was something like that. "You and Othel, and I guess further back you and my uncle, y'all would just have pie and talk about who was coming and who was going from the camp? That's how it was explained to me."

"That's about it. Anything going on I need to know about, well, now would be a good time to know it."

"And same for my side, right? Anything I need to know about—anything out here what might threaten the camp or the people there?"

"My side? There's no sides here. We're all one community here." The sheriff finished off the pie he'd been nibbling on. "One happy family."

Cottonmouth took a bite of the chocolate pie in front of him, picked up a loose flake of crust from the table, watched as a little pressure from his fingers broke it into a thousand pieces, each piece falling away into dust, the dust falling away into nothing. "And is there anything I need to know, you know, speaking as a member of the community here?"

"Now that you mention it, some men from up in Hazelton would like for me to gather up some of your guests and ship them up the road to them."

"Hazelton?"

"Oh, I'm sure you've heard of it," the sheriff said. "Nice little town just a little to our north. Known for their watermelons. Had a little trouble at the bank few days back."

Cottonmouth said "Oh, that Hazelton" and added how he did, in fact, enjoy their watermelons.

The sheriff figured the men in question had made it to the Tomlin camp but couldn't be sure. Othel hadn't mentioned it during their little chat, but maybe they had yet to arrive. Or maybe the sheriff hadn't used enough vigor in the asking. Strong-arming people for the Rudds was getting less and less appealing, but that was a thought he could dwell on later. The sheriff asked had Cottonmouth seen any men fitting that description.

"What description was that?"

"Criminals. Hazelton."

"I haven't seen any men who have broken any laws in our county, Sheriff. I can assure you of that." Cottonmouth drained his coffee, nodded a smile toward Miss Phoebe, who walked right over and refilled his cup. "And how much did these men in question make off with?"

The sheriff said he hadn't heard, then added "But speaking of money" and raised his eyebrows.

Cottonmouth slid a folded copy of the *Banner-News* across the table to the sheriff, through drips of coffee, detritus of pie. "I believe there's a little good news in the paper worth looking at."

"I like to see good news for a change," the sheriff said, sliding the money out of the paper, holding it below the table, and counting. "Seems like there's not much good news in the paper after all."

Cottonmouth said it had been a slow news week.

The sheriff cleared his throat, shook his head. "So it seems. Few more weeks like this, I'm not sure anyone is going to be too interested in keeping up with this paper. Might not be worth the trouble."

Cottonmouth said to not worry about it, said there wouldn't be any trouble.

"Needs to be enough trouble to give the paper some heft," the sheriff said. "But not so much that it, well," he said, losing the idea.

Cottonmouth said he understood. "A paper that has enough good news for our community, even though there's a rash of bad news in the other counties."

"That sounds about right," the sheriff said.

"Have to give your employers what they want," Cottonmouth said.

"Keep the citizens of the county happy," the sheriff agreed.

Cottonmouth stood. "I meant the Rudd sisters."

~

Cottonmouth pushed the pirogue to the edge of the water. The Dorcheat's water eased toward the land in soft suggestion as he pulled in, then lifted the shallow boat, set down the bag, flipped the pirogue to drain the water.

Two of the Catahoula curs his uncle had brought in ran across to greet him. He called the white one with black markings Romulus, which left the black with white being Remus, though he'd switch back and forth, as the pair was never separated, so it hardly mattered. He pulled two strips of dried meat he'd brought from Moon's, passed one to each dog, said "Off you go now," and walked on to the main cabin.

"Did you bring the paper?" Beans asked as Cottonmouth stepped through the door.

Cottonmouth tossed him the *Texarkana Gazette*, the pages opening, fluttering like an inebriated condor falling from flight.

Beans unfolded the paper, scanned the front page for the latest Ray Hamilton update. "They convicted Ray again."

"For the Bucher killing?" Jimmy asked.

"Yeah. Last year in Texas. Been more than a year ago by now, figure."

"He with Clyde on that one?"

"Naw. The Clause boy."

"Santa?"

"Frank."

"If you say so. I can't keep track of these no more."

"You and me both, pal."

"What are you two hens squawking about?" Everett asked.

"The Ray Hamilton trial."

Everett pulled for the front page. "How many times can they give one little man the chair?"

"He gets one more, he'll have a whole dining room suite," Jimmy joked.

Everett read through the story as quickly as he could. "He still with that O'Dare woman?"

"Long as her old man is still in prison, yeah."

Beans tapped his chin. "Born in 1914. Makes him, what, nineteen?"

Jimmy shook his head. "Lord, I got hemorrhoids older than that."

"Everything go OK with that banker?" Cottonmouth asked.

Everett found the story. "Looks like they got twenty grand for him."

"Christ on a cracker," Cottonmouth said. "That worked out well. And quick."

"Those guys know what they're doing," Everett said.

"Twenty grand," Cottonmouth repeated, looking around the mostly empty cabin.

Beans looked up from the funnies, asked, "What now?"

"Dinner, I reckon," Cottonmouth said.

Beans said all right, but he'd meant what about a job.

"What job?" Cottonmouth asked.

Everett looked up from his cards. "We all were thinking, while you were out, how your uncle would sometimes hear of things, work to do, and pass that on to us. Now that the banker's gone, the question is what's next."

"Something to think about after dinner," Cottonmouth said.

"What are we having?" Beans asked.

Cottonmouth said he'd brought back some pork and some cabbage.

"Pork *and* cabbage?" Jimmy mocked. "Is Mr. Rockefeller coming over?"

Everyone laughed except Cottonmouth, who went into the kitchen to pull the skillets from cabinets and help Othel with the cooking.

~

When he was done and each man had food on his plate, Cottonmouth asked if anyone knew how much bankers usually went for. Was twenty grand normal?

Beans said twenty grand was a lot of cabbage.

They all laughed, and Beans looked around to find the joke.

"Cabbage," Everett whispered, pointing to his plate, and Beans laughed along with them, though just a little too late.

"They got more than that for that man down around Monroe," Jimmy said.

Cottonmouth set down his glass. "And all they did was set a man somewhere for a few days and take him back."

Jimmy said, "When you think about it, all they did was borrow something and return it."

Cottonmouth said, "Twenty grand. Or more. How much room does that take up?"

"You'd need a suitcase, wouldn't you?" Jimmy asked, and they all said that sounded right.

"And a banker," Beans said.

"Another banker," Jimmy said. "We just let ours go." He looked at Cottonmouth.

"Or a banker's kid," Everett said. "That's what people are doing. People can get more for a kid. It's one of the things Hyer was saying."

Cottonmouth said to tell him.

"You grab the Lindbergh baby, only older. One you don't have to take care of, seeing as how none of us wants to change diapers."

They all nodded in agreement.

"Baltimore," Everett said. "They got this ice cream man's college boy. Kid was on his way home from a dance. Stashed him in a cottage out in the county, but they got scared, let the kid go."

Jimmy said he remembered that, asked, "Didn't they get some painter up in New York for it?"

"That was just some idiot who heard about it, thought he could make some money pretending to be the kidnappers."

"What?" Jimmy asked. "The nerve of some people. Lie about something like that. That ain't right."

Othel Walker stepped from the kitchen to ask what was the world coming to, and they all said they didn't know.

Cottonmouth asked about the real kidnappers. "They caught them?"

Everett said they did. "Was in the papers last month. Kid recognized where they took him, figured out how to identify one of the men. That's why you use a blindfold or some goggles, drive him around in circles, take him someplace quiet."

"So grab a college boy?" Jimmy said. "Aren't they likely to put up a fight?"

Cottonmouth said that was a good point.

"But grab the son," Everett said, "and Mom and Dad are going to want him back. They'll pay more. Grab the banker—maybe the wife doesn't want him back."

"That's a good point too," Cottonmouth said.

Everett said, "Wait a second. Are we discussing hypotheticals?"

Jimmy said he sure hoped not.

"Make-believe," Everett explained, then turned to Cottonmouth. "Is this just talk, or is this something we're doing?"

Cottonmouth said he didn't know any bankers or bankers' sons. "Haven't been back long enough to be invited to any fancy parties," he joked.

Everett said he didn't know any, either, though they could start looking. "We could ask around, but that just puts us in more danger of people finding out it was us."

"In case anyone was wondering," Cottonmouth said, "it has to be outside this county."

Everett said not to worry; that was a given. "We understand the rules."

Othel Walker asked did it have to be a banker.

The other men looked at each other, shrugged. "Just what got caught in our heads," Everett said.

Cottonmouth asked did he have someone in mind.

"You know the Stoneciphers over in Union County?" Othel asked.

"Not going near a Stonecipher," Cottonmouth said.

"No," Othel said, "there's a man did some deals with them, a banker lives over there, at least has a house there. Name of Henderson Deal. Only reason I know of him is he did the Stoneciphers dirty—they were looking for some help dealing with it."

"Banker?" Everett asked.

"Way I hear it."

"And he's across the line in Union County, not here?" Cottonmouth asked.

"All the way across. Has a house overlooking the Ouachita. Probably see clear across to the Mississippi on a clear day."

"Othel," Cottonmouth said. "I thought you were the one preaching about keeping things the same around here."

Jimmy looked at Othel. "Yeah. That does sound like you."

"You tell me," Othel said to Cottonmouth. "Your camp now."

Cottonmouth said he just wanted to know what he was getting himself into.

"Providing hospitality to an oilman for a couple days," Everett said. "Least that's what it sounds like."

Cottonmouth said to keep talking.

Everett asked how old the man was, and Othel said around sixty.

"Well," Jimmy said, "looks like we should figure out how to get the old geezer before he drops dead."

16

Cottonmouth walked from the big cabin to the storage shed, began moving the boxes, the crates, the dynamite, making stacks along the outside wall.

Othel came up behind him as the other men were still in the main cabin talking out the plans, the ideas.

Othel asked was he sure about this.

"I'm sure if we're ever going to make anything of this, we can't just keep following orders from the sheriff and the Rudds."

Othel said he'd never felt like it was following orders.

"Maybe it didn't seem that way to you," Cottonmouth said. "Just never been my experience that the people who follow orders are the ones who make the money."

Othel said it was just a matter of keeping the peace, keeping the county safe. "We got a good thing going here," he said. "We make money off the robbings and shootings going on, and none of that gets here. You sure you want to put all that at risk?"

"You're the one came up with the idea of keeping the banker they brought in."

"I'm the one who had the idea for getting rid of him as soon as we could."

"You're so worried about the Rudds and the sheriff—why don't you go tell them what we're doing?"

Been asking myself that same question, Othel said to himself.

Cottonmouth had finished stacking the crates, with no help from Othel. "And why is it I'm the one moving all these crates?" Cottonmouth asked. "How come I'm not getting any help from you?"

"You asking about help for the crates or the kidnapping?"

Cottonmouth shook his head, said they couldn't go on the way they were going on. "Othel, I need you to be with me on this. Come here," he said, stepping into the now-emptied storage cabin. "This here is where we can set up the man they're bringing in. The guest. We'll have him a bed of some kind, a chair. I'm getting us ready for the next step."

Othel asked was the step they were taking likely in the right direction. "Just taking a step don't make it the right thing to do."

"This is what we have to do," Cottonmouth said. "The only thing we have to figure out is how to get ready for this. A bed. A chair. A slop jar."

Othel asked couldn't they just walk the man to the Roosevelt Room when he had to go.

"See," Cottonmouth said, patting Othel on the shoulder. "I knew I could count on you. Thanks for volunteering."

Othel looked into the storage cabin. "Won't he need some kind of light in here?"

"Likely."

"Is the idea to tie him to the bed? Chain him there?"

"Figure something like that. Keep the door locked. Someone sitting out here on watch. Like the sheriff in that movie few years back. What was it? *Law of the West*? *Justice of the West*? Sat in a chair outside the jail."

"Didn't he get shot in the gut when he fell asleep?"

"That's right; he did," Cottonmouth remembered. "Best not fall asleep."

17

Cottonmouth stood at the front of the auto shop on the south end of town, rapped on the wall near the bay doors.

Lorena Whaley stepped out into the windowed sunlight, working an oily rag across her palms, around each finger, thumb. "Help you?"

"Morning."

"Why, Cottonmouth Tomlin, as I live and breathe. What's it been? Ten years?"

He scratched the back of his neck, lowered his eyes. "Ten days."

"Ten days? Is that all? Well, when you crawled out of here that morning . . . ," she started.

"Yeah, about that. I'm sorry about that. I should have . . . well, I'm sorry about that."

She grinned, threw the rag at him. "Don't worry about it." She told him to come on in, and he did.

He said he wasn't worried about it. Not really *worried*—wasn't the right word. He looked around her shop. Looked at his feet. It was just, well. Not worried.

"Look," she said. "When you came back, we said nothing serious."

He said he knew that, but, well.

"One night. It was one night."

"Well, it was the afternoon and then the night."

She said OK, OK.

"And after midnight too. So technically . . . ," he said.

"Fine." She looked around for something else to throw at him. "If you've come for more of that, you'll have to wait. I have work to do," she said, widening her arms and turning to show the cars in the garage. "And no, I haven't finished the car your people dropped off to me. Haven't had a chance to start on it."

They stood silent for a few seconds, caught between.

Cottonmouth looked around at the pistons and tire rims hanging from the ceiling rafters, finally pointing to a steering wheel hanging from the wall. "Been meaning to ask if there's a story in that old steering wheel."

"Willie Carraway's," Lorena said. "Flipped his roadster racing Duke Emerson's Cadillac."

"Willie Carraway and Duke Emerson?"

She said yeah.

"Car racing?"

"It was a while back," she said. "We were kids. Twenty years, reckon. Hit a rut in the road. Car flipped right over. First wreck in the county—you believe that? Uncle Hilliard fixed it up. A Partin-Palmer. Four cylinders and twenty-two horsepower. A thing of beauty. You know much about cars?"

"Only enough to bring them to you."

"Well, this one had a Gray and Davis electric starter. Can you believe that? Back then?"

Cottonmouth said he couldn't believe it, not matching her level of excitement.

"Guess if you're not a car person, that don't mean much to you."

He shrugged. "Means something to you, so it must be important."

She nodded as Cottonmouth reached across the shelf of metal car parts he didn't have names for and rubbed his fingers along the unwanted bend in the steering wheel.

"They don't make 'em like that anymore," she said. "Anyway, after he replaced some of the pieces and parts, he kept the steering wheel as a souvenir. You must remember the wreck. You were here then."

"Nope," he said, turning away from someone else's wreck. He looked around the shop again. "Things going good?" he asked her. "Enough wrecks to keep you in business?"

She said she'd seen better, seen worse.

She asked what had brought him by the shop. Said she hadn't been sure he'd ever come by again, had thought he might've gotten scared off. Said she'd figured he'd just keep sending Othel or the boy to drop the cars off, pick them up.

"Of course I was coming by here," he said. "Lot going on. Thought I'd figure some things out before I came by."

"Figure anything out?"

He said he hadn't.

"You're here now," she said. "And I don't see a bottle of wine in your hands, so you come to talk business?"

"Got some crates of things in the trunk, was hoping to stash them here for a bit."

She asked what kind of things.

He said things he didn't want his guests getting into.

She said he could rent a corner of her shop, in the back with the mice.

He asked would she add it to his tab, and she reached into the air with her fingers and scribbled.

She asked was that it, figuring it wasn't.

"Also had some ideas in mind. Modifications."

"What sort of modifications? Kinda shorthanded now. Don't know if you heard, but we lost JD couple weeks back."

"Hadn't heard." Cottonmouth couldn't remember JD. John David? John Daniel? "You lost him?"

"Ran into trouble with the Stoneciphers. Caught up between them and the Bulgarians over at the mill in Mohawk. Nasty way to go, you ask me."

"The lumber mill?"

"The Stoneciphers."

"Was it Punch Stonecipher?"

"That's right," she said. "That's right. Him and his brother. Pribbles in there, too, of course."

"Of course."

"Doing a spot of time up at Tucker. Anyway, can't nothing be done about it now, don't reckon." Lorena leaned against a shelf. "Being around Little Rock still better than being in the ground, even if not by much."

The sunlight was coming in through the front door now, breaking through the clouds, through slats in the wall.

"So you say you need modifications. You mean more than a paint job? More than the usual I been doing for you?"

"Extra gas tank."

"Oh, sure. That's easy enough. I can get that done for you in a week, soon as I settle couple other jobs. Just leave it with me."

"Maybe some bodywork."

Lorena shook her head. "Patching bullet holes again? You keep on, sounds like you're trying to get us both in trouble." She laughed the way she'd done in school, three years his senior, when a handful of them would get into something they had no business fooling with and she'd just go along with it, nothing better to do, always able to get them out of whatever trouble he'd gotten them into.

"You never minded trouble," he said.

She moved closer. "Didn't say I minded it. Just like to know what I'm getting myself into."

He said life was full of surprises, moved a little closer to her, feeling his heart beat, thumping in his ears.

"Isn't it, though?" she asked, turning from him and walking back toward the car she'd been working on.

She said he was right to bring her the work, seeing as how she was the best mechanic in town.

"Right near the only mechanic in town, at the moment," he said.

She said then maybe she should raise her rates.

"How much I owe you so far?" he asked.

She raised an eyebrow. "You mean for the cars?"

He grinned, said yeah, that was what he'd meant.

She told him, and he said all right. He said it after he'd whistled through his teeth, taken a breath, but he said it just the same.

She asked was he wanting to pay any of it now, and he said sure, reached into an envelope in his coat pocket, pulled out some of the money he still had from the card game at Moon's, handed it to her.

She said it wasn't much.

He said it was what he had now but that he'd be getting more. Asked wasn't his credit good anymore.

"Maybe. You know what a Chevrolet Independence looks like?" she asked, and he said he didn't, so she explained it to him, told him about the chrome-plated wire-mesh radiator guard, the chromed bumpers, the wire wheels. He said it sounded fancy, and she said it was. Said if anyone he knew happened to come across one, she knew someone in town who was interested. Said there might be money to be made.

"Seems I'm racking up quite a bill with you lately."

She said it seemed that way. "And whatever else you got planned. Can't tell you how much it's gonna cost, neither. Ain't no way of telling the cost of a thing at first. Sometimes you get going on a thing seems like a good idea—afore you know it, you realize you're two steps away from disaster, but you're too far in to go back."

He asked was she talking about the cars, and she said yeah, that was the thing that seemed to be important to him, so sure enough she was talking about the cars.

So he went on about the cars. "Had a thought about another modification. And I'm just thinking out loud here, but what about a strap or two in the back seat?"

"A strap? Like for holding something or tying something off?"

"Something like that. Like for keeping an unruly kid tied to the seat, keep the kid safe. Restraint."

"You never were one for much restraint, Cottonmouth."

"Times being what they are, you know."

"I could think of something, I guess. How big a kid you figure?"

"Maybe six foot, couple hundred pounds."

She shook her head, took a breath. "Pretty much what I was figuring."

He nodded, said there was another thing. "The back of the cars. Need that lined with lead."

"You're kidding me."

"I'm not. Heard about it getting done across the Louisiana line, down around Vivian. It's a thing can be done."

"Extra tank, paint, lead in the trunk, restraints in the back. You need me to mount a repeater on the hood?"

Cottonmouth told her not yet, but he'd let her know. Seemed like a good idea.

"Seems like a terrible idea," Lorena said.

He said if she could get it done a little faster than a week, he'd be able to get the money back to her sooner.

"Come on in here," she said and opened a door to a little room, couple of chairs, upturned bucket, table for cards.

Cottonmouth walked in, sat upright on the front edge of a chair, took the bottle of orange soda she offered.

"See, this shop, I worked years here before it come to be mine. Nice shop. The loft above us with a bed, place to wash up. I think you've seen that recently, come to think of it. Anyway, I can work during daylight, turn on some lamps and work at night. Lotta folks get to fixing their own cars under the trees. When they can find what's broken, find the right parts to fix it."

"If you're offering me a job, I get weekends and weekdays off."

"I'm just trying to tell you how things are. This has been life for me, this work. After three years, you come back, and, well"—she waved her hands wide at all the world she'd known—"I can't have you coming back and throwing it all whompy-jawed for no reason."

He looked down at his orange soda, kept his eyes off her. He said he understood what she was saying. Then he looked up at her. "While I been gone, I been working too. Seen a lot of . . . well, seen a lot. And now I'm back, well, some things are different, and some things are the same. The whole point of going off—the point of coming back after going off, I guess—is to take what I picked up on out there and make it better back here. Otherwise, what's the point of going off somewhere?"

She said sure, what was the point?

He said he needed to get going, set down his bottle, and moved to the door, said he'd bring the car around the back of the shop and leave it.

Lorena stood, took what little money he'd given her to the back of the room, opened the safe, reached inside, shifted clear the pistols.

"Oh, and Cottonmouth?" she asked as he turned to go. "Next time you leave like you did, at least wake me up to say goodbye."

18

Henrietta Rudd asked the sheriff about the Morris problem, was it taken care of, and he said it was not. "They plan on auctioning off the Morris farm. Nothing much I could figure to do about that."

She asked what the problem was, and he said it was still the bankers.

"Our bankers?" she asked.

He said no. "From over to Dallas."

"Texas," she said, shaking her head. "Texas." She asked was the deal done, was it over.

The sheriff said best he could tell, it would be after the auction.

Henrietta Rudd nodded along, said well, she'd see about that. She asked when was the auction, and he told her.

Then she asked after Claude Umbach.

"Claude gave it some thought, felt that he wanted to avoid what happened to poor Mr. Shewmake up in Brister when he tried to set up his, well, his entertainment establishment. I'll stop back by in a few days, check on how well business is going."

"Always nice to have a new business start off well in our county," Henrietta said. "A right shame what had to happen to Mr. Shewmake."

The sheriff said it was, said he felt Claude Umbach understood how things were a little better than Mr. Shewmake had, now that Mr. Shewmake was some sort of a learning example for folks. "I suspect," the sheriff said, "that Claude will be stopping by in the next few days to impress upon you his commitment to working with you."

"Good, good. And the Tomlin camp?" she asked as Abigail excused herself into the back rooms of the hotel suite, a drink or two an hour making her more ambulatory than one might have expected.

He fumbled a little with his new sheriff's hat, hoping to find a way around the matter, knowing that saying too much too soon to the Rudds was probably a mistake. Knowing that his power extended only as far as the Rudds allowed. He'd tried a couple of years back to work with the Pribbles and Stonecipher, the first for the grunt work and the second from over the county line to provide a little financial backing, to regain a little more control over the county. After all, his own family had as much right to it as the Rudds, as anyone. But that had all gone wrong when Punch Stonecipher had wanted more than anyone had a right to ask for, certainly anyone from an outside county. If they hadn't been able to lay the whole thing at the feet of the Becketts, no telling what would have happened. At least most of the Beckett family didn't suffer much. Small consolations, he told himself. He rocked back and forth a little, turning his hat, convincing himself that it was best just to come right out with it. "Had another chat, a follow-up chat, with our friend Othel, and it seems they got the makings of a snatch camp brewing up."

Henrietta leaned back as Abigail returned to the room just in time to overhear, asking, "A what?"

The sheriff repeated. "A snatch camp."

Abigail fanned her face, feigned being flustered, asked if he'd meant a brothel. Though she and her sister had established a few rooms in the Culver for just such a purpose, Abigail never missed an opportunity to put on appearances, especially with her father watching from the enormous portraits along the walls.

"Oh, no. No." The sheriff stuttered the same syllable over and over. "No, no, no."

"Because, Sheriff," Abigail explained through the day's bourbon, "a snatch is how a man not quite a gentleman refers to . . ." She stopped speaking, raised her eyebrows until they nearly fell off, her eyes loose buoys on an overfilled sea.

"Kidnapping," the sheriff managed to say.

"Kidnapping? In our county?" Henrietta asked.

"Who has he kidnapped?" Abigail asked, moving around the room, a slight stutter in her step.

The sheriff said it was a banker.

Henrietta shook her head. "This seems to be a common question lately, but one of our bankers?"

The sheriff said no. Out of the county, though he didn't know where.

"And they just have him tied up there?" Henrietta asked.

"They snatch them off the streets," Abigail said, having read about kidnappings every few months in *Black Mask* or *True Crime Monthly* or whatever was left lying near the drink cart. "Then they hold them, take their shoes, and hog-tie them to the bed. Sometimes they take their shoes, pants, and shirt so they won't get away. Some of them perform such depravities the likes of which have not been seen outside the continent of Asia until only recently."

Henrietta asked did she read about the naked, hog-tied men in the newspaper or in one of her magazines.

Abigail, not bothering to lower the glass from her face so that she was speaking from the other side of her whiskey blur and into the far side of her whiskey cocktail, just said, "Yes."

Henrietta asked was the man still there or had they made the exchange, gotten the ransom.

The sheriff said he didn't know.

"Whatever it is," Henrietta said, "whatever the status of this is, you need to stop it now. The last thing we need is men from Little Rock—or, worse, Washington—coming here and waving around their badges.

This is not the way of our county, Sheriff. This is a peaceful community. I thought we understood that."

The sheriff said he understood her.

Abigail set down her glass, eased herself toward the sheriff, who shifted to stand, but she waved him off, then took two steps to him, placed her hand on his shoulder. "When Cottonmouth Tomlin came back here, we were sorry for his loss, for the reason of his return, but we were happy to see someone return from the war back to his home and ours. Much the same as you, Monroe."

Henrietta shifted in her chair, enjoying the show while Abigail continued. "Monroe McCollum, now sheriff of our county. Much like Sheriff Jefferson Hendricks before him. Of course," she said, moving behind the sheriff and placing a hand on each of his shoulders, "not too much alike, we hope, considering what happened to Sheriff Jefferson Hendricks—God rest his soul."

Abigail reached around to the sheriff's lap, took the man's hat, walked back to her chair. She sat down, raised her feet to the ottoman, stretched out her legs, and tossed the hat to spin around, then rested it on her outstretched feet. She looked to Henrietta, nodded, and then reached for what little was left of her drink.

Henrietta took a sip, set down her coffee cup. "Cottonmouth Tomlin's uncle always proved to be an honorable man. Well, not always, come to think of it." She looked to the distance for a moment. "But lately he had been, once he'd seen reason and admitted he needed a little . . . shall we call it *financial assistance*? Beurie Tomlin turned that hunting lodge into a nice camp for outside miscreants, taking money from their dirty little hands and helping guarantee the safety of our county. And I don't expect any trouble from the nephew, you understand? We expect everything to run smoothly. When you come to visit us, it's a much nicer day for us if you're ticking off a list of everything that's going well." She looked to the sheriff. "Understand?"

The sheriff said he wasn't sure what she meant, but he'd do what he could and keep her informed of everything that was happening.

"Sheriff," Henrietta said, rubbing her temples. "Do you know the little Dillard boy they call Tuck?"

He nodded.

"He keeps things running around here," she said. "Sometimes he finds a plank on the stairs has cracked or one of the nailheads has popped. Sometimes there's a door to one of the rooms that doesn't quite shut right. The building shifts; the ground shifts. Oh, who knows how these things happen. But can you guess when he tells us about the problem?"

The sheriff shook his head, though he could have guessed the answer.

"When he's taken care of it. He'll say we had a problem, and he took care of it. See, that's what we pay him for. Any piker can complain about a problem, Monroe. We keep the boy around because he keeps the little things in this place," she said, waving widely to mean the hotel or the town or the county, perhaps. "Keeps the place working well enough, running smoothly so that we can enjoy life."

Sheriff Monroe McCollum stood, said it looked like he needed to take care of some problems.

Henrietta nodded. "Always a pleasure to see you, Monroe."

Abigail said, "Absotootly," then laughed.

He walked to her feet, thought for a second about reaching for his sheriff's hat.

Abigail reached down to her feet, took the hat, set it upon her head as she and Henrietta walked into the back rooms for their afternoon naps.

Sheriff Monroe McCollum turned, wiped at the front of his shirt, then shuffled, hatless, to the door, which opened and closed without issue, then down the perfectly maintained staircase and into the sun-drenched town square.

19

Cottonmouth pulled the pirogue to the bank, looped the rope around a root, settled the small box of canned meat he'd gotten from Moon's on top of the Rudd family whiskey Earl had set aside for him at the hotel, and carried the groceries toward the cabin. He'd made it to the porch steps when he saw a matted, brown-haired pup of some kind dart off toward the woods.

He looked back at the road that had once brought cars to the cabin, could again. Wouldn't take much to open it back up, clear it. *Maybe throw some planks on it, make the drive easier. Could get Othel on it. Must be other folks around looking for a little roadwork.*

As he got closer to the main cabin, he could hear the men inside arguing.

Cottonmouth opened the back door, set the box of supplies on the counter, walked through to the main room.

It seemed a few of the men had heard on a Texarkana radio station that Davey Herron, who'd been known to run with Everett Logan and Beans, had a price of five thousand dollars on him on account of killing a lawman in Paragould.

Everett Logan said he hadn't seen Davey Herron in a dog's age. Said he could do without seeing him for a while.

"Why's that?" Othel asked.

"Fellow thinks he's still in vaudeville."

Jimmy asked what was so wrong with that.

Everett sighed. "He's friends with Arthur."

Jimmy asked, "Arthur who?"

"Arthurmometer," Everett said.

"That's terrible," Jimmy said, throwing something near Everett.

"That's the kind of joke he tells."

"How come nobody's shot him before now?"

"Guess we're all too nice."

Cottonmouth asked did anyone need anything, whiskey or beer, as he was fresh from town and had some local liquor.

Othel asked was it Rudd liquor from Lamartine.

Cottonmouth said not to worry about it, said it was Captain Warnock's finest.

Othel worried about it.

Jimmy said he could use a ginger ale, so Cottonmouth opened a bottle, walked it over to him at the poker table.

Everett Logan was cutting circles from the newspaper, pressing them into a set of goggles. He put on the goggles, turned his face to the light, waved his hand in front of his eyes.

Beans said Davey was from up north, Illinois or Indiana. Maybe Iowa. One of those.

Jimmy said he was pretty sure it was Illinois.

Everett took off the goggles, peeled strips of tape, and placed them inside, running his fingernail along the creases. "I think that'll do. Can't tell if it's day or night you've got these on." He tossed the goggles to Jimmy, who put them on.

"Can't see a thing," Jimmy said.

Cottonmouth asked were they staying for supper, staying the next day—asked did they decide because he'd brought back enough food.

Everett said they had been talking, had come up with an idea of who to grab.

"Already?" Cottonmouth asked.

Jimmy said there was no time like the present.

Everett watched Cottonmouth's face start doing weird things as he was going to say something, then stopped.

Everett walked to a table, rolled out a map. "Notice this lake, which is not in this county and therefore should not worry your friend, the sheriff, so there's no need to get that look."

Cottonmouth said he didn't have a look. "Not in this county is a good start."

"An oilman and a banker are having dinner here," Everett said, pointing to a circle he'd made earlier on the map. "So we grab the oil-man, bring him back here to the camp for just a little bit."

"Why the oilman and not the banker?" Cottonmouth asked. "I thought y'all said you were getting a banker."

"Excellent question," Everett said. "Jimmy was over at the race-track, heard there was money to be made, ended up talking to a college boy, son of the banker. Well, the oilman visiting the banker is from Louisiana, which, as you know, is also not in this county." He grinned, and Cottonmouth raised an eyebrow, said to get on with it, so he did. "From Cotton Valley, to be exact, which is here," he said, pointing to another dot a little south of the Arkansas-Louisiana line.

Cottonmouth asked who controlled that part of Louisiana.

"Ain't that Martello's corner?" Jimmy asked.

Cottonmouth's eyes widened. "He has a whole corner?"

Jimmy looked to Everett to explain. "He has a few parishes there," Everett said, dragging the pencil along that area of the state. "Mostly he's in Shreveport."

Cottonmouth asked how they knew all this.

"We didn't run off to Mexico for a few years," Jimmy said.

"Honduras," Cottonmouth corrected.

Jimmy shrugged. “Mexico. Honduras. Either way it’s so far off this map it’s on the floor. Rest of us stayed around here, learned what’s what.”

Everett said that was a fair assessment. “Now can we get back to the oilman and the banker?”

“Just a quick question,” Cottonmouth said, thinking about Martello, about how he’d become the man in charge in just a few years. “How did the area there go from being not Martello’s to being his?”

Everett looked to Jimmy and Beans, no one wanting to take the lead. “He owned a couple clubs in Shreveport,” Everett said. “Havird’s downtown on the river. Another one north of there. Pretty sure that was his.”

“Which one?” Jimmy asked.

“The Black Rabbit,” Everett said. “Up the road from Shreveport a piece.”

“He owned two clubs,” Cottonmouth said, “and now he runs the whole corner of the state? I’m in the wrong business.”

Everett said he couldn’t say how he’d gone from that to where he was now. “My guess would be there were people in his way who aren’t in his way anymore.”

Cottonmouth was looking off toward the wall of the cabin, seemed to be looking at something, but Everett could tell his eyes and his brain weren’t connected at the moment.

“You having thoughts?” Everett asked.

“Just thinking,” Cottonmouth said, looking at the map. “Couple clubs here, Campbell’s place about here.” He pointed to a spot halfway between Shreveport and the Arkansas state line, close to the Texas line. “And all this area,” he said, moving east and north, to the Arkansas state line, the line that separated the county they were standing in with Louisiana. “Wonder if there might be some sort of partnership worth discussing with the man.”

Everett asked didn't he have a local partnership already with those ladies in town, the sheriff.

"Not really much of a partnership," Cottonmouth said.

Everett cleared his throat, looked to Cottonmouth, who handed the pencil back, started pointing to all the spots he'd spent the morning marking on the map. "Now, Cotton Valley is here. We grab the oilman at the lake house. Here. Stash him here while we set up the swap. Make the swap along the railroad tracks here, north of Cotton Valley near Springhill. Already know a place. We get the money, then turn the oilman loose near his place. By next week, we're sitting in butter."

"Which is good?" Beans asked.

"Which is good."

They all said "Good" and nodded, while Cottonmouth thought of a partnership to replace the Rudd sisters.

20

In the summer of 1926, when Abigail and Henrietta Rudd had traveled to Memphis to meet with a businessman named Clarence Saunders, they had stayed in the Peabody Hotel. This, it should be noted, was not the Peabody Hotel on Main and Monroe, home to President Jefferson Davis just after the war. Abigail and Henrietta, registered as Abby and Henri Rudd, had stayed the week in the new Peabody, built on top of what was left of the old Fransioli Hotel. Though they would stay at the Peabody Hotel seventeen more times, it was said by those who claimed to know that 1926 was the last time they would register as Abby and Henri Rudd, as the hotel manager, soon replaced, had mistaken them—on the written register only, it should be mentioned—for a French husband and wife, or wife and husband, if the order of the registration card were to be believed, which, oddly enough, it was, though further assumptions pertaining to the card were, in fact, not.

Mr. Saunders had been working as a grocer in Memphis for two dozen years when the Rudd sisters met him that evening in 1926. This was during the time Saunders and Governor Peay were beginning their quarrels, with Peay running for a third term. Saunders had warned his friend not to run for that third term, had backed another man, and had even, so the story goes, issued threats against Peay's life. Pure hogwash, of course, but when Peay had won and soon died in office, the Rudd sisters had used the meeting to make suggestions.

"No," Henrietta said. "I can't say that Mr. Saunders ever asked us to help him remove Governor Peay from office. I declare, can you imagine two little old ladies from Columbia County, Arkansas, with that kind of power?"

In truth, they had traveled overnight to Memphis to speak with Mr. Saunders about a business proposition and about his need for investors. What they'd gone in with was a plan to help him finance his next wave of grocery stores, his having gone bankrupt in his last run causing some bit of a problem for him. What they came away with was a detailed history of how it had all gone wrong for him, how he had reached—not too high but too wide. How he had taken his Piggly Wiggly stores, the name of which still caused each Rudd to sneer and chortle, to towns across the country, had even listed the business on the stock exchange in New York City as a man of success was told to do, only to have Wall Street and the bankers pick him to pieces. Saunders had entertained the two sisters with stories of the ravenous beasts of Wall Street, those fattened men in carriages who looked for openings, for weakness, for worth someone else had created. Saunders had just been forced to sell off his Memphis mansion, and whether he blamed Governor Peay for not stepping in to help and whether that had caused their friendship to sour was of no concern to Abigail and Henrietta.

"Tell us about these Wall Street types. They sound dreadful," Henrietta said, though she meant *delightful.*

"You can't imagine," Mr. Saunders said, though soon they would be able to.

Which had taught them that Memphis was a nice place to visit, though you wouldn't want to lose a fortune there. New York City, they could tell, was not even a nice place to visit.

Seven years later, the Rudds were receiving visitors in a suite at the Culver Hotel. Claude Umbach had come by after the sheriff had called on him a couple of times. Umbach was sitting on a pale-blue Duncan Phyfe sofa, his left arm draped across one of the dips in the back of the sofa, then pulled back into his lap, holding his right hand. Feeling a little foolish then, unsure what to do about his elbows now moving away from him, now back, he lifted his left arm to the dip in the back of the sofa once again, the dip an odd angle for him at the moment, his arm moving back into his lap, starting the process all over again. He hadn't slept well since Sheriff McCollum had visited him, asking after his business and giving him the story of what had happened with Archie Shewmake the year before. He crossed his legs at the ankles. Uncrossed them.

When he had visited, the sheriff had been telling him about Archie Shewmake, how the man—rest in pieces, the sheriff had said—had tried to run a little brothel and card parlor down in Brister, just up the road from the one Umbach was working on starting in Emerson.

The sheriff had said it was a small world, and Claude had agreed, wondering how far along he was on whatever path Shewmake had been on, whether he could do anything.

"A small world and difficult times," the sheriff had said, and again Claude had agreed. Small and difficult. That covered so much of it. The sheriff had gone on about how the trouble with Shewmake was that he thought the world was bigger than it was, that the county was bigger, and that making your way in the county was easier than it was, Shewmake not recognizing the importance of community in these troubling, difficult times, and so Claude had agreed again, saying how these were difficult times and how community was important.

The sheriff had said it was a shame what had happened to Shewmake, adding how bad he felt for Widow Shewmake and how difficult it must have been when her husband had gone missing and how she must have felt once they'd found most of him, but that he was glad to see she'd moved on.

On that day with the sheriff—*Was it just a few days ago?* Claude thought. On that day, he'd felt a drop of sweat bead its way down his side, another bit of what might have been sweat moving down the back of his thigh as the sheriff had walked around the now-emptied house Claude had been using for cards downstairs, barneymugging upstairs.

"I mention all this because I've been feeling a might guilty," the sheriff had said. "I explained to Mr. Shewmake how he needed to follow the laws around here, the ones we write down and the ones we don't, but he was thinking he didn't need any help there, that he had it all under control. I just should have done better by him, that's all. And I wanted to come by here before you ran into any trouble, remind you that the best way to keep safe around here is to remember the importance of community. No room for selfish fellas thinking they're the big cheese themselves, you understand?"

The sheriff had been looking him in the eye, Claude had said he understood, and then the sheriff had suggested he stop by and talk to the Rudd sisters in town, make sure they were there to help him.

And here he was now, eating chilled cucumbers and drinking rickeys with the Rudd sisters, watching the sun drain away over the Magnolia skyline through the window of their second-floor suite at the Culver Hotel, it being the hotel they'd bought when they'd returned from their visit to Memphis, feeling right at home in a building filled with people they could order about.

Trying to make small talk, Claude said he appreciated the bourbon in the drink, said how most people these days made the rickey with gin.

"If the good Lord had intended the drink to have gin," Henrietta Rudd explained, "the drink would have started with gin. Its natural state, however, is bourbon. Though my sister disagrees."

"If the writers of our day suggest gin, who am I to argue?" Abigail Rudd asked, raising her glass in a toast to the portraits of her father hanging about the suite's sitting room: first to the one of him sitting in a rocking chair, top hat and cane held across his knee; then to the one of him standing in front of blurry trees, his hands deep into his pants pockets, the vest of his suit one deviled egg away from popping a button; and then to the maroon-and-olive one of him perched on, rather than sitting in, a straight-backed chair, his legs crossed at the knees, his dressing gown draped precariously, covering his otherwise naked body, this being the painting that tended to draw the most looks and the fewest comments. Abigail slurped a little from her glass, said, "If Mr. Fitzgerald, in his eminent wisdom, suggests gin, then gin it shall be."

"You're drinking bourbon," Henrietta said.

Abigail leaned toward Claude, placing her hand against the side of her cheek in confidence, whispering, "I didn't want to make a scene."

"We have a couple bottles for you to enjoy later, of course," Henrietta told the man.

He said he appreciated that; he really did.

Henrietta asked did Claude know the Hutcheson boy, and Claude said he did. Reuben's boy.

"He's restarted his beverage business after a little setback," Henrietta said. "We've been trying to help him with it, you know, community being so important. We'd appreciate it if you'd do your best to help support him."

Claude said he understood, said that made sense. Bourbon from the Hutcheson boy. Not a problem.

"No problem with gin either," Abigail said. "Some of the finest parties in New York start with gin they bring from England, of all places. Plymouth Gin. It's what they serve in the Royal Navy there. And they ship it all the way to New York City."

Claude said New York City sounded nice.

"We've never been. She reads," Henrietta said, shrugged. "I can't stop her from it." Henrietta nodded back toward the bookshelf and table at the edge of the room, piled high with creased copies of *Argosy*, *Black Mask*, *Oriental Stories*.

"I like to be entertained," Abigail said. "It helps me forget that life doesn't have any meaning." She winked. "I need my stories."

"And gin," her sister said. "Don't forget the gin and the bourbon. If those stories are the boats that carry you through, then gin is the river." Abigail had spent her last seven waking hours with one drink or another in her hand, which Henrietta had noticed.

"Thank you, ladies, for seeing me," Claude said and began to stand, considering the matter over.

It was not.

"You can't change the recipe because of what's abundant," Abigail said. "You can't change the makeup of a thing on a whim. You can have all the bourbon you want, but that doesn't mean gin isn't better. I know you want to push the brown stuff because it's what we have around here, but London gin is a goddamn delight."

"Because some jazz novelist said so? Isn't that what you were going on about?" Henrietta asked. "As if what we have here isn't enough. As if some Princeton dropout from Minnesota knows better than we do. And he thinks he's too good to even respond to your, what is it now, thirty-three letters of invitation?"

Claude wondered should he leave, was this a conversation best had without him.

Abigail snorted. "If Scott won't correspond with me, it's clear he's of no great use. Bad taste in women. He wants to spend his time with his wife in the nuthouse—they can make all the bathtub gin they want." She took another drink. "Fine. You've convinced me. Give me a bottle of Old Rip Van Winkle and a Frank Owen story, and call me in the morning." She reached to the side table; poured herself a little more bourbon, moving into her eighth hour of continuous lubrication; raised the glass in a toast: "May the good Lord be with us as we pass from strength to strength." She took a swig.

"Amen," Henrietta said, standing, causing Claude Umbach to stand. She thumped her walking stick on the floor. Claude flinched.

"Now, we want to make certain that everything runs smoothly in the county, you understand?" she said, walking him to the door.

"Yes, ma'am." He opened the door to leave, took a step to the hall.

"It's good to work together through these difficult times," she said. "We don't want them to get more difficult, you understand?"

He said he did.

"You have a good head on your shoulders," she said. "Make sure you keep it there."

21

Cottonmouth set a bag of hamburgers from Brewster's on the garage counter, asked Lorena if it was going all right.

She pulled herself from under the sedan, stood, wiped her hands on a rag from her pocket. "Come here," she said, walking around to the back of the car, then lowering herself so that she could reach underneath.

Cottonmouth followed, and she said, "Look here. Right here."

He knelt with her but didn't see anything. She said, "Reach here, right here," and took his hand, which startled him a little, though it shouldn't have.

"Feel this long box underneath the car here, right here?"

He said yeah, he did.

She asked had he ever heard of caltrops, but he thought she'd said cow traps, so he repeated it back to her as a question.

The sun was coming in from the windows now in triangles and squares, oranges and yellows, so that he had to squint even more when looking into the darkness around them.

"Yeah. Figured you and the boys could drive these cars around the county and catch some cows." She looked at the bag he'd brought in. "Old Man Brewster offers ten dollars a cow." She shook her head, and Cottonmouth tried to follow along. "They call it a jackrock, a crow's foot. Romans used them against horses and chariots. Australians or French or someone used them in the Great War against horses."

He stood, walked to the bag of burgers, pulled one out, asked was there much trouble from horses attacking soldiers over there.

"Not as much trouble as I'm having with a horse's ass right now," she said.

She walked toward him, set down the rag while she pulled a caltrop from a box on a shelf, handed it to Cottonmouth.

"Sharp little thing," he said, moving it around in his palm while he ate his burger with his other hand. "Looks like a couple nails folded on each other." He dropped it onto the floor of the garage, used the bottom of his boot to move it around. "So it always lands with a point up. Good against horses, chariots . . ."

"And cars," she said, finishing his thought. "Rigged it so there's a release just near the steering wheel," she said, leading him to the driver's side of the car. "Up through the floorboard. Flip that, and the bottom falls out, literally—all these little buggers come spilling out behind you, leaving some split tires in your wake."

Cottonmouth asked how do you close the flap after, and she showed him the latch, said the closing might not be as important as the opening.

"That's a fair point," he said, the back of his hand wiping mustard from the corner of his mouth.

She asked did he know there was a goat's leg under the car he'd brought in the other day.

He said he'd heard there'd been trouble with a goat but hadn't known there was still goat under the car. "Sorry about that."

"Wonder would Old Man Brewster pay for goats? Might be some extra money. You haven't found me a Chevrolet Independence yet, have you?"

He said he hadn't.

She asked what brought him in, asked what it was he needed.

He scratched the back of his neck, said that was the question, wasn't it?

She said she believed it was, yes, seeing as how she'd just asked it, for god's sake. She closed the distance between them, said "You missed some" as she thumbed mustard from the corner of his lips. "So what was it you needed?" she asked, using the tips of her fingers to trace his cheek.

"Seems it was one thing," he said, "but I can't remember. Now seems it's another thing."

"Promise not to run away this time, and we can go upstairs and see if there's something up there you need."

They closed the bay doors behind them, the inside of the garage moving to shadow, her finger along his forearm as they moved upstairs.

~

Afterward, he asked her if she had anything to drink.

"Not much point in getting me drunk now," she said, added there was some rye on the counter.

"You're still drinking rye?" he asked.

She asked, "What about it?"

He asked did she remember that time they'd found her father's bottle of rye and snuck off to the woods by the old Gaines place.

She rolled over on her elbows, put her head on his chest. "Don't know what you're getting at, but I remember you spent the next day dog sick."

"I remember I took the beating for both of us," he said, pushing her hair from her eyes, trying to tuck it behind her ear, "once your old man found out."

She said she hadn't thought of that, asked again what he was getting at.

"Been thinking about that, the old days, thinking about that the other night here when I was out looking up at the stars. Same stars we were under that night. I don't know. I mean, the trees at the camp are the same trees I built forts out of as a kid. That stuff's the same. Just had a flash of it in my mind is all. Was just thinking how back then, we didn't know there were things we couldn't do. But it wasn't overwhelming, like it should have been. I mean, we didn't know enough for it to be overwhelming. Anything being possible."

She asked for him to wait a second, stood, walked across the loft to the counter for the bottle of rye. She held the bottle up, tilted it. "You been sneaking up here and getting ossified when I wasn't looking?"

"I'm just talking. That all right?"

She sat down on a stool, reached to the corner of the bed for a blanket to cover herself, said to go ahead, sure.

"Just been thinking—that's all."

"Seems like a fair habit to get into. Go ahead."

"You ever get the feeling people have this idea of you that isn't you? Like it's this painting someone did, and they show it to you, and you think, 'That what I really look like?'"

She said, "Sure, figure people see a piece of you, see you from a certain angle, like who you are to them. How you fit into their world, not your world, you mean?"

"Yeah, maybe so."

She nodded. Gave it a second. He'd come to a stop, so she went on without him. "You're their banker, say, or you're the grocer, the mechanic. They see you as what you do. Functional." She stood from the stool, draped the blanket shawl-like around herself, and walked to the small window in the loft. "Like . . ." She looked around, thought for a second, said, "What do you think Bill Moon had for breakfast?"

"What did Bill have for breakfast?" Cottonmouth repeated. "No clue."

"You got a feeling he doesn't eat breakfast?"

"No. Just can't hazard a guess right now."

"OK. How about Miss Phoebe?"

"Probably eggs. Biscuits."

"You've had eggs and biscuits there?"

"Sure, give me a few minutes to feel my legs again, and we can walk over and have some."

"Well, there you go. People fit their function; that's the simplest way to see it, I guess."

"Yeah," he said. "It's been a long year." He looked off, then back. "Long decade. Whatever."

She asked what had really brought all this on. "You sure you haven't been drinking?"

"Only a little bit, honest. Look, I feel like I'm supposed to be someone I haven't met yet, you know? Like when I meet him, I'll know. I'll say, 'Well, that's me, then.' Something that fits. I don't know. That's the way I'm supposed to be going about this. I'll know how to react, how to act. Right now I'm just floating around, I guess. That's mostly why I ended up in Honduras after New Orleans, after here. Just going along, trying to find a place to fit. I'm thinking about what you've got here, thinking how you seem to be right at home. And I'm just thinking about that night back with you and that bottle of rye, our backs against that tree, looking up at the stars and talking whatever nonsense two first-drunk kids talk about. And now it's like we're not supposed to question any of it. Just keep forward; do the thing you're supposed to do, I guess. Keep moving. Seems like back then—back before we knew any better—back then we were just kids asking questions. Now, well, I feel like I've stopped asking questions, but I still don't have the answers. Least not my answers."

"Bill Moon," she said. "Miss Phoebe. Hell, any of us. Think anyone's different? They've all got their stories too. I get why you're lost, if that's what it is. Going away and coming back and wondering about where you fit into the big machine. And I get about your mom running off with that man and your dad going after her—eventually, mind you, but still. I get that. And Bill Moon, he's got his troubles. Lost a wife and son. And Miss Phoebe, well, there's a story there I'm sure we'll never know about her and that man from Tulsa. And yet, there they are if you need them. Toothpaste. Lemon pie. They're right there in town where we can count on them, in spite of whatever they've been through or whatever they're going through. Don't really matter what's wrong; what matters is the getting on with it. Hell, everybody's got something."

He took a deep breath, said, "Sure, everybody's got troubles."

"Everybody feels a little lost sometimes," she said. "You come back after being away like that, takes a while to find your place, feel your way around."

Cottonmouth cleared his throat to say something as someone he didn't know knocked on the front door downstairs, walked on into the garage.

"I thought you locked the door," she said, glaring at Cottonmouth as she walked by.

"When would I have—" he started asking.

She motioned for him to be quiet, threw a long shirt over her naked body, leaned over the loft railing. "Mr. Thrailkill," Lorena said. "What can I do for you?"

Thrailkill said it sure was dark in there, and Lorena said it sure was. "How can I help you?"

He said he was having a problem with his Buick and could she take a look.

She asked if he wouldn't mind waiting outside with his car—could he give her just five minutes?—and he said that was fine as he walked outside.

Cottonmouth was putting his boots on, asked what time it was.

When she told him, he said he had to get back to camp. Expected some hungry people there soon.

She said she was glad he'd stopped by, and he said he was too.

He kissed her on her cheek as he walked by.

"Oh my," she joked. "That's a little forward, don't you think?"

He said he was just checking for mustard.

She turned her face, said he'd better check the other side as Thrailkill hit the car horn twice.

22

As he was walking through town to his car, Cottonmouth was waved down by Sheriff McCollum.

"Hey now, hey now," the sheriff said.

Cottonmouth turned, nodded to the hatless sheriff. "Evening."

"I was just on my way to see you," the sheriff said, nodding to a bench in front of a vacant storefront.

Cottonmouth shrugged, sat down next to him. "Only spare a minute. Expecting some men back at camp soon."

The sheriff said that was just what he wanted to talk about, pulled a hard candy from his pocket, offered the candy to Cottonmouth, who waved him off. The sheriff peeled the candy as he spoke, working free a side that had melted to the wax paper. "Was just speaking with Miss Rudd and her sister. Seems to be some concern, word getting around, about a banker tied up at your camp down there. I said probably just someone got their telegraph wires crossed."

Cottonmouth asked who had the concern.

"Doesn't really matter who has the concern. Just want to make sure that's not what's going on, seeing as how there's this agreement in place, keeping the county safe, free from all that."

"Sure," Cottonmouth said. "Sure it matters who has the concern. If it's you, then we can talk about that. If it's the Miss Rudds who have the concern, I'll go talk to them. I know that you and my uncle—and I figure you and Othel—I know y'all had it all worked up the way you liked it, but if the Rudds have a concern, I think it's likely best to speak directly with them."

The sheriff shook his head, sucked a little harder on the candy, the cinnamon tingling his breathing. "If they've got a concern, I've got a concern. And right now the concern is you." The Tomlin boy coming back, pulling this. The sheriff had explained to Othel Walker, had let him know that Othel needed to deal with the sheriff, to not go around to the Rudds. He was the one who dealt with problems; he was the sheriff, goddamn it. And here Tomlin was being a problem. He'd be goddamned if he was going to let Cottonmouth Tomlin come in and push him around, bow to the Rudds, and brush him aside. Though maybe it was more a problem of where he himself stood with the Rudds than where he stood with the rest of the county. He'd thought being named sheriff meant something. Turned out it did—just not what he'd thought.

"I appreciate your concern," Cottonmouth said, standing to go. "Does this count as our next meeting?"

The sheriff set his jaw, moved his lower teeth out just a little, scrunched in one eye, the way he'd practiced when he was just a deputy. He looked up, letting Cottonmouth know that he had all the power he needed right here on the bench, that he didn't need to pretend he was tough, that he was the sheriff. Because he was. "My concern is that the county stays safe and peaceful. My concern is that the story about you people having a banker down there is just that. A story."

Cottonmouth didn't sit back down, didn't want to get into it with the sheriff. He had to get back to camp, to get set for the boys bringing in the oilman from the visit to Union County. Maybe he and the sheriff would have to fight this one out, but it wouldn't be today. Cottonmouth said he understood the concern. "Look, there's no banker at the camp.

You have my word that there won't be a kidnapped banker at the camp." Which was true, as far as it went. Oilman, yes. Banker, no.

The sheriff stood, thinking maybe he'd made an impression on Cottonmouth after all. "Then we've got no problem," the sheriff said, standing, turning to go, reaching to straighten his missing hat.

23

“I can’t breathe in this thing,” Beans said, standing behind Henderson Deal’s Union County house.

Everett said to just stay calm, pull the cloth down to his chin for now, until they had to go up to the house. He stood, looked over the stone wall that separated the backyard from the land that led to the lake. “Shouldn’t be long now.”

Beans said that was good. “And all we have to do is grab the oilman, drive away.”

“That’s it for tonight,” Everett said.

Beans looked behind the house, across the lake. “Don’t think you could see Mississippi from here.”

“Well, it’s night, Beans.”

Beans said he knew, he knew. “But I mean in the day. Seems like a long way away.”

Everett said it probably was. Said to stay ready.

“And how would you know it was Mississippi anyway?” Beans asked. “I mean, you could see lights or a building, but how would you know it wasn’t just more of Arkansas?”

Everett said he didn’t know. “Not sure what the difference would be, ’cept you’d be on the other side of the river.”

Beans said that made sense. "What are you going to do with the money we get here?"

Everett said he didn't know.

"You opening a business when you get the money and finish the college classes, right?"

Everett said that was the plan. "What's your plan for the money?"

"Kinda thought you might need a partner," Beans said, and Everett said that sounded like a good idea.

"Hold up," Everett said as lights flashed from the car parked to the side of the house. "That's Jimmy's signal. Time to move."

They stood, raised their masks, walked toward the house.

~

Henderson Deal and his wife, Eliza, had spent the afternoon getting together the cards and drinks, had enjoyed an early evening meal of fried chicken and potato salad from Milliken's, and were sitting down with the Gorhams for a night of bridge.

"Can I help you with that?" Joe Gorham asked, lighting his pipe as Eliza Deal poured another round of drinks.

She said she had it, sat back down once she was convinced all the glasses were filled to the brim.

Francis Gorham asked what kind of punch had they been drinking, and Henderson said, "One to the face," and they all laughed, faces spread wide to let each other know they were having a good time.

Eliza dealt the cards around the table, and each of them settled in again after a little break before the hand.

"So tell me about Benjamin," Joe said, then looked down at his cards. "Pass. He's staying with you for a while? Do I have that right?"

"Well, he's off at the horse races for a few days," Henderson said after he'd bid one heart.

"Henderson is worried he'll get kidnapped," Eliza said.

Francis blinked a few times. "Kidnapped?"

"It's all over the news," Henderson said. "And he said he felt like someone's been following him."

"Have they?" Joe asked, blowing smoke across the table. He reached for a tumbler of whiskey to blunt the sting of the awful punch.

"Of course not," Eliza said. "That boy thinks he's as important as the Lindbergh baby or that fellow in Denver or that lady in Chicago. He has an inflated sense of ego, that boy. And we know where he gets that from."

Joe and Francis raised their eyebrows, peeked over their cards at Henderson.

"She means Amelia," Henderson said. "The first Mrs. Deal."

Eliza raised the back of her hand to the side of her mouth and, in a stage whisper she'd often used five years ago when she had been a twenty-three-year-old actress, said, "His practice wife."

Henderson asked did they hear something, and Eliza said she was just fooling, didn't mean anything by it.

He said no, at the front of the house.

"Oh no," Eliza said, pretending fear. "We better hide the Lindbergh baby." Joe and Francis weren't sure whether to laugh, so they looked at each other and gave a slight "Ha ha."

"I'm going to have a look," Henderson said, standing.

Francis gave Joe a look, and Joe said, "I'll come with you," and followed.

~

Henderson Deal opened the door, the barrel of a pistol suddenly pressed against his chest.

He said, "What's the meaning of all this?" as he stepped back into Joe Gorham, who was stepping back into a cabinet.

Gorham reached around, flailing for something on the cabinet, only knocking off hats and a lamp, which fell to the floor, the thin patterned glass crashing against the hardwood, shards of painted flowers in fingernail shatters along the floorboards.

From the back of the house, Francis bellowed, "Is everything all right?" before saying "Oh no, oh no, please God no."

Deal watched a sling-armed man shoulder the door closed behind them. The man motioned for them to move to the back of the house.

Jimmy the Hook shifted his pistol to the hand of this slinged arm, helped Deal into his chair. The other three cardplayers sat in unison.

Beans and Everett stood over them with Jimmy, and the three men shifted their aim from Deal to Gorham, back and forth.

"Nobody move, and nobody gets hurt," Everett said. "Now which one of you is Gorham?"

Joe Gorham and Henderson Deal looked at each other while Eliza Deal grabbed and squeezed Francis Gorham's hand.

Henderson Deal stood, said, "I am. Now what's this about?" He looked to Joe, shook his head. "There's obviously been some misunderstanding," Deal said.

Francis Gorham's jaw shook as she watched her husband sitting, waiting. She wasn't like Eliza Deal, women like that. Those women took what they wanted, knew they deserved it. Francis had been waiting for something like this, something to take everything away from her. This was it. This was the night. She sniffled, unsure whether she was allowed to wipe her nose, whether she'd be shot. She looked across the card table to her husband, knew he'd reveal himself to the criminals, knew they'd take him away and kill him and her life would be over. There were times she'd forgotten to worry, and she thought about those times now, when for a moment she'd believed, hoped, that life would work out for her. An hour ago, she'd had no idea. She thought about that, how she should have known what was coming, something awful—how she should have felt it somehow but hadn't known that was the last time she would be happy, at peace. She waited for Joe to stand up, to say no, he was the man they wanted. But for now, he was safe. In whatever seconds were left, he was still her husband, her wonderful, brilliant husband she didn't deserve, had never deserved. She'd been lucky, she knew, so lucky to have had these years with him. She would miss him so much. Without thinking, she reached into her pocket for her handkerchief, then wiped her nose.

Did none of the bastards notice that? Eliza Deal thought. Francis could have been going into her pocket for anything. *What a bunch of saps.* She looked them over, the three men. One had a busted wing; one was sweating so much the pistol was about to drop from his hand. That left the one who seemed to be in charge, the one standing a little farther away from everyone, surveying. She'd dropped a handsy patron in Kansas City who was twice the man this fellow was. If she took him first, the sweaty one would panic. Maybe Joe and Henderson could handle the one with one good arm. She looked to Francis, who'd pulled her hand away from Eliza's and was nose deep in a handkerchief, making sounds from her honker Eliza hadn't heard since her own dyspeptic father had cleared the house after a bout of volatile indigestion. Christ, the woman could honk. And yet none of these gate-crashers was looking, as they were all three moving their pistols back and forth between the two men. Eliza reached to the table, brought an emptied tumbler to her side, and felt the weight, the heaviness of the base. She ran her thumb along the bottom of the glass, looked at the man in charge, looked at the side of his face, just by his eyebrow. There was no chance she was letting these morons walk out the door with her meal ticket. No, sir.

24

Henrietta Rudd leaned on her walking stick, moved along the yard, along the Morris family's front porch, in what appeared to be a deliberate pattern, each step the same distance apart, measuring, calculating. The sheriff had said the bankers were still the problem with the farm's auction. She'd seen bankers in the county cause problems, but more and more the bankers outside the county were coming in, taking things that didn't belong to them. Coming over from Texarkana, down from Little Rock, taking what the local folks had worked for their whole lives. In fact, just a mile or so down the road from this very farm was a tree where her father and Herschel Beckett had hanged what they'd left of a Yankee banker. She mumbled under her breath, thinking back on watching that, saying she hoped it didn't come to that again.

She looked out at the gathered crowd, held back the frumpy rim of her hat, the light breeze a flicker never amounting to much that morning, a few miles outside Emerson proper.

She looked from face to face across the gathering, yammering crowd—Stoneciphers from Union County, the Blackburns from up around Buckner, the Futch boy orphaned in the Camden fire a while back, a couple of the Gaines boys from College Hill, though it had idiotically been called Godbold for a while, most folks who'd remember that thankfully dead now.

For a moment, she gave thought to the story of the Gaines brothers, seven of them, coming from Wales to Virginia more than a hundred years back, then across Tennessee and on down to what was Union County until December 1852, when Little Rock had cut off pieces of Hempstead, Ouachita, Lafayette, and Union Counties, which before that had just been Hempstead, which before that had been called Missouri Territory. Families coming across and down, dying along the way—some that managed to stave off death and disease to settle here, just to have their family land taken from them because a banker said so.

From the front steps she watched the young auctioneer, one of the Chisholm boys, walk from person to person, glad-handing so much like a new preacher in town that everyone was checking their pockets when he moved to the next person. Past him, Curtis Nipper and J. D. Garth, two twenty-odd-year-old boys who'd come with her, owing her and her sister some indeterminate favor down the line, about to be repaid today. Curtis and J. D. followed behind the auctioneer, explaining to those in attendance what was about to happen, what was expected of them. Henrietta watched as a man who seemed to be in his forties shook his head in an argument, until Curtis nodded toward Henrietta, who looked back down at the man. For a few moments, their stares to each other seemed solid enough to build a road on, each not taking eyes off the other, the possibility of being able to walk through the air, on that look, from one set of eyes to the other right near palpable. The man turned away, spit, wiped his chin, and walked through the crowd to his car, then drove away through curses and dust.

After he'd reckoned he'd met everyone there, the Chisholm boy checked his watch, walked to the front steps of the porch. He waited for Henrietta to step aside so that he could get on with auctioning off the farm for the bank. She didn't move. *These Rudds,* he thought. *Just because they've been here near the longest, probably stole the boots off de Soto's corpse,* he thought. *Being around longer doesn't mean you're the most important—no, sir.* His grandmother had an armadillo they called Old

Stink that lived to be thirty-six years old, but no one ever cooked it Sunday dinner, not at all. He shook his head. *These Rudds.* He was the auctioneer, after all. His name was on the handbills, in the paper. He'd auctioned off quite a few farms the past few years, and if anyone had a right to stand on this porch, it was Henry D. F. Chisholm Jr., by God.

"Afternoon, Miss Rudd," he said, motioning for her to step down into the yard. "You mind if I get to work now?"

She grinned. "Why, young Master Chisholm, what delightful manners you have. Your mama must be so proud."

As she walked to the patch of yard at the corner of the house, she gave herself a good view of Chisholm, of the crowd. She saw J. D. Garth looking her way. He nodded to her, and she smiled.

Chisholm blew a whistle, cleared his throat. Said "Welcome, glad you could all come," added that he was here on behalf of the bank. He listed off the acreage, the number of outbuildings, the size of the main house. He said there was some livestock left, what hadn't been sold off, been slaughtered, or just outright dropped dead, and that was up for negotiation with the bank, following the successful closing of the sale of the property. He pulled a sheet of paper from his coat pocket, read a couple of paragraphs of legal jargon no one paid much mind to, and then got to the business of auctioning off the Morris farm as Henrietta Rudd turned to face the crowd.

He started by asking "What'll you give for this tractor?" and waved his arm to the side of the porch where the tractor in question sat. Like most everything around it, excluding maybe the little Talley boy who'd come with his grandfather to see the farm, the tractor had its best days behind it.

As Chisholm kept lowering the bid to try to get things going, a McLure in the front row said he'd give five cents. Chisholm stopped stark, waiting to see was someone pulling a joke on him. Someone else in the crowd said, "Too rich for my blood." The auctioneer, not knowing what to do, stood there, just stood there, and you couldn't even tell was he looking at anything.

Someone else in the middle of the crowd said, "Sold, to D. C. McLure for the sum of five cents. Next item."

It went on like that for a while, raising a total of a dollar and thirty-five cents after a half hour of equipment, until a man from Texarkana decided he'd had enough, started raising the bids. The way the story was told for years after, all Henrietta Rudd did was turn her shoulders in a way, or maybe it was a look in her eye to someone, but the population of Texarkana was decreased by one inhabitant that day, the story goes.

By the time a shaken Henry D. F. Chisholm was helped down from the porch, the bank had raised nearly seven dollars total.

As she made her way past the auctioneer, Henrietta Rudd paused. "Well, I suspect Mr. Morris will be able to work something out now, don't you?"

Chisholm said something that sounded like "I, um."

She tapped him lightly on the chest with her walking stick. "I suppose I'll be seeing you at the next one of these auctions. Always nice to get out and about. And it was lovely to see you again, Henry. Say hello to your mama and 'em for me, mind," she said and made her way to her sedan.

As Henrietta was getting into the car, one of the Morris boys came up to her, handed her a little green-and-brown crocheted purse. "Daddy told me to give this to you and to say thank you."

She took the purse, felt the weight in her hand. "Oh, I can't accept this," she said, opening the clasp, looking at the jewelry inside. "Was this your mama's?" she asked, setting the purse onto the seat of the car behind her.

The boy nodded, having said everything he'd been told to say to the nice lady and not knowing what to do now but wait to be dismissed.

Henrietta sat down next to the purse; closed the door; told the boy to tell his pa that she was only there to help keep the community together, only doing what was right; then drove away.

25

"We take 'em both," Jimmy said to Everett, his voice booming deep from his throat, rattling everyone in the room. "When we figure it out, we shoot the other one."

Henderson Deal said, "If it is all the same to you, let's not be shooting anyone," said everyone should calm down. He knew he had to get these men away from everyone else. If he could get one of them alone, he could start there, then figure it out. Come up with a plan—that was what he usually did. Then do the next step. After that, do the next one, and so on. While he didn't have much of a plan, he did have the next step, and that was separating the men. "I have five thousand in cash upstairs," he said. "Take that, and call it a night. You can tie us up after. By the time we get loose, you'll be long gone and safe. Five thousand," he said, his eyes on Everett, identifying him as the man in charge. "Split three ways? That's still a good night's work."

"A little over sixteen hundred each?" Everett asked, doing the math and remembering he still had homework due for his finance class. "Reckon an oilman could bring more than that."

So there are only three of you, Henderson Deal thought. *No one waiting in the car outside. No one waiting wherever you're taking Joe. That's good to know.* Feeling he had a leg up, he looked at each man's face, cataloging eye color. Their hands. Shoes. "Think about the risk," he said.

"I go upstairs with one of your men while the other two stay here and guard these three. We come back down with the money. You tie us all up and leave. Ten minutes. Tops." He liked his odds with the other two men, either of them. The wounded one or the nervous one. Upstairs to his private study, to his grandfather's Colt Peacemaker, locked away in the cabinet. Locked away but loaded. He'd subdue one of them, somehow. If he had to fire a shot up there, he'd count on one of the others to come running. Whatever happened, he had to throw these men off their plan. Get them off balance. *That's a plan, isn't it? Force the other guy to fumble the plan he came in with? Sure.* He was starting to see it. Get the three men separated. Next step, get one of them upstairs with him. He nodded slightly while Everett watched him, hoping the slight nod would somehow encourage the outlaw.

"Fine," Everett said, turning and pointing his pistol at the sniffling Francis Gorham. "You. Get up."

Francis shook back to the moment. "Who? Me? What?"

"Tell the woman where the money is," Everett said to Henderson. "Tell her. We get the money, I'll bring her back without any extra holes, and we'll be on our way, like you said."

Joe Gorham shifted his weight to stand, to stop these men from taking his wife. It was him they wanted, after all. Why had he let Henderson go on like that, pretending? Francis probably thought him a coward now, letting another man take charge like that, take a risk like that. As he stood, he started to tell them he was Joe Gorham but only managed "I'm" before Henderson took charge again.

"I'm afraid," Henderson Deal said, stepping in front of Joe, forcing the other man back to sitting. "I'm afraid there's a combination lock to the money. You'll need to take me."

Beans, shifting his pistol from hand to hand every few minutes so he could dry one palm at a time, looked at Henderson Deal, then at Joe Gorham. "Wait. If you're the oilman, then why do you know the combination?" he said before Everett started talking over him.

"Tell her the combination," Everett said to Deal. "Tell it to her. Or me. We'll come back down with the money."

Henderson Deal shuffled, said, "Well, there are things, um, in the safe, you know, private things, that—"

Eliza Deal stood; said, "Oh, to hell with this"; threw the whiskey tumbler across the room at Everett, hitting him squarely in the forehead; then kicked up the table, cards and glasses flying everywhere.

Henderson Deal moved for the staggering Everett and shoved his way through Joe Gorham, who was once again attempting to stand. The oilman and the banker fell into each other, knocking Jimmy the Hook on top of them in the process.

Eliza Deal stepped across the upturned table, past the curled-up and sobbing Francis Gorham, and reached for Beans's pistol.

~

Everett Logan stumbled back, a hand on his pistol, a hand reaching for his forehead. He seemed to mumble every swear word he knew, all at once, feet taking short, quick backward steps. Below him, he saw Jimmy the Hook, the banker, and the oilman rolling about, all elbows and chins. He reached down, pulled Jimmy up by his shirt, used the tip of his shoe to push away the one who seemed to be in charge, the one claiming to be the oilman.

Jimmy standing to his left, Everett looked to his right to see one of the women lunging for Beans, whose sweaty, panicked hands were in the process of dropping his pistol, which fell, hitting an upturned table leg, firing a bullet that somehow hit nothing but a window behind them, the shot and shatter calling everyone to attention.

Jimmy drew his gun on the men, said for everyone to calm down, calm down.

Pistol pointed at the women, Everett picked up Beans's pistol, handed it back to him.

Beans thanked him, apologized. Everett nodded to the women, which brought Beans back to focus, and Beans raised his pistol to guard the women. “Oh, right,” he said. “Right.”

Everett walked over, searched the one not claiming to be the oilman, found a silver case with business cards inside. “Brooks Oil Company, Joseph P. Gorham,” Everett read. He turned to Beans. “Keep a gun on Mr. Gorham here while we tie up the other three.” Ten minutes later, they were five minutes down the road.

26

At camp, Cottonmouth handed out the plates with the sandwiches.

"Egg and cheese," Jimmy said. "Really, you spoil us."

Cottonmouth faked a grin.

"Starting to miss your uncle's cooking," Jimmy said. "God as my witness, never thought I'd say that."

"This snatch business goes through, the big guy in Shreveport gives us a little more business," Cottonmouth said, "we'll be eating steaks and, well, whatever else you fellows want." He lined up the bottles of soda on the table for the men.

Jimmy took a ginger ale, said "Here's hoping" as a toast, and walked to a table to join Beans and Everett while Othel helped Cottonmouth with the cleanup in the kitchen.

"Tell me again about the oilman," Jimmy said. "You and Beans took care of it?"

Everett said, "Yeah, yesterday and today." Two trips across to Louisiana in two days. "Gorham gave me the name of a man he trusts. I left an envelope with instructions for him at the Jefferson Davis Hotel."

"And you're sure they agreed."

Beans nodded on behalf of Everett. "They put a flower in the window of the hardware store, like we asked."

Everett said, "Yeah, they're good."

"And getting the money?" Jimmy said. "You still haven't explained that to me."

"I did," Everett said.

"I mean, not in words I could understand."

"Which words were giving you trouble?"

"Not so much the words, I guess," Jimmy said, talking around a mouthful of sandwich, "but what it all meant."

"Train tracks. Money. Celebrate. Those words?"

Jimmy said he didn't have to be like that about it.

Beans said it had been a long day, long couple of days.

Jimmy nodded. "All right. Would it make you feel better to go punch that oilman in the teeth?"

Everett said it might, but maybe save that as a last resort.

"Find out how you did on that college test the other day?" Jimmy asked, looking for a change of subject.

Everett said he hadn't. "Need to get to the post office, but I wasn't sure how long we were staying here."

Beans asked how long they were staying, now that Everett mentioned it.

"Up to us," Everett said, "far as I know. Hoping we get this oilman taken care of, have some cash to spend. Like to make sure this camp is still in business next time we need it."

Jimmy said it didn't look like there was much other money going to be coming into Cottonmouth's camp anytime soon.

"Hate to see it shut down," Everett said. "His uncle was the one helped us hold things together when we got the wrong side of Eddie Strawn's crew over in Nashville."

"You never told me you've been to Tennessee," Jimmy said.

"Arkansas."

Jimmy asked was there a Nashville, Arkansas, really.

Beans said there was a Paris, Texas.

"What?" Jimmy asked.

"There's a Paris, Texas, I said," Beans repeated.

Jimmy asked why he was telling him that.

Beans said he thought that was what they were talking about, thought he'd want to know.

Everett said that was fine, said, "Yeah, Paris, Texas."

"And Tennessee," Beans said. "A Paris, Tennessee."

Jimmy asked was that right.

"It's on the way to Nashville, Tennessee," Beans said, "if you're going that way."

Jimmy said they probably weren't.

27

Cottonmouth and Lorena were having dinner in Emerson at a small family restaurant neither knew the name of.

"It used to be McKamie's place," Cottonmouth said, leaning across the table to whisper to her, not wanting anyone around to know that he didn't know where he was.

"They sold it couple years ago to that Eubanks fellow from Mount Holly," she said.

"So Eubanks, then."

"No, I heard they got rid of it and moved to Lewisville."

Cottonmouth asked, "Well, who owns the place now?"

"I do," the man standing behind him said, then introduced himself as Daniel Lebow.

Cottonmouth stood, shook the man's hand, introduced himself, and said it was good to meet him. Said this here was Lorena Whaley, who nodded.

Lebow said he was charmed, and he was. He said to please sit back down, sit down. Asked what he could get them.

Cottonmouth surveyed the room to see were they causing any commotion, but the four or five groups around them just kept on eating, pretending they weren't listening out of the corners of their ears to all this. "We were just asking what the specialty of the house was," Cottonmouth said.

Lebow said he had some good greens and some chicken, if that would interest them, and they said it would. As he was leaving, Lebow said he had known Cottonmouth's uncle and was sorry he was gone.

"He was a good man," Cottonmouth said, having figured out that was usually a good enough thing to say to get through this type of conversation where someone felt the need to offer condolences.

"He was at that," Lebow said. "You must be the nephew he was saying nice things about all the time."

Cottonmouth said he was the only nephew, far as he knew.

"Well, there you go," Lebow said, then nodded a "Ma'am" to Lorena as he walked back to the kitchen.

Lorena said he seemed nice, added it was good to have the ownership of the place settled.

Cottonmouth took a sip of his coffee, said it wasn't easy taking over a family business.

"I'm well aware," Lorena said. "And anyway, how goes the business?"

"Getting better, I hope," Cottonmouth said. "Some of the fellows are off now doing some work. New line of work. Should be a good profit in it."

"So you say. Hopefully they can line up a whole string of easy jobs."

"Even better than that."

"How's that?"

Cottonmouth said they were working out a new business plan, working on moving forward. "Heading into the city to let a businessman know we're open for business."

She said that seemed like the way things ought to work.

He realized he hadn't explained it well, tried again. "When I took over, everyone there was just following orders. Making money for people who already had money."

Lorena said she could do with a little of that money.

He said that was the point. There wasn't enough. It was all coming to an end. That way of life. "Sending letters. Then sending messages over the wire. Then the telephone. You have to keep moving ahead, keep working on new things. This man I used to work for down south, he was always looking forward."

"He in the telephone business?"

"If that's where the money was, he would be. Anyway, with all this change, goddamn Roosevelt, we have to move forward."

"Caltrops. Straps in the seats. Lead reinforcements."

"Exactly. And now that we have that figured out, it's time to let this businessman in the city know we're open for that business."

"Guess you can't just put an ad in the papers."

He said that probably wasn't the best idea.

"But do you have to go all the way to . . . where? Kansas City? Chicago?"

"Shreveport."

"Oh, when you said *city*, I thought you meant *city*."

He looked around the room, at the three groups left at tables, raised his hands.

She asked what Shreveport had that they didn't have here.

"The man I need to talk to," he said.

"The other afternoon at the shop, you needed something much different," she said, then hid her eyes in her coffee cup.

"Lorena Whaley," he whispered sharply as he leaned in, and they both laughed.

Lebow stepped in from behind, set their plates of chicken and greens on the table, asked if they needed anything else.

When he'd gone, Lorena asked Cottonmouth if it was a good idea reaching out to someone down in Shreveport to help him out in this county.

"I'm done taking orders from people in this county," Cottonmouth said, checked his watch.

28

Everett Logan eased to a stop a couple hundred feet from the crossing, left Jimmy behind in the car as he and Beans stepped out with lanterns in hand. They'd crossed into Louisiana a while back, through Springhill; come on down a little farther into Webster Parish; found the spot Everett had talked about using. The ransom notes had gone back and forth, but the family had finally agreed.

"Think they're going to hand over all of it?" Beans asked as they closed in on the money spot.

"If they want us to hand over all of the oilman," Everett said, lantern bobbing side to side as he walked through the tall grass.

"You sure it was smart leaving the oilman back with Cottonmouth and the other one?" Jimmy yelled from the car.

Everett stopped, turned back, walked closer so he wouldn't have to yell. "The other one is named Othel. You know his name. And that's the whole plan, isn't it? Can't have the oilman and the money together. We get the money, drive back to where they're parked, flash the lights to let them know it's good. They drive the oilman to the drop spot, with us behind. They drop the oilman. Then Othel drops off Cottonmouth, heads back to camp, and the rest of us go to Havird's in Shreveport to throw some of the money around. Can't make it any simpler. Now can I walk over to the tracks, or you want to go over it a fifth time?"

Beans said he'd be glad when this was over. "One of us is getting mighty grumpy lately. And by *one of us*, I mean you."

~

Beans walked back from the embanked tracks to the sedan. "How much longer?" he asked. He and Everett had walked back and forth a dozen times.

Everett twisted the cap back on his hip flask, stashed it, stood from leaning on the hood of the car, and said, "Oh, so much sooner than the last time you asked me."

From behind the wheel, Jimmy the Hook said, "So if it keeps getting sooner the more he asks you, then you gotta figure he should keep asking you to make it even more sooner, right?"

Everett said, "That may be the dumbest thing you've said."

"Or the smartest," Beans said, standing near the car.

Everett shrugged, nodded along in a soft grudge. "Considering the things he's said these past few years, yeah, maybe it is the smartest, as dumb as it is."

Jimmy said, "Thank you very much, Professor College Boy."

Everett said, "Let me ask you something. Either one of you ever hear of Adam Smith? The invisible hand?"

Beans shook his head in the starlit dimness.

Jimmy looked up to his left. "Invisible hand. That the Italian gang took out Fat Louie in Nashville?"

"Economics," Everett said. "Coursework I'm starting. Have a quiz to send back, but it got me thinking about something."

"Well, then it's money well spent," Jimmy said.

"How about John Maynard Keynes?" Everett asked and could hear the rattle of both men shaking their heads.

"Economist, wrote a thing called *A Treatise on Probability* that I just read. Or read some of."

"Probability?" Jimmy asked. "Like gambling?"

Everett said not exactly.

Beans said it sounded like the kind of book that made him sleepy, then asked had anyone heard a car, and they said they hadn't.

Jimmy asked what was the point—were their odds looking good or not?

"Just got me thinking about economics and economists is all," Everett said.

"What about them?"

"They've got these big ideas, these big books on world economies and monetary reform and financial institutions, right?"

Jimmy shook his head again. "If you say so. It's all Greek to me, Professor."

"We kidnap some beer baron or oilman or banker, right?"

They said right. "Pretty sure we already got us an oilman," Jimmy said. "Didn't know we were starting a collection."

"In fact," Everett went on, "all goes right in a few minutes, we're about to see a train come down those very tracks behind me and a satchel of cash come flying off into this field, land at our feet for the taking."

They said that sounded about right, sure.

Everett turned to the men. "And what is the plan with that money?"

The men shrugged. "Buy ourselves happiness?" Jimmy asked.

"And a Buick," Beans said, and the two men stared back at Beans.

"Just as a sidenote," Jimmy said, "we're keeping you away from the car. We all agreed. Keep the goats safe."

Beans slumped.

"Good dinner," Jimmy said. "I could go with a good steak."

Everett's thoughts were back with the oilman, back with the banker at the house on the lake. He was walking back and forth, building a rhythm, the grass a flattened path as he went. "Did you notice the banker's house, the one where we took the oilman?"

They said sure they had.

"And did you notice how he was in charge of the situation, or felt he was, even though we'd come in with pistols in his face?"

Jimmy nodded. "I did kinda get that impression."

"I feel like if a banker had kidnapped an oilman, he'd be doing more than just getting a bag of cash."

Jimmy said he wasn't sure what Everett was getting at. Beans didn't say much of anything, just waiting to catch on.

"Right now we have this asset, this oilman, and we exchange him for a bag of cash, and we exchange that for goods. It's come from our work here, so it's work for cash for goods is what the book says." He was pointing at the air now, drawing invisible lines in the sky. "Now, we could use a barter system and just trade our work—our time, as it were—for goods. Instead of going to work taking money from people by robbing them and kidnapping, we could, theoretically, just use that time and effort in exchange for the steak you want, but we've agreed that these rectangles of paper have value, correct?"

"He's gone goofy," Jimmy said. "Beans, did you give him any of that rotgut whiskey Cottonmouth was passing us?"

Beans said they'd run out of that whiskey, said all he had was some brandy.

But Everett kept walking. "Since we've allowed cash to enter the equation, we should use it to its fullest potential, correct?"

Jimmy said, "Sure, Professor. Keep talking. We ain't got a radio, so you just keep going." Jimmy leaned back in the seat, reached into the back for his hat, rested his head, and settled the hat on his face. "Keep talking. Wake me when we're rich."

Everett said, "What if, now I'm just laying this out here, what if instead of snatching an oilman or a banker and setting him in the corner of the shack for a few days, ungagging him just long enough to feed him fried chicken, what if we take an economist, and he can tell us the best way to use this money, where it should go, what we should do with it."

"Kidnap an economist?" Beans asked.

"Can you imagine?" Everett said. "We grab John Maynard Keynes; he can tell us whether we should save or invest or spend the money. He could tell us whether to put it in dollars or pounds or gold coins. Do we buy jewels now to sell in five years? Stock up on whatever gold we can find?" Everett was really going now. He was making quick stuttering steps, his hands nearly a blur at this point. "Do we invest in a business? Now that they're going to allow liquor again, is it wise to invest in a bar? We should grab Keynes or Alvin Hansen or any of these. We benefit from them while we have them; then we get the cash when we give them back. It's a win-win. We grab them, and we're getting free economics lessons. Or, better, we're making money while they're telling us how to make money. There's no downside to this at all. We use the money to make more money, just the way the good Lord intended."

Beans asked where those men were, the economists. "Never met one myself. I mean, I don't think I have. Saw some pictures of some of them in your books, and I think I'd remember a guy who looked like that."

"London, I think," Everett said. "Find them in London. At least I figure that's where Keynes is. Don't know about Hansen. New York or Chicago? Wherever economists go, I suppose. Maybe that island off Georgia? I'm sure we could ask around."

Beans said he hoped it was London, said he'd never been to London, asked how that would work—where would they put the guy?

Jimmy lifted the hat off his face; said his brother-in-law had spent a summer in Paris, if that was any help; and then settled the hat back down again.

Everett said they'd have to start planning it out. "This could be the one that sets us up, boys. Just the start."

They all nodded, and Beans asked how much longer.

Jimmy looked at his watch, and Everett said any minute.

Then they saw the lights coming down the tracks.

"See," Jimmy said. "Good thing you kept asking him, or we'd've been here all goddamn night."

As the train got closer, Jimmy flashed the car's lights off and on, off and on, as they'd planned.

"Here we go," Everett said, walking the fifty or so yards toward the edge of the tracks.

As the train drew next to them, they crouched, hidden in the ditch, and saw two men in lantern light standing in the flat of one of the cars. Then they saw a satchel flying up through the flashing headlights of their car, then disappearing into the blackness of the sky.

The satchel hit the ground, clasp breaking open, loose bills flying softly from the opening, the wind picking the little rectangles of paper from the bag, floating them along the air; the three men chased the paper around, yelling "I got one! I got one!" here and there.

29

A few hours later, Jimmy pulled up to the sedan where Cottonmouth and Othel were waiting with the oilman, goggled and tied in the back seat. Jimmy flashed his lights to let them know everything was fine, and Cottonmouth flashed back, the two of them the only cars on the road.

Jimmy eased the car next to the other, pulling onto the logging road, doing his best to avoid the ruts. True to plan, Everett got out and joined the oilman in the back seat of the other car, and the outlaws rolled on.

The first few miles next to the oilman in the back seat were quiet enough, Everett figured, with Cottonmouth keeping a steady hand on the wheel, Othel up front with him, Jimmy and Beans coming up behind.

Everett leaned out the back window, saw above them thin tissue clouds moving to cover, uncover stars across the blue-black sky. Around them, clumps of pine broken by fields and occasional houses, water easing to the edge of the road, cypress trees spotting the horizon.

The oilman had tried to get them to say something around Porterville, but back at camp the men had made a pledge to keep quiet, already putting too much of their own voices in the man's head. Jimmy had read a story in the Texarkana paper about two men getting arrested because a woman had recognized their voices. Every day they'd kept her, she'd gotten them to talk a little more, about the food they were feeding her, about the weather, even about the baseball scores in the paper. She'd pieced together where they were, which team was the home team for the men, and so forth. They had been as good as caught before they'd let her go, but they just hadn't known it then. So Jimmy had tried to disguise his voice at first, even trying out an accent, but had sounded like Greta Garbo impersonating an inebriated Maurice Chevalier, so he gave up to keep the other men from laughing.

The two cars took a side road near Sarepta, crossed the bridge they'd set as the drop spot. They pulled in a few hundred feet later at a burned-out church, circled back the way they'd come.

When they came back to the bridge, they slowed. Saw the creek beneath the bridge, saw the oilman's car parked in the pull-off spot folks used for fishing, camping, petting.

Getting word to the oilman's people had been easy enough, just finding someone near the man's office to take a note to leave with someone at the office. But you could never tell with these things. Hodge Rollins had been nabbed in Wichita because of a leaky ink pen he'd used on the ransom note, a trail of stains connecting him to everything, so you never knew.

Cottonmouth stopped the car at the edge of the bridge, only now thinking how maybe doing this and having to cross a bridge wasn't the best plan, though having the receiving party below and the delivering party above had made sense when Everett had suggested it.

Everett stepped out of the car and pulled the oilman out behind him. Beans got out of the other car just as the road lit up behind and in front of them, a voice booming, "Stay where you are. Stay where you are."

Everett kicked the still bound and goggled oilman between the legs and jumped back in the car with Cottonmouth and Othel as Cottonmouth spun the wheel and accelerated, with Othel hanging out the window firing a pistol.

Beans fired two shots into the air, then jumped back in his car with Jimmy, and they took off.

Both cars were a couple hundred feet down the road before the law started after them.

Cottonmouth and Jimmy drove side by side, each car giving a little and gaining a little, two old mares coming down the backstretch at some forgotten racetrack.

Shots pelted the cars as they passed two police cars trying to pull onto the road to block their path, lawmen with pistols and shotguns taking their turns. The men ducked low. Cottonmouth went off and then back on the road, hardly able to tell the difference. Jimmy kept on the road, taking the lead.

Othel switched his pistol for a Browning, leaned his head out, and fired back at the lawmen, the automatic threatening to shake loose from his hands, his shots wide enough to debark a dozen Louisiana pine trees along the road but sending the men behind them scurrying, rolling their cars back, taking cover—but only briefly, for when Othel leaned back in, shots dinged off the trunk of the car.

Cottonmouth was nodding a silent thanks to Lorena's work when he was forced to swerve just off the road to miss a deer by a foot and a half. The lawman's car chasing him wasn't as lucky—it, too, swerving, then slowing suddenly enough for the car behind to ram into it, flip it, send it blazing into the tree line.

"Should we go back?" Beans asked Jimmy. "Should we go back and help?"

"Beans," Jimmy said without looking back. "They just tried to kill us."

Beans said, "Well, even still," but Jimmy kept driving, Cottonmouth closing the distance.

A few miles down the road, Cottonmouth pulled alongside Jimmy, signaled that he was pulling off.

Underneath the glimmer of a dozen stars and the white thumbnail of the crescent moon, the two cars pulled off somewhere east of Plain

Dealing. Jimmy and Beans stepped out of one car—Cottonmouth, Othel, and Everett from the other—and each man walked to the back of the cars to see the damage.

Jimmy had a flask he passed around as they walked off the rush of the chase, shook loose their legs and arms, eased their chests back to normal breaths.

"Uh, guys. Guys," Beans said, stepping away from one of the cars.

"What?"

"I got bad news."

"What?" Everett and Jimmy asked together.

"Uh," Beans said, "I think the oilman stole the goggles."

They told Beans not to worry; with the money they'd just made, they'd buy a dozen sets of goggles, and Beans said OK.

"Now," Cottonmouth said, "let's head down to Shreveport and cause a scene."

30

"Take a chair, Monroe," Henrietta said as the sheriff entered the Rudds' sitting room.

Abigail walked along the back of the room, tumbler in hand. "Anyone need a drink?" She waited a beat. "Just me, then, is it? All right."

"Would you care for some lime gelatin?" Henrietta asked the sheriff.

He said, "I wouldn't; thank you."

Henrietta carved away another spoonful, watched the slivered piece shake, settle in her spoon. Only when it had stopped moving did she continue. "Did you know that fruit gelatin flavors can lose fifty percent of the flavor in just a month on the shelf?" she asked, eating.

He said he didn't, shifted, standing.

"Was reading about that in *Ladies' Home Journal*," she said, setting her gelatin to the side.

He scratched the back of his dampening neck, said he must have forgotten to pick up the latest issue.

"Bill Moon keeps it for us—the gelatin, I mean. Also, the coffee, you know," she said, then took a sip from a coffee-filled teacup that had been resting unseen on the side table. "Chase and Sanborn. Yankee coffee but quite good, if a little expensive, though I suspect that's more to do with the rush in getting it here, Bill's cut, and all that." She sipped again. "Do you know what I like most about this coffee?" She paused but not long enough for him to answer. "It's dated coffee. Comes with a freshness date." She held the cup of coffee up higher, looked at the brittle china flower decorating the outside. "I believe the can this came from is guaranteed fresh until the middle of July." She took another sip, held the bottom of the cup in the palm of her hand, feeling the heat.

He nodded, asked "That so?" to fill the gap as best he could.

"It is, Monroe, it is. Now." She set down her cup, the delicate clink of the china sharp against the room's silence. "Now," she repeated, "wouldn't it be nice if people had a stamp like that, right on the label?"

He said he didn't follow. "Freshness?"

"More of a 'good until' date, don't you think? Each person who worked for you—well, for me and my sister, I mean—each person would have a guaranteed 'good until' date, when you could tell that the person would be no longer useful. The gelatin, as I was saying, they tell me that in a month the gelatin loses half its flavor. Now if I'm expecting lime gelatin and don't taste the . . . Abigail, what's the phrase I want?" she asked, turning over her shoulder.

Abigail, standing by the liquor cart, wiped the underside of her bottom lip, said "Piquant tartness" between sips.

"Yes," Henrietta said, "if I want lime gelatin, then I want it to be tart. Piquant, even. You see? It's how it has been advertised to me. What I expect. This agreement we've made, the gelatin people and me, as to what's expected. If it's lost its taste, why am I even bothering with this gelatin? Do you follow?"

He said he thought so, but he wasn't sure. In truth, he was thinking of all the places he could have been. He was fishing in most of them—or at least sitting on or near the water with a fishing pole in his hand. When people talked about things he didn't understand, which he felt was becoming more and more common, he would find himself thinking about other things, things he understood, places he'd rather be.

During the war, an Italian local had taken a few of the soldiers to a spot on the Adige, where they'd each pulled in near about their own weight in trout. There was nothing like a warm afternoon, he figured, of loafing about, dragging your line along the water, waiting for that snap to tell you that you'd won this round. He was letting his mind wander now: a small cabin somewhere; sitting down to the breakfast table with someone, maybe Miss Phoebe; and deciding which trail they wanted to walk along, deciding where they wanted to be when the sun set.

"Bill Moon sends over a box of food and drinks," Henrietta said, bringing the sheriff's thoughts back to the room. "Always the freshest he can find. It's what we've asked for, what we expect. If what he sends us is no longer good, then we no longer do business with him, because he's become useless to us too. If my coffee has lost its taste, I might as well be drinking a cup of that swill in the pie restaurant across the square. That clear enough?"

He said that was clear enough, yes.

"And yet here we are again, with the ever-expanding Cottonmouth Tomlin problem, and I'm wondering if we need to check you for a freshness date."

A rattle from the back of the room, and the sheriff turned to see Abigail watching with interest.

"I think with his uncle gone," the sheriff said, "he's just settling in, feeling his oats, as they say. He'll settle in and settle down."

Henrietta shook her head. "Seems everyone leaves that boy, doesn't it?"

The sheriff shuffled. "Well, I think he's just trying to make a good business. A successful business."

"Never minded success," she said. "Even someone else's. As long as it doesn't disturb the peace and order we've worked for here. We're told that they've taken care of their involuntary guest."

"You have good information," the sheriff said. "Just found out about that myself."

Henrietta raised an eyebrow. "Just found out? Well, I wouldn't go around bragging about that."

"No, ma'am," he said. "That's not what I meant. He's making changes, growing his camp."

"I appreciate that, Monroe. I do. The right kind of change, well managed, this county has no problem with. And growth—again, well-managed growth—is a pleasure to observe. But I'm afraid we're back to limes again."

"Gelatin?"

"Trees," she said, and as she started talking about lime trees, he faded back to the trees along the water in Italy and those trout, those magnificent trout. She was saying something now about tree limbs: "Which sometimes must be pruned to save the tree, to save the entire orchard."

Just as Henrietta Rudd stopped talking, Abigail set her hand on the side table by her sister, then stepped back to reveal a Colt Vest Pocket pistol next to Henrietta's teacup.

The sheriff's eyes widened, and Henrietta said, "Oh, Abigail. No, no. It won't come to that, I'm sure." She reached to the table, handed the pistol back to her sister, who shrugged and walked back to a chair against the wall, next to the liquor cart, the pistol disappearing in her dress as she moved.

"Sheriff," Henrietta said sharply, the sheriff realizing he'd been watching Abigail walk away with the pistol while Henrietta had been speaking to him.

"Yes?"

"I was saying that other matters will likely have to be dealt with. If the Tomlin boy believes he can expand and grow and change, well, that's a thing we need to make certain is managed properly. If he's thinking he's going to grow himself into this county, he needs to understand his place too."

"I suspect," the sheriff said, "he's just trying to settle into some sort of success. Something solid. Times being what they are."

"I am counting on you to see that success and order can coexist, Monroe."

He said he understood.

"Are you sure you don't want any of this gelatin?" she asked. "I suspect it's good for a while yet." She stopped, looked him in the eye. "Until it isn't."

31

The horn playing onstage at Havird's in Shreveport was coming in steady now, reaching the bar where the men from camp were drinking. A tall thin kid in a dress shirt and vest, maybe fifteen years old, was squawking out the notes for "Exactly like You," with a stout old man pitter-pattering his way across a small set of drums.

Jimmy had volunteered Beans to walk around the club, finding out information.

"What time's the main act come on?" Beans asked a man who was leaning against the bar, looking to be the sort of man who could often be found leaning against this exact corner of this exact bar.

The man turned to Beans, adjusted his cap, shrugged. "That is the main act."

Beans looked at the kid onstage, listened to see if he was missing something until he felt the horn's squeal in his back teeth. When he was done wincing, he asked, "That's the main act?"

"Should have been here last Saturday," the man said. "Vinny Booberg was here tickling the ivories. Had one heck of a crowd."

Beans was thinking how many people he knew—four or five he could think of right away—was thinking of how many men he knew who would stab the man in the throat for saying a phrase like "tickling the ivories" and thinking he could get away with that. Beans had seen men stabbed for less than that. He was glad Jimmy and Everett weren't within earshot. In Wichita, he'd seen a man carried out of a club like this one for saying "bee's knees" a third time in one evening. "Never heard of Vinny Booberg."

The man straightened himself from the bar, set down his drink. "Never heard of Vinny Booberg?"

Beans shook his head. "Sorry, no. What's he done?"

"He only played with Paul Whiteman on *The Victory Hour* is all."

"Who's Paul Whiteman?"

"Who's Paul Whiteman?" the man repeated. "Who's Paul Whiteman?" The man looked closer at Beans, at the men with him leaning against the bar, drinking. "Say, what are you fellows doing at a jazz club if you don't know jazz?"

Beans shrugged, raised his eyebrows. "Here to impress a man."

"How's that going so far?" the man asked, then took his drink and walked to the far end of the room, looked back, saw Beans watching him, kept walking.

Behind Beans, Jimmy the Hook drained his glass, then said to no one in particular but everyone in general, "Bring me another one of these, these, what did you call it?"

The man behind the bar put his hands palms down on the counter. "It's a Bunny Hug."

"The hell you say. No wonder I forgot what it's called."

"You want another one or not?"

Jimmy said he did. "Just don't call it that. Ain't you got another name for it?"

"Like what?"

"Tell me again what's in it?" Jimmy asked, holding the empty glass up to the light, looking at its bottom for secrets.

"Gin, scotch, absinthe. You said you wanted a drink with liquor, liquor, and liquor."

Jimmy shook his head, blinked his eyes clear, set the glass down in front of the barman. "That's one hell of a rabbit."

"You still want another?" the barman asked.

"Christ, man. I'm not even sure I wanted that one."

Cottonmouth looked around the club, told himself he could get used to owning a place like this, if things went his way. Have the camp come along, have the business improve, let Martello see what he was capable of—then maybe there would be a club of his own soon enough. That place he and Lorena had dinner. Lebow's place? The joint Claude Umbach had started up. He could have a place like that, a place like this. Something steady. Something you could count on. Who knew?

The music stopped, the stage clearing as Beans got back to the group.

The man he'd been talking to had gone behind the stage, to what must have been an office, and was now standing at the far side of the room, behind a table and just on the edge of shadows, with a man who looked pretty well put together, Cottonmouth thought, wondering vaguely if you could get a nice-looking fedora like that around these parts.

~

"Where'd they say they were from?" the club's owner, Victor Martello, asked.

The man, by happenstance named Calvin Coolidge and called CC, said they hadn't told him, but he'd heard them talking, and he was sure it was that crew from over the line in Arkansas, the one Old Man Campbell had been going on about the other night, with the nephew coming back to take over for the dead uncle.

"I remember the uncle. So that's the Arkansas boy with the camp?" Martello asked.

CC said he thought so.

"I wonder if they still have the run of the entire parish?"

CC said "County" and immediately leaned forward, shaken, trying to pull the word back into his mouth, trying to slow time, reverse. Good Lord. What had he just said?

Martello turned to him. "Excuse me?" he asked, reaching into his coat pocket. CC watched the man's hand, not noticing the nod Martello made, so slight.

Two men standing next to CC escorted him to the back of the club after Martello gave them a look. Martello sat down at the table, now fully in the shadows; lit a slim cigar; and watched the men at the bar.

"When's the music supposed to start back up?" Everett asked the barman.

Before he could answer, Jimmy asked Everett, "You even know who we came here to see?"

Everett picked up his beer bottle. "Wasn't you, I can tell you that."

Beans said Vinny Booberg had been there last weekend.

"The piano player?" Jimmy asked.

Beans said yeah, wondering how Jimmy knew about jazz. How he had time. Well, people could surprise you, as his grandma used to tell him all the time.

"I was in Dallas last year," Jimmy said, "when you boys were up in Kansas on that job for the Dutchman. Heard a couple fellas from Arkansas. Snub Mosley. Alphonso Trent too. Thought there might be a chance they'd be here tonight, but this don't seem to be the year for things breaking my way."

Everett said he had that right, looked around the club. "Guess we came all the way down here for a bottle of Coors and Ben Selvin on the jukebox?"

Jimmy said not to worry, cleared his throat, stood up, thought better of it, sat down. Another Bunny Hug had appeared in a glass in front of him, so he had a swig. Cleared his throat again. "Just friends," he started, high and nasally, imitating the way he'd heard it. "Lovers no more, drifting apart." He mumbled lines, moved to a muffled trumpet, his hands over his mouth, wah-wah. "We loved, we cried. Suddenly you died—just friends." He raised his glass. "Barkeep, another Bunny Hug for me and my friend. We're just friends," he sang, falling off his stool and into the side of a man walking past, who stopped and shoved him back against the bar, saying, "What's all this about?" All the men around stood, reaching for blackjacks and blades, until someone said, "Hey, break it up. Show's up there, show's up there." Then a handful of men walked onto the small stage in the corner, the lights going off and on, but the men only rolled a piano onto the stage.

Jimmy dusted off his coat, settled himself at the bar, held up his glass, just a few drops of the drink swirling around the bottom of the glass. "Dry. Simple. Packs a wallop. Could call it a Jack Dempsey."

Cottonmouth said, "Pretty sure there's already a drink called a Jack Dempsey."

"You know," Everett said, "speaking of Jack Dempsey, Jimmy knocked out Harry Greb at a club in Hot Springs a while back."

"What were you doing with Harry Greb?" Cottonmouth asked. "Some prizefight I don't know about?"

"No," Everett said, "just wasting some money at Leo McLaughlin's place. Got into a scrape with some boozehounds out of Joplin. Harry Greb happened to be with them."

"And Jimmy ended up knocking Harry Greb out?"

"Well," Jimmy said, waiting for a grumble in the back of his mouth to pass, something trying to make its way out of him. He squinted, shook his head, settled. "I didn't know at the time it was Greb."

Martello had seen what he needed, stood, walked to the back of the club.

Cottonmouth turned to Everett.

"That was him, right?" Cottonmouth said.

"That was him."

"Think he saw us?"

"Couldn't have missed us," Everett said, looking around the club, counting maybe six other people.

"So what now?" Cottonmouth asked.

"Only one thing impresses a man like that."

Cottonmouth nodded, felt the money in his coat pocket. "You get the boys. I'll meet you outside."

Everett gathered Beans and Jimmy.

They walked out of the club, Cottonmouth lingering at the bar.

The barman came to collect the glasses, asked would that be all tonight.

"Thanks for . . . ," Cottonmouth started, then realized he didn't know what to say, wondered what the Banana Man would have said here, wondered what anyone who knew how to do this sort of thing would have said here. "Thanks for the drinks and show," he said, confident that was not what he should have said and certainly not what the Banana Man would have said. He reached into his pocket, pulled out a wad of cash. "Tell Mr. Martello that Cottonmouth Tomlin of Columbia County, Arkansas, appreciates his hospitality."

The barman watched him but didn't move. Finally, when Cottonmouth started to leave, the barman nodded, reached for the money. Cottonmouth walked to the front door as a man onstage introduced Snub Mosley.

~

Outside the club, Cottonmouth joined alongside Jimmy, the other men a little ahead of them, and walked west along Texas Street, turned onto Spring for a block, and saw a Ford and a Buick parked at the curb, then spotted a Chevrolet Confederate parked around the corner, all three cars with Texas plates.

"That's my dream car, right there," Jimmy said when they spotted the Confederate.

Cottonmouth said, "That so?"

"See the Town and Country horns there on the front?" Jimmy asked, and Cottonmouth did, squatting to look at two long horns, one under each headlamp.

"Classy."

"Run on the ol' Stovebolt Six, you know," Jimmy said.

Cottonmouth said he didn't know that.

"Not a car person?"

Cottonmouth shrugged. "Seems like everyone else is, though."

"Well, all you got to know is that little engine in there has been souped up so it's like you've got sixty horses under the hood. Now you tell me a cop that can outrun sixty horses."

Cottonmouth said he couldn't think of one.

Everett and Beans came back with two plates while Jimmy knelt to pull the plates off the Confederate.

After they'd pulled the license plates from the cars, they walked back toward Havird's.

Cottonmouth asked about the Texas plates.

"Old trick I learned from a friend of mine used to work with the highway patrol," Everett said. "They see a car with out-of-state plates, they figure it's somebody out of state. That's how their minds work. We hit a place a hundred miles away, and they're off looking a thousand miles away."

Cottonmouth said that was a good trick.

"And see how he didn't find that in one of his fancy college books," Jimmy said, laughing.

"Could be we write our own," Everett said. "Stealing cars could be good business."

Jimmy said that was true. A car turned the corner toward them, and they eased into an alley off Spring Street.

The car slowed as it rolled by, but it was only two men in the front who thought they were swell, two women in the back who thought they were flappers. The car rolled on, turned another corner, and was gone.

Everett signaled Jimmy to wait. Jimmy raised his arm in acknowledgment, forgot he hadn't completely healed, let out a little squeak.

Cottonmouth asked was he all right, and he said he was.

Jimmy and Cottonmouth stepped back into the alley as Everett and Beans walked on, seeing whether there was anything on the road worth taking.

"More plates?" Cottonmouth asked.

"Plates, cars. Maybe there is good business in that; I don't reckon Alfred Marshall will be writing a textbook on plate swapping anytime soon."

"No idea who Alfred Marshall is," Cottonmouth admitted.

"Name on one of Everett's textbooks. You travel around with an overgrown college boy, you end up seeing all the books he keeps in his satchel. Day after day. You saw he made me quiz him on economic theory?"

"Sounds like maybe you're picking up some book learning too."

"Never got past the first sentence. Read it so many times—ended up memorizing it on accident."

Cottonmouth said, "Well, let's hear it, then."

Jimmy cleared his throat. "Economics is the study of mankind in the ordinary business of life."

"That so?"

"It is. Same in both copies. I checked."

"Both copies?"

"Yeah. Up in Kansas City last month, we had to find a new copy. A thousand fun-filled pages. First copy took a bullet when we were getting away from a couple cops in Topeka."

"A bullet? That's one tough book."

"That bullet made it all the way to page three hundred before giving up, which is pretty impressive."

The other men came back, another plate in hand.

Cottonmouth looked around, standing on the edge of an alley in Shreveport, Louisiana, wondering what had happened to bring him here. *Head back home from Honduras, and the next thing you know, you're running a kidnapping ring out of your family's hunting camp. What a world,* he thought. *What a world.*

Everett said they should be getting on back. "We got the money, got rid of the oilman, visited the big man's club, and picked up a few Texas plates. I'd say it was a good day."

Cottonmouth looked up the street at a car that had caught his eye. "Jimmy, what kind of car is that?"

Jimmy said it was a Chevrolet Independence. "You can tell by the—" he started, but Cottonmouth cut him off, walked a little quicker to the car.

"Gentlemen, this good day just keeps getting better."

32

Two days later, after Cottonmouth Tomlin had delivered the Chevrolet Independence to Lorena, he walked into Miss Phoebe's to meet Victor Martello, who was at a table in the back, a piece of buttermilk pie on a plate in front of him, the slice missing one bite.

Cottonmouth walked across the room, tipped his cap to Miss Phoebe behind the counter, stood across the table from Martello until he waved him to sit.

"How's the pie?" Cottonmouth asked.

"About what I'd expect from a place like this," Martello said, pushing the slice minus one bite to the center of the table.

"Not a fan of buttermilk pie?"

"Not this buttermilk pie," Martello said. "My grandmother used to make a buttermilk pie you'd talk about for weeks." He looked at the slice of pie on the plate between them. "Of course, my family has been passing recipes down for generations, perfecting them. They didn't just find a recipe on a tub of Crisco." He pushed the plate farther away.

Cottonmouth hadn't heard of anyone disliking Miss Phoebe's pies. There was a story that Mr. Joseph Frisbie of the Frisbie Pie Company up north had come down south looking to start a new bakery but had gotten a taste of a lemon meringue that Miss Phoebe had made and hightailed it back to Connecticut. Cottonmouth knew that was more than likely just a story. More than likely.

"Have you tried a slice of the butterscotch?"

"Would have to be an inordinate amount of scotch in it," Martello said.

Cottonmouth felt the need to say something in defense of Miss Phoebe but let it go, not wanting to upset Martello, risk anything that might be coming. He felt good things were coming, and Martello accepting his invitation to come visit was a good sign.

"This could be so much more," Victor Martello said, the pie fork still in his hand, sweeping a wide arc. "You ever been to Saint Paul up in Minnesota? Great little spot called the Green Dolphin."

Martello nodded, and a dark-suited man from two tables over popped up, walked over to take the slice of pie, the napkin.

Cottonmouth said he hadn't been to Minnesota.

"Cedar Rapids?"

Cottonmouth said he didn't know where that was.

"Iowa," Martello said. "See, up north, you get far enough outside Chicago, you've got these towns, bigger than this one we're in now—they're outside that direct influence but still get the trouble now and again. The towns have come to an understanding like you say you've got here, where you keep any trouble outside the town limits, and Johnny Law leaves well enough alone. Only, it's the whole damn county here; do I have that right?"

Cottonmouth said that was the understanding.

"And there's none of the difficulties they're dealing with in New Orleans and New York and Chicago, the big places, with the Irish families or the Italian families cutting everything up into pieces."

Before he could stop himself, Cottonmouth asked, "Aren't you Italian?"

"Only by blood," Martello said. "And this place could be so much more. Haven't you ever thought about more?"

"Hasn't everyone?"

"You'd be surprised. Some people find a place where they can settle in," Martello said, turning a sneer around the restaurant, "scratch around some dirt and twigs and call it a nest. A place where they're comfortable, mistaking comfort for happiness."

Cottonmouth asked wasn't that happiness?

"Challenges. Overcoming challenges. Growth. 'Amazing Grace.' You know that song?"

Cottonmouth said he did.

"'When we've been there ten thousand years, bright shining as the sun.' That line. You know it?"

Cottonmouth said he did.

"The next line, that's the part that has to chill you to your core. 'We've no less days to sing his praise than when we've first begun.' Dear Lord, does that sound like a heaven to you?"

"Living forever?"

"Can't call that living. Doing the same thing you were doing the day you crossed Saint Peter's gates? Give me a Saturday night in Saint Paul, Minnesota, over eternity at Saint Peter's gates."

Cottonmouth nodded, but Martello could tell he wasn't quite following him.

"How's this? Take the yellow-faced American beaver," Martello said. "Ever heard of it?"

Cottonmouth shook his head, trying his best to follow Martello's words. From church songs to a beaver. "No, can't say I have."

"They burrow. More like a groundhog, I suppose. Settlers encountered them, years back. Along the rivers. Missouri. Up to South Dakota. North, too, far as I know. Montana. Points north and west. They'd burrow down—not far, you see, just sort of hide themselves in the shallow water, little warm spots along the banks. Just settled in. Families coming across them found out soon enough they made good stew meat. Not great stew meat but easy to find. *Easy* being more important than *great* sometimes, to some people. The beaver burrows, you see. Bunkered in, just waiting to be somebody's dinner."

Cottonmouth said he didn't remember ever eating yellow-beaver stew or whatever it was called.

"No," Martello said. "You wouldn't have. Hunted to nothing. Can't find them anymore. But at least they were comfortable, right?"

Cottonmouth nodded along.

"You've shown the promise of this place, your camp in the woods. This town without trouble. Could use a good restaurant, some upgraded choices at the brothel, but what you've got now is potential. Potential. Growth. A thing to look forward to. And you can grab that or keep talking about it. Does the name Benny Garvey sound familiar?"

Cottonmouth shook his head, realizing he was spending his night saying how little he knew.

"Worked with the men in Chicago. Had a place in Wisconsin, lot like yours here. Folks would stop in on trips to Saint Paul. Had a good thing going there. This was just a couple years ago. Chicago offered to help him expand. He said he liked the way he was set up. Said if he expanded, he'd have to hire more people. You hire more people, you have to pay more people. You have to pay more people, you have to make more money. Said he was happy the way things were. Any idea what happened to him?"

Cottonmouth thought he finally had one. "They made stew out of him?"

"Not a bad guess, but no. They built a new road, goes around his place completely."

"So they just left him alone and forgot about him?"

"They did," Martello said. "After they burned it to the ground, obviously."

Cottonmouth said, "Yeah. Well, obviously."

"All depends on what your goal is," Martello said. "Money? If money is all you want, what's keeping you from it?"

Cottonmouth shrugged. "Mostly it's the locks."

Martello laughed. "Timing. See, this year, this Roosevelt—Yankee, of course—this Roosevelt threatens to ruin everything we've spent the last decade building. People have been paying top dollar for alcohol, for coming in the back door of clubs, for having a secret phrase to get through the door. They're in on a secret. Freemasons. Knights of the Golden Circle. Illuminati. Half the men we work with think the Chicago Outfit has a secret handshake. You take all that away, you let people go back to buying a bottle of gin when they get their eggs, you've lost your margin. Put a bottle of bourbon on the store shelf, and everybody walks right by. Hide it behind the counter, and people come looking for it. You understand what I'm telling you?"

"When they make it legal, the illegal side gets cut out."

"The profit gets cut. They get rid of our side of the alcohol trade, everything goes back to hitting banks, kidnapping the ones with money. Not but so many ways to make that kind of cash."

Cottonmouth said he thought he understood.

"Cash business. I have the club in Shreveport, the one you visited. Have another one up the road from there in Vivian called the Black Rabbit. And I own seven laundromats around. Some on my own, some with other people. I'm a businessman. All that gives me pull. Also gives me a way to move however much cash I need. Now, what are you charging here, per night?"

Cottonmouth told him.

"See, there's your problem. You're leaving money on the table. Men come through here making thousands on their jobs, and you're walking out with five bucks here, five bucks there. Can't have that. Leave that kind of money on the table, and someone else takes it. That's your money."

"I agree with you," Cottonmouth said. "I do."

"You should be talking about taking a percentage of the jobs, don't you think?"

Cottonmouth nodded.

Martello continued, not waiting for a response. "Guys come in here, spend a few days planning a job, bring in this guy, pick up that guy on the way, maybe they steal a couple cars, maybe they buy some guns. I know this guy—Angel Acosta, they call him. So Angel and his men steal this Ford up around Memphis, I believe it was. Then they drive it to this car guy and sell it to him for probably half what it's worth. Fine. No problem. So they steal another car down the road, use the money from the first car sale to buy some guns from this dealer in Memphis—fine, yeah, now I'm sure it was Memphis. So they drive back to where they'd sold the first car, use the guns to steal it back." Martello stopped, pulled a cigarette and lighter from his jacket.

Figuring the story was over, Cottonmouth said, "Sounds like they made out fine."

Martello scowled his disappointment. "Sounds like too much running around for a couple cars, some cash, and a handful of guns, you ask me. You ever give much thought to moving on from this place?"

Cottonmouth looked around. "The county or the camp?"

Martello nodded. "That's it, isn't it? One and the same. You were down in New Orleans, down in Honduras, I hear. Working? Moving guns around?"

Cottonmouth said sure, something like that.

"Imagine instead of taking orders, giving them. Being the one making the money instead of the one doing all the work."

Cottonmouth nodded.

"I have some men I work with, men who own businesses in New Orleans, in Texarkana, up in Hot Springs. Figured they'd like to know a little more about this place. Might like to have a little business of their own. A good restaurant. Hotel. A good place for drinks, dancing, playing cards. That sound like something you might want to be involved in?"

Cottonmouth smiled, thinking how quickly things had turned around for him. And why shouldn't they? He'd played this right. Christ, he'd forgotten to say anything. "Yes," he managed. "Sounds good."

"The time to expand is when people are dying to sell," Martello said. "New avenues, new revenues. You have to be ready for whatever is coming. Did you know a friend of mine had fifty thousand barrels of beer ready to roll down the ramps as soon as Roosevelt was sworn in? You can imagine what that little move will do to my private clubs."

"Figure it won't be good."

"Good? It will be a disaster. You know what a private club is when it becomes public and anyone can visit?"

Cottonmouth shook his head.

"A church," he said, then caught himself. "Of course, there's good money to be made in running a church, but not for me."

"Seems you're busy enough already," Cottonmouth joked.

"Speaking of which, have you ever thought about a partnership for your camp?"

33

Everett Logan pulled out a tumbler and a bottle of brown liquor, poured a fistful, raised his glass. "Cottonmouth Tomlin, didn't think you had it in you, but you've set up a nice place here."

Outside the main cabin was some barking, but just the yaps here and there, dogs testing their voices, nothing yet to worry about.

Cottonmouth nodded, took a quick swig of beer, said "Only the beginning" with a look in his eye that caught Everett.

"How's that?"

Cottonmouth took another swig, said, "Never mind that. Still too early to tell."

Everett said maybe it sounded like he ought to tell.

A few new men had come to the camp, just for the night. Word was spreading, Cottonmouth thought to himself. *Everything is coming up, Cottonmouth; that's for sure,* he thought. He looked back to Everett. "Just pieces coming together. Thinking everything is going to be all right." That look in his eye again.

Everett set his glass on the table between them. "Don't do anything too quickly."

Cottonmouth smiled, said some things were being currently discussed.

"Just be careful," Everett said, standing up, then walking back and forth. "You know much about Martello? Other than he's 'the big guy' supposed to set it all right?"

"Can't say I do," Cottonmouth said. "You're the one who told me he ran so many things. You're the one said he seems to be doing all right for himself."

"Couldn't have said it better myself. Doing all right. For himself."

"And you're the one taking all the college courses in business. Ain't the goal to make yourself money? Ain't that what we're all trying to do?"

Everett said that was an excellent point, said everyone he could hit with a rock from where he was standing was out to take someone else's money. "I'm just letting you know you should be a little sensitive for a hand in your pocket. It's true I said he was a good man to know. But I never thought anything would come of it—not so quickly, anyway."

Cottonmouth said, "Thanks for the vote of confidence."

"It's not about that," Everett said, then took another drink. "Martello never has business partners for very long, from what I've been able to find out in the last day or so. When I asked around about his place in Shreveport, to make sure he was there—well, you hear things."

One of the new men standing nearby perked up, turned an ear to the conversation.

Cottonmouth said it was time they all started looking forward. "Roosevelt," Cottonmouth spat, "has it in his Yankee head that the best thing for this country is to take away our gold and open up the bars again. Now, I'll grant you I haven't been back in the States too long, but even I can see that isn't a good recipe for the bootleggers. And with the bank robbing getting tougher, it's all leading to finding these new ways for a man to make a living. Now you and Beans and Jimmy and who knows who else seem to have figured out this snatch business. Like

I said, I think we're better off not housing the marks here, but that's something we can work on. Mr. Martello is in a position to make all this here work even better so we can keep up with it all. It's looking like good business to be a businessman."

Everett took a drink. "Isn't all of this sounding too good to be true? Suddenly everything working out like this?"

"Suddenly nothing. I was in Honduras running around making one man richer, just because he was the businessman, and I was getting the business. High time to grow up, have some tapestries of my own on the wall, if you know what I mean."

Everett didn't. "I'm telling you you can't trust Martello. You know that fellow Moyet? Clark Moyet? Said he heard Martello struck a deal with a Louisiana family name of McKenney. The man inherited a restaurant, married a woman from Chicago, and brought her down here. Ended up turning the place into a drinking-and-dancing place, down along the Red River. That's the Black Rabbit."

Cottonmouth said, "Yeah, you already told me about it."

The new man who'd been eavesdropping moved closer still.

"Well, the husband and wife get a visit from your new friend Martello; few months later, husband and wife disappear. Martello owns the place."

"Maybe he paid them so much for the bar," Cottonmouth said, "they moved to Paris. France, I mean, not Texas."

"Doesn't explain how a man found most of their bodies in a clump of dogwood trees outside Plain Dealing."

The man who'd been listening from the edges perked up again.

Cottonmouth winced, had some beer, wiped his mouth with his sleeve. "Could have been anything."

"Could have been."

Cottonmouth asked was that all he had.

Everett said he wasn't saying anything, except to just not rush into anything. "He comes in, maybe it's exactly like you think it is. Or maybe he wants a little more control. I'm just saying it's worth taking your time on the deal—feel him out. When Jack Morgan was loaning money to the French," he started, but Cottonmouth waved him off.

"This isn't the night for a college class to scare me from making a deal with Mr. Martello," Cottonmouth said.

"I'm just saying, and this is just from looking around and asking a couple people here and there recently, I'm just saying be careful. I've been working with your uncle for years, been coming here off and on. And I want you to be able to make something of this place. Just saying you have to be careful who you trust is all. That's all I'm saying."

"Can I trust any of you?" Cottonmouth asked.

Everett wanted to say he could, but he didn't.

"That's what I thought." Cottonmouth patted his shoulder. "Have another drink. I appreciate your worrying, but my mother walked out a long time back, and I'm not looking to replace her. So maybe you just keep to scaring bank managers and reading textbooks about business, and I'll keep to running this business."

As Cottonmouth started to walk away, the eavesdropping man came over, introduced himself as Charles. "Came down with Victor," he said. "Victor Martello," he continued, as if there might be another.

Everett and Cottonmouth nodded to him.

"I was about to head out," Cottonmouth said. "Good to meet you, Charles."

Everett set his glass down, then stood up. He'd tried. Tried to get the man to look at what he was doing, what was going on around him. Would Cottonmouth's uncle Beurie have told him any different? Everett wasn't sure exactly what he owed to Beurie but felt it was something. But he'd been dismissed now. *You warn someone, what else can you do? It's on them at some point, isn't it?* The question now was whether to stick around for a few days planning the next job or to move on. Things were changing. That was all he knew. Even the air felt different.

"Yeah, it was nice to meet you," Everett said, starting to turn away.

"Everett, one second," the eavesdropping man said. "Was just wondering if you had a few dollars I could borrow. Wanted to head over to El Dorado for some of the stronger stuff."

"Plenty around here, if that's what you're after."

Charles squinted. "Honestly, there's this gal I been seeing on the sly. Her man found out, and he's lammed off with their money, so I was going to head over there and, well, you know. Only I don't have the cash. I have this, if you want to hold it until I get back and can repay you. I'm good for it."

The man pulled a ring from his pocket.

Everett looked at the ring, turning it in his fingers. "Don't try to tell me this is an emerald ring from some prince."

"Not at all." Charles laughed. "It's jade, to be honest with you. Jade and fourteen-karat gold. If it were emerald, I suspect it would be in a museum, not Arkansas."

Everett said he didn't know much about jewelry, asked what it was worth.

"More than the few dollars I'm asking you at the moment, I can assure you."

"Why don't you just get the cash for this from a hockshop or maybe a jeweler? Sure there's one in Texarkana or Shreveport you can use."

"No time. I can take it somewhere and sell it, sure. But that's a tomorrow problem. Today I need the cash. I don't get to El Dorado tonight, there's no telling what she might do. Go after him, which wouldn't be a good idea for her. Take off somewhere else, which wouldn't be a good idea for me. I just want to head over there, be with her tonight, stay with her. She's a good woman. Deserves better than the hand she's been dealt. I'll be back in a couple days—give you back the money, plus a little for the trouble, and you give me back the ring."

"Don't see how I can lose," Everett said, handing the man a few dollars. "You sure you can trust me?"

"If we don't have trust, what have we got?" The man tipped his hat, walked out the door.

"Looks like things are looking up," Everett said, turning over, then pocketing the jade ring.

34

The next morning, Victor Martello stopped by the camp, was ferried over by Othel.

He left his drink untouched on the porch rail in front of him, looked around to see the men he'd brought up to the county with him, looked to the men who had been there with Cottonmouth. "It certainly is a nice piece of land you have back here. Quiet. Secluded."

Cottonmouth said it had been his family's, used as a hunting lodge when that had been the thing to do.

"And you grew up here?" Martello said.

"I did. Spent time over there." Cottonmouth motioned toward a clump of bushes. "That was the Alamo for a while, then Camelot, then back to Alamo, I think. Spent some time as the Wicked Witch of the West's castle too."

Martello said he'd meant the county overall, and Cottonmouth said sure, sure.

"You must have seen the places change quite a bit."

"They've changed," Cottonmouth said, "but I didn't see it. Been away past few years."

"Thought you'd said you grew up here."

"I did, sure. But things don't change while you're looking at them. Matter of perspective and all that."

"Perspective?"

"Like . . ." Cottonmouth thought for a second. "Being on a train. You don't notice you've moved until you go to get off or get back on, and suddenly you're in Tennessee."

"And you've noticed changes?" Martello pulled a cigar from his pocket, chewed the tip, spit, rolled the end around his mouth. The morning sun was coming up pretty good now, easing above the tops of the cedar trees, cutting through the tips of the pines.

"People come and go. Came and went."

"Your mother, as I understand it?"

"Right."

"I heard she left with the man who sold extracts and spices from a wagon."

"Funny," Cottonmouth said. "That's what I heard too."

"Your father went after them?"

Cottonmouth nodded.

"Dead?" Martello asked.

"Or might as well be. My uncle was the only family I had after that, aside from pretty much everybody else in this county."

"And you left?"

"Overstayed my welcome."

"And you came back."

"When my uncle died, yeah. Came back to take over."

Martello said it seemed to be going well, seemed to be making money.

"It's a good business to be in," Cottonmouth said. "Times being what they are, our kind needs a safe space, for planning and recovering."

"My friend Campbell has a place like this down around Vivian," Martello said.

Cottonmouth said he'd heard about it.

"Hard to get to," Martello said. "Bit like this place. Keeps the law away."

Cottonmouth said it was the same here.

"But you have a deal with the sheriff in town, right? Keeps the law away, this agreement, without the need of boats and bayous?"

Cottonmouth nodded, said he supposed it did. "Long as we stay out of trouble inside the county, then the county won't bring trouble to us."

"So what's the point of making this place hard to get to? Seems it would be bad for business."

Cottonmouth said he hadn't thought of it that way.

Martello pointed to a slight opening in the woods. "Wouldn't take much to get that road open. Long as the law is set on staying away, don't see the point in having to dodge snakes and gators to get here."

Cottonmouth said more than likely there weren't any gators out there.

"I'm aware," Martello said. "I was making a joke. Not exactly the Louisiana swamps here, is it? This is Arkansas, after all. So clear the road. Easy."

Cottonmouth said all right. He had thought about the road, sure, had even considered maybe clearing it. But Martello was going to do something about it. That was the way the Banana Man was too. Deciding on a thing and doing it. *How does it come so easy to them?* he thought.

Martello said it was no trouble. "Be glad to work with you, call in a favor to get that road cleared for you, bring in some more business."

In a split second, Cottonmouth pictured it. Cars coming right up near the cabins, a little hidden motor court here, this place building up. Improving the cabins. Driving in crates of food from Moon's. He said that sounded like a good idea.

"I think we can work this out," Martello said. "Get the road cleared and stable, make some improvements to the accommodations."

Cottonmouth said that sounded expensive.

"Let me worry about that," Martello said. "I have the cash to get that started." He snapped his fingers, and a man Cottonmouth hadn't noticed handed Martello a large envelope. "I went to the trouble of having some paperwork drawn up, just to make sure everything is on the up and up." He handed the envelope of paperwork to Cottonmouth.

Cottonmouth weighed the envelope in his hands. "Feels heavy."

Martello grinned. "Fairly straightforward. We enter into a partnership. I'll take care of funding the improvements, which will be a large portion of the investment, you see."

Cottonmouth didn't see. Maybe he would when he had a chance to look at the paperwork. Or maybe he could get Everett to look at the paperwork, he thought, hoping one of Everett's business classes had been in contracts. Though Everett would likely as not just look for a reason Martello was trying to cheat him.

Martello was going on about agreements with the businesses in towns, about negotiating better rates, about offering protection. "And the cars," he said. "You'll want to think a few steps ahead. You have a mechanic in town you like to use, I hear. Move him down here, have him set up shop right here. Surely you could keep him busy, all the increased traffic."

Without thinking, Cottonmouth said, "The mechanic's a woman."

"A woman? Even better." Martello laughed, scratched his jaw in thought. "Even better." Laughed again.

Cottonmouth didn't laugh.

35

"Are you sure you don't want the sheriff?" Deputy Dolson asked Henrietta Rudd. "Earl said you wanted to see me, but I figured you wanted the sheriff."

"Sit down, Deputy," Henrietta said, herself seated on a divan they'd had brought in last year from Memphis when their old friend Clarence Saunders had been selling off some of his estate to raise money for some soon-to-fail idea or another. She assured the deputy that she'd sent for him, not Monroe.

Deputy Dolson sat down, fidgeted, stood, sat back down. "Yes, ma'am."

"Would you like a drink, Deputy? My sister usually plays bartender, but she's lately taken to afternoon walks about the town for some reason or another."

He said he'd heard that walks were nice.

"Nice," she said, smiling at his nervousness. "Yes, indeed. So, a drink?"

"No thank you, ma'am."

She said that was fine. "The reason I asked you here is that I've heard a number of unsavory miscreants from down Shreveport way have made their way to our county, invited here by our very own Cottonmouth Tomlin."

Dolson had been staring at the paintings on the wall, the portraits. He was lost in the colors, lost in the depth, in the face of Old Man Rudd.

"Deputy," Henrietta said, drawing his attention.

"Yes," he said. "Shreveport miscreants. We had a couple of them in town this morning. There was some disagreement at Mr. Moon's store."

"I trust you settled the matter?"

"I had to talk to the men, yes, ma'am."

"Talking," she said. "And you have some level of confidence that we are still at the talking stage with these outsiders?"

He started to say something, realized he didn't know what to say, so he just said "Yes, ma'am" again.

She ran her hands along the lower part of her dress, straightening as she stood. "Deputy Dolson," she said, then stopped as he stood.

"Yes, ma'am?"

She shook her head. "Oh, do sit back down. I'll let you know when it's time for you to stand."

He sat back down.

"Now, as I was saying, the man named Martello is not unknown to us. We read the papers. We know what he's been into. We are aware of his dealings."

"Yes, ma'am. If he does anything illegal," Dolson started, then stopped when Henrietta turned on him.

"Illegal?"

He nodded.

"Legal and illegal," she said, walking to the edge of the room. "That does not concern me in the slightest. Those are courthouse matters." She looked out over the courthouse square. "Do you ever wonder why you have to drag people to that little jail of yours to hold them? Then you have to take them up to the courthouse, to the courtroom, floor to ceiling covered with the laws and the paintings of old dead men in robes?"

He said he didn't.

"The papers in the courthouse only matter to the courthouse. If there's an argument to be made, to say that it says such and such in these court documents, then that argument must be made in court, where it's binding, you understand."

He nodded along, as if he did.

"You follow the rule of law in a court of law. But when you're an outlaw, as these people are, well, do you know what that means?"

He said it meant they'd broken the law.

"Deputy Dolson," she said, sighing. "I can see we're not understanding each other, and by that I mean that you are not understanding me, which is what concerns me. An outlaw is someone who lives outside the protection of the law. Dates back centuries. They have done something, certainly, but their present state of being, as it were, is that of outlaw. Outside the law. Outside the reach of the law, fine. But also outside the *protection* of the law, do you understand? They are no longer allowed to hide behind bailiffs and courts and sheriffs, even deputy sheriffs."

He nodded. "Outside the protection of the law."

"Which means that they have what they think of as their own code, you see? They live outside the law and therefore must be honest, as someone once said. For years, there was an agreement about behavior in our county. And then Cottonmouth Tomlin comes back. And this man from Shreveport that Tomlin brought here, this Martello, as we've been given to understand, is of the belief that he is able to work even beyond these, well, let's call them agreements or understandings. So threatening a man such as that with jail time is of little value, as someone will just come along and blast a hole in the wall to free him. Do you understand?"

He was beginning to understand. "If you can't stop a man with the law, you have to resort to other means?"

"I'm glad we understand each other," she said. "I'm not convinced that Sheriff McCollum understands this."

36

Cottonmouth stepped down from Miss Phoebe's, walked toward Lorena's.

He nodded as he passed two women he didn't recognize, then a man he'd seen recently but couldn't place. *You blink and you miss it,* he thought. Growing up with Cliftons, McMahens, Cranks. He tried to remember all the names, the faces. The Willis store over in Sharman. The depot in Waldo where he'd nearly lost his left hand. He looked up and down the road, at the drugstore, Miss Phoebe's behind him, Moon's place, Lorena's garage down at the end. Should the town have changed more than it had? Less? Were more people coming in or going out? People comfortable, like Martello was saying. People making wages at the lumber mill, then spending it at Moon's store, that same dollar then going back to the lumber mill for supplies. A dollar being passed from one person to the other, never leaving the county, until it was ground to dust.

Cottonmouth walked through the open door at Lorena's garage, his eyes adjusting to the change in light, and saw a man with a gun. "Looks like you walked in at the wrong time," the man said.

"He's got a gun, Cottonmouth," Lorena said, and the man turned to her, then back to Cottonmouth.

"I thought that was you," the man said.

Cottonmouth took off his hat, moved sideways toward a workbench against the wall. "You all right?" he asked toward Lorena.

"So far, so good," she said.

"You try to sell this man some of those cheap tires again?" Cottonmouth asked, still moving sideways along the workbench.

"You're Cottonmouth Tomlin, right? The one what runs the camp," the man said.

Cottonmouth said he was.

"I'm Moose Malone," the man said. "Came up from Shreveport on Victor Martello's suggestion. Said there was snatch work to be discussed."

"A real honor to meet you, Mr. Moose," Cottonmouth said. "What say we set the gun down and someone tell me what's going on here."

Not putting the gun down at all, Moose said, "The lady and I were talking business. Wanted to see one of these cars for myself—people speak so highly of them, so we came by to see could we borrow one, take it out for a drive. But then the lady here got a bee in her bonnet about it."

"Here, here," Lorena said, turning to the safe behind her. "Let me get the keys to the coupe. Some cash too. Just don't do anything stupid."

"Looks like it's good you stopped by," Moose said, laughing. "Suddenly the princess has some sense."

Lorena pulled her pistol from the safe, turned, leveled it at Moose Malone. "Good time for you to leave."

He turned. "And what do you plan to do with that, little lady?"

"Hoping not much more than this," she said, shrugging, "but you never know."

He turned his gun from Cottonmouth to her, held his other hand out, palm up. "Best hand that to me before you get hurt."

"Maybe you're right. This was my brother's," she said. "I'm not even sure it still fires."

She spun the grip toward him, stepped forward.

As he reached for it, she loosened her grip, let it spin back into her hand, the barrel leveling toward him as she pulled the trigger, and he jerked back, twisted, fell toward Cottonmouth, who'd eased behind the man for a move that wasn't needed.

She tossed the pistol to Cottonmouth, shrugged, said, "I guess it still fires."

The man was still falling, taking his time about it, holding the wound in his hip, staggering; then he spun toward Cottonmouth. Cottonmouth hit him in the temple with the butt of Lorena's gun, and the man crumpled like a bag of flour, dust clouding up from the floor.

"Friend of yours?" Lorena asked.

"Who knows anymore?" Cottonmouth said, stepping over the man and picking up a rag from the workbench as he set down Lorena's pistol. He turned to the wounded man, pressing the rag to the man's bleeding hip, the .22 not doing too much damage but enough. He picked up the man's pistol, which he knew was a Colt M1911, having sold hundreds of them in Honduras. He held the gun in his palm, looked over to Lorena. When he'd sold these, he'd praised the power of the pistol and the fastest pistol bullet available. She'd pulled a .22 on the man while he was holding something that fired a .38 caliber bullet at thirteen hundred feet per second. *Christ, that was close. Men with this kind of firepower walking through town now?* Maybe he could speak to Martello. Maybe Moose Malone had just gone rogue.

Lorena walked to the window, tried wiping the grime from one of the panes but only managed to smear a pane of grime to thinness. She leaned forward, looked left and right through the window. "You'd think someone would come running for the gunshot."

Cottonmouth didn't say the pop from her pistol wouldn't have been noticed. He stood next to the man on the ground, pocketed the man's pistol. "He said *we*."

"What?"

"He said 'We came to town to see about borrowing a car.'"

"Oh. We."

"Was anyone else with him when he walked in?"

She said there wasn't, but he had seemed to be in a hurry. "Maybe his friend was waiting outside." She looked farther up the road, then down the other way.

They heard a sound Cottonmouth knew was a shotgun blast, and each ran to the front door, Lorena with her pistol, Cottonmouth keeping the man's pistol in his coat pocket.

Cottonmouth eased open the door, said he'd go see what was happening, that Lorena needed to stay inside with the shot man, and she said the hell she would.

They eased into the street; people were running into the square when another shot from across the street stopped the crowd from moving.

Pistol shot, Cottonmouth thought. *Damn sure bigger than a .22.*

Cottonmouth and Lorena stepped between a Packard and a Buick, looking through the car windows as they did, then leaning out into the street once they'd gotten to the back of the sedans. They kept close to the backs of the parked cars as they moved, hunched.

Two hatless men in dark suits walked out of the bank, trying to force another into a car, the crowd standing around, stuck in place. Each man was holding what looked like a Browning Automatic Rifle.

"Those are BARs," he said to Lorena. "Five hundred rounds a minute."

"You sound impressed." She knelt, had her back to the sedan's tire while she checked her pistol.

"It's a good gun."

"You trying to sell me one?"

"I can get you a good deal. Discount if you take a whole crate. Even throw in some free rounds for you."

"I'm good," she said. "This pistol can fire five shots a minute, unless I want to go back to the garage for more bullets."

Cottonmouth dared another look around the car, saw the two men with the automatic rifles, the driver aiming a pistol out the window. He looked back to the bank to see where the shotgun blast had come from but couldn't tell.

"Five shots a minute? Good thing there's only three or four of them," he said.

She nodded. "Good thing."

Cottonmouth looked up to see Earl Withers Jr., the barman from the Culver Hotel, kneeling near the front of the car, looking at the gathering crowd near the bank, then back to him and Lorena.

"What's going on?" Earl asked.

Lorena said it looked like a couple of gangsters had grabbed someone from the bank.

"Oh, thank God," Earl said. "The Pribble boy said it was another goddamn bank run."

"Your money's safe, Earl," Cottonmouth said. "Might want to head back to the bar. I'm sure folks could use a little refreshment once this is all over in a few minutes."

He said that sounded like a fine idea, left the two of them by the car.

Cottonmouth and Lorena eased across the street, coming up behind the men and the car.

Lorena asked what he wanted to do, and he said he didn't know.

She said he needed to help, and he said, "Help what? Help who?"

"Mr. McLeach from the bank," she said, tugging him toward the trouble, just as McLeach broke free, running back into the bank.

Sheriff McCollum and Deputy Dolson came around the corner as three men jumped into the getaway car, nothing but a split lip for their troubles. The sedan spun around and headed south on Jefferson.

"That was Hank Moon's car," Lorena said.

Cottonmouth asked if that was Bill Moon's brother.

"Same. Plymouth. Worked on it last week. Had to rebuild the fuel pump."

Cottonmouth shook his head. "They stole Hank Moon's car?"

"At least they didn't get Mr. McLeach."

Deputy Dolson ran into the bank to help McLeach while the sheriff fired two shots well above the retreating car. The car made a shaky, stuttering left turn, headed out of town, a few townspeople following it like a parade.

Lorena eased to standing, looked toward the commotion: people walking around, people stopping, everyone talking to each other.

Cottonmouth said it looked like everyone was safe.

Lorena turned to him. "Safe? Is that what you call this?" She looked around the square again.

"It's safe now. Safer. The trouble is gone."

Her hands were shaking. "The trouble hasn't gone. It's gotten worse. It's here. The trouble hasn't gone at all."

"You should hand me the pistol."

She asked, "What? What pistol?"

"The one you're pointing at me," he said as she continued to wave her arms around, her hands still shaking.

She set the gun down on the running board of the Buick they were next to. "I was working on a car," she said, moving her hand along an imaginary line in the air, stopping with each sentence as if she were making a list. "A man comes in. He wants a car. I won't give him a car. He pulls a gun on me. Those men find another car. I shoot the man. The man they sent for a car." Her eyes weren't focused on anything in particular. "So I shot the man. He had a gun. You came in. So I shot the man. He had a gun."

"You handled that," Cottonmouth said, picking up the pistol. "You did great."

She quickly shook her head a few times, waved him off. "I don't need you patronizing me."

He said he wasn't.

Her hands were still shaking. She held them to her face. "Cold. My hands are so cold."

"All the blood rushed to your heart, your head," he said. "Happens like that, times like this. All the blood is trying to settle back."

"Settle back? Settle back? There's no settling back." Neither of them knew what she was saying. She started to shake her arms out, lower her arms, shake them out.

"Are you OK?" he asked her.

"Do I look OK? No. I'm not. I'm not." She took a breath, stepped away, then stopped, turned back. "How are you OK? I was working on a car. I was looking for the half-inch manifold wrench. For the '29 Chevrolet. I turned to the table, and there was the man. He said he wanted to talk about the cars I was working on. Then he wanted to shoot me. Then you walked in, and he knew you," she said, waving her hands, "because of course he knew you."

"And you handled him."

"He wanted to shoot me. Of course I handled him. I could have died."

"You're safe now."

She said again how she could have died, leaned against the Buick, started shaking, heaved, threw up along the side of the car, the splatter hitting her shoes, his shoes.

Cottonmouth walked toward her to put his hands on her shoulders, as if that would help. "Are you OK?"

She wiped her mouth, eyes watering. "Do I look like I'm OK?"

Down the street a bit, the sheriff walked along the road, trying to settle the townsfolk, asking was everyone all right, speaking to them about what they'd seen, taking notes in his notebook. He saw Cottonmouth Tomlin standing to the side.

The sheriff yelled, "Anything?"

Cottonmouth thought about telling the sheriff about Moose Malone, coming clean about Martello, but knew he couldn't explain it without it looking like he was involved, and he'd wind up in jail or, worse, having to explain himself in front of Henrietta Rudd. Cottonmouth shook his head, shrugged to say he didn't know.

The sheriff nodded, went back to listening to witnesses already misremembering what they'd seen.

37

Cottonmouth walked Lorena back toward her garage, pulled a small flask from his coat pocket, asked her if she wanted a drink.

She took a sip. "Probably need more than one. Have you ever seen anything like that?" she asked—rhetorically, she thought.

He stopped just before they got to her front door. Looked back the way they'd come, the way he'd come, what he thought he'd left behind. "I have," he said.

She said she'd have something to talk about for a while as she moved to step through the door. She turned, saw Cottonmouth left behind in the street, looking backward. "You coming with me?" she asked again, not thinking she was really asking a question.

"I have," he said, and she asked, "Have what?" and he said, "Seen that kind of thing." He leaned his back against the outside wall of her shop as she stopped and waited for him.

Back down the street, stories were already being carved out, heroics on display, threats heightened. In a few hours, the stories would contain more bullets than a Chicago garage on Saint Valentine's Day.

Or a nameless Honduran village on a random Thursday.

"I thought," Cottonmouth started. "I thought just, you know, with the camp, the men coming in. I didn't think," he said, then stopped. "Moose Malone."

"Oh," she said. "Right." She closed the shop door she'd started to open. "What do we do with . . . ," she said, not wanting to finish the sentence. The body.

Cottonmouth exhaled, stepped in front of her, pulled his pistol from his pocket, and walked into the garage.

Lorena followed, then stepped to his side as they both looked at the spot on the ground where Moose Malone had fallen. The dark stain was there, but no Moose.

"What?" she asked. "What?"

Cottonmouth looked up to the lofted area above them, then to the walls. He raised the pistol, then reached out his arm to keep Lorena behind him as he walked. A crash of parts was on the floor ten feet past where Malone had fallen, so Cottonmouth worked his way there, his head turning to any creak or shard of light in the garage.

"The door," Lorena said, pointing to the back door of the garage. "It's open."

They walked toward the slash of sunlight coming through the back of the garage, each of them nodding or pointing as they passed a new stain on the corner of a table, a clump of parts knocked to the ground.

"Stumbled his way to freedom," Cottonmouth said as they looked out the back door, the empty lot behind the garage leading to dozens of houses, streets.

Lorena asked should they try to follow him.

Cottonmouth turned, took Lorena's hand, and pulled her inside the garage, then shut and latched the door behind them. "I think we've had enough excitement for the day."

~

The first couple shots of whiskey were medicinal, and they were each settling in to sipping their third drink, her setting down her glass to let her hands shake a little every so often.

She asked again had he ever seen that man before, the man she'd shot, who had gotten up while they were gone, dragged himself away to, well, who knew?

Cottonmouth said he hadn't.

"But he was with those men at the bank. That was . . . ," she started, took another swig. "We've never had anything like that here. Not that I've seen." She looked across at Cottonmouth, who seemed to have drifted. "You've seen that sort of thing, though."

"I did this," he said. "Brought this here."

"Brought what?" she asked, but he wasn't listening.

"Happened so quick," he said. "It was just weeks ago. Months? I got the wire about Uncle Beurie," he said, his thoughts back in Honduras now. "I thought I could just start clean or come back here, start over. Start again. Pick up where I was. I don't know. It just, it just seemed like I had a chance, you know? With people who weren't there, who didn't see. There were families in these villages," he said. "Where they wanted to put down rails, wanted to clear the area. But there were people there."

She said it was all right. "You don't have to talk about it. I don't need to know anything you don't want to tell me. It's fine."

"It's not. Maybe it was too much to ask, the coming back. Thinking I could settle after what happened. After what I helped happen. These men, too, they've . . . ," he said, then shook his head. "Look, I shouldn't drop all this on you."

"You're not dropping anything on me. You can tell me whatever you want."

"No," he said. "I mean all this." He pointed toward the bank, waved his hand to the mess in the garage. "I shouldn't have brought these outlaws to your door, to your garage. Shouldn't have brought them into your days at all. I'm sorry about that. I've let things get out of hand."

She said it wasn't a problem. She said he shouldn't worry. She said it was fine. "At least they clean up after themselves," she joked.

He finished his drink, set the glass on the table. "You seem to be feeling better."

She said the whiskey was helping, asked if he wanted her to see about another bottle.

"After I see about getting some of this"—he pointed around him—"chaos settled."

They stood up, and she walked him to the door. "I'll find that bottle for when you're done," she said.

38

Sheriff Monroe McCollum looked around Miss Phoebe's from his table. Across the way, he saw the Henager woman trying to talk her little boy into eating some scrambled eggs as the McWilliams newlyweds sat a few tables away, looking at each other, wondering if they'd run out of things to talk about already, him starting and stopping a couple of times, her wide eyed and encouraging.

"Another piece?" Miss Phoebe asked at his elbow, bringing him back.

"No, those were good enough," he said.

She asked if he was after the men who'd caused all the trouble.

"Always," he said. "It's my job to stop the trouble, straighten things out."

"And you have some things straightened out?"

He said he had some straightened out and had to go deliver an update on those things. "Of course, I could always stop by here later." He wiped crumbs from the corner of his lips. "Not sure how late you're planning to stay open."

She smiled. "Hadn't planned to stay open late. Hadn't been given a reason. Figure I might stay around some, given a good enough reason. Girl's got to have a reason she's making plans like that."

He nodded. "It's plans like that I wanted to talk to you about. Not so much just tonight but the days to come. Lot of what's been going on here got me thinking. If you ain't got anything better to do, wouldn't mind thinking some of it over with you once you're closing up here, when I'm done over there," he said, nodding across the street. "Would be nice to talk about what we're going to fill our days with—I mean, when those days come, maybe we can, I mean." He scratched his head, looked away, then back. "It would be nice to spend those days with you I think is what I'm trying to say."

She'd had better offers, of course, but not recently.

And she knew, whatever else people said about Sheriff Monroe McCollum, that he was a nice enough man, nice enough to the townsfolk, nice enough to her. He was nice enough, she figured. And, if she was being honest, it had been a while since a man had been lost for words around her. "If I'm here, I'm here," she said, already thinking of a grassy flat piece of riverbank that would make for a nice picnic when the weather cooled. Maybe a fishing boat set right in the middle of a lake.

He said that was good enough for him and walked away, nearly running into one of the Hayes boys as he crossed the street.

The sheriff said, "Careful now," and the boy turned, hand holding his cap on his head. He said "Sorry, Sheriff" and kept running.

The sheriff crossed the streets, held open the Culver Hotel doors for two strangers leaving, and then doffed his hat to the bartender.

Working a dishrag around a chipped tumbler, Earl Withers Jr. said, "Evening, Sheriff. What can I do you for?"

"Just a whiskey. Here to see the sisters."

Earl set aside the dried glass, poured the sheriff a couple of fingers of the cheap stuff, said the sheriff ought to tread lightly up there. "Seems the elder Miss Rudd is in a foul mood."

"So what's new?" The sheriff smirked, raising his glass but not drinking.

"The Williamson girl finally had her twins this morning."

"How's that?"

"Beulah's youngest. Over in Brister."

"Did I ask about the Williamson girl?"

"You asked what was new. I just thought . . ."

"That's fine, Earl. You keep your ear to the ground."

"Occupational hazard."

"Figured. Now can I get some decent whiskey in this place?"

Earl shook his head, drank the sheriff's whiskey, poured him some of the slightly better stuff. "And the Tomlin boy. The one that's come back. Saw him at all that commotion across the street," Earl started. "Talked to Othel Walker a few minutes ago. He'd heard they found one of the men what tried to kidnap Mr. McLeach shot dead a block from the bank, over by Archibald Henry's old place."

"Never mind that," the sheriff said, smelling his glass of whiskey but not drinking. "Ain't a thing to worry about."

"Never said it was," Earl said, setting a glass aside, picking up another, and starting the drying routine all over again.

The sheriff asked how business was, and Earl said he couldn't complain. "Since when?" the sheriff asked, taking a little sip of his drink.

Earl Withers nodded to the stairs. "Might want to head on up there. The Dolson kid went in about twenty minutes back now."

"Jarvis?" the sheriff asked. "My deputy?"

"One and the same."

The sheriff set down his glass. "What do they want with Jarvis?"

"Reckon they could tell you, you stop stalling and get on up there and let me get back to my business."

The sheriff turned, looked across the emptiness of the room.

"Fair enough, Earl. I'll let you get back to your fan club." The sheriff winked. "You leave my drink there, and I'll finish it when I get back. This shouldn't take long."

"Just be careful up there," Earl said.

"I know, I know." The sheriff waved him off. "Everybody's in a rotten mood."

The sheriff shook his head going up the stairs. He'd been planning to take a little more time to himself, maybe hand off some of the heavy lifting to Jarvis. Fishing. That was what the sheriff wanted to do. Row out in a little boat, drop a line in the water, and fade off to sleep with birds flying overhead and supper swimming underneath, perfectly at peace with the world. But if Jarvis was going behind his back to the Rudd sisters about something, well, that would have to be dealt with immediately. As he hit the landing, he began running through a list of candidates to replace Jarvis.

He walked down the hall, got to the Rudds' door, straightened his hat, knocked.

The door eased open, Deputy Jarvis Dolson pulling the knob.

"Deputy." The sheriff nodded.

"Sheriff," the deputy said, then mouthed "Sorry, sorry" to him as the sheriff entered the room.

As Dolson stepped into the hall, Henrietta Rudd told him that he should stay, and so he did, avoiding the sheriff's look. "So kind of you to join us, Sheriff," Henrietta continued as the sheriff walked to the center of the room to stand in front of where she was sitting.

"The Pribble matter is solved," the sheriff said, air of the peacock about him, chest out as he listed off his recent wins. "The Thrailkills too. And I was able to collect the money owed from Mr. A. C. Kendrick as well. All taken care of, as requested."

"That where you were while these outlaws came into town to nab Ambrose McLeach right out of his bank?"

Confused, the sheriff said they'd stopped that. "Me and Dolson here. Put a stop to that foolishness."

"Not before the entire town was terrorized by these men. I thought you were taking care of the Tomlin problem, which has grown into a

Martello problem, and here you are shaking down A. C. Kendrick for pocket change."

"I'm able to do both."

"Apparently you're not," Henrietta Rudd said, standing, then leaning on her walking stick as she worked her way along the walls of the parlor, circling the sheriff as she spoke. "Tomlin's partners are now attempting to kidnap bankers in broad daylight in our town? And Dolson here tells me that one of Tomlin's men turns up shot to death in the middle of the day."

"Those weren't his men. They were strangers to him," he said, "if I'm not mistaken."

"Oh, I think we can assume you're mistaken," Henrietta said. "I think we can assume we've all been very mistaken." The *all* dragged along for five or six syllables as she slowed her perimeter walk. "Broad daylight," she repeated. "We are on the verge of having Governor Futrell send down carloads of badged bumblers or, even worse, that Yankee president setting loose God knows what on our little county."

The deputy stood still next to the sheriff, turning his head to watch Henrietta circle the room, while the sheriff watched as Abigail walked across the room to the drink cart, poured herself a few fingers of gin.

The sheriff said he'd have a word with Cottonmouth right away, get it settled.

"Oh, this will be settled; there's no doubt about that," Henrietta said, "but we're well past words, at this point. We've been through this, explained things, been very patient—I think you'll agree. Lime gelatin, as you'll recall."

"I'll take care of it," the sheriff said, and in the back of his mind, the fishing boat drifted farther and farther away.

Henrietta Rudd walked directly behind him until he turned to face her. "No, you won't."

"I'm the sheriff," Monroe McCollum said. "I'm the law here."

"You're neither of those," Henrietta said, stepping to the side.

Deputy Dolson watched Abigail Rudd step behind the older man, raise her hand until it popped with light. McCollum's head jerked forward—one knee buckling, one stiff—his mass moving toward the floor.

In shock, the deputy reached around him but had nothing to hold as Monroe McCollum thudded at his feet. Dolson took a step away from the body, turned to where Henrietta Rudd had been standing, but she'd moved. Quickly, he thought. Everything was moving quickly. The smell of the gunshot, the burn in the air. Someone was speaking. Was it him? Was he speaking? No.

"Did you hear me?" Henrietta asked him.

He turned to face her.

"You're the sheriff now," she said, taking the gun from her sister. Abigail sighed, walked back to her chair, her glass.

"I'm what?" he asked.

"You're the sheriff now, and your first job is to arrest the man who killed Sheriff Monroe McCollum in cold blood."

The deputy looked at Abigail, who was sneering at him over a highball glass she was draining. He said, "Man?"

"The man's name is Cottonmouth Tomlin," Henrietta said, raising her arm to him. "And here's the gun he used," she said, handing him the Vest Pocket pistol.

Dolson said, "Tomlin?"

She said to get on with it, lock up his men, too, if he could find them. It was time to get this county back under control.

Downstairs, Earl Withers had heard the shot, shaken his head, and set the sheriff's glass in the wash bin.

Outside the Culver Hotel, men and women walked through the dulled night, moving dimly from place to place, while a few stars here and there shone on no one in particular.

Across the street, Miss Phoebe, filled with thoughts of riverside picnics, put away the last of the cleaned bowls, the clatter of porcelain echoing in the emptied restaurant. She pushed a chair under a table as she walked across the room, stood for a moment looking through the glass out onto the street, watching other people for a few moments, smiling as the McWilliams newlyweds held hands as they walked along the courthouse square.

She turned her door sign to **Closed**, sat at an empty table, and waited for days that never came.

39

Cottonmouth stopped the sedan a hundred yards from the opening to camp, pulled off to the side of the road that was being cleared.

He wasn't convinced about Martello. He had been, but then he wasn't. The Banana Man with the tapestries in New Orleans, the one who seemed to own half of Honduras. The Rudds, seeming to own the county. *Is Martello a partner to getting me there?* Cottonmouth thought. The incident in town—maybe that was just a onetime mistake. That couldn't be the way things would go, not with the Rudds and the sheriff in charge. Maybe he and Martello could work together. That had been the plan, hadn't it? Bring Martello in; bring in business. All he had to do now was go over some ground rules with Martello, let him know that when he came to the county with his men, he himself was welcome to stay as Cottonmouth's guest. And, slowly, Cottonmouth could extend his reach from the camp to the town, maybe even taking over a business in town. He could look at expanding into Union County, maybe. Work with the Stoneciphers there. Reconnect with the men he knew in New Orleans. A case of Brownings would go a long way. Could probably still move that dynamite in the storage shed at camp. Three or four cases, minus the few sticks he'd put in his car to show Lorena, see could she make something for one of the cars. But then that botched kidnapping of the banker. And Moose Malone, back in

Lorena's garage—he'd said he'd come from Shreveport on Martello's suggestion, hadn't he? One of Martello's men? He'd have to speak with Martello; that was clear. Cottonmouth would have to make it clear that none of that was acceptable. Rules. Order. He'd have to explain to Martello the lines that couldn't be crossed. If he had to, he could always get Sheriff McCollum to help Martello find his way out of the county, he thought. But hopefully it wouldn't come to that. Hopefully Martello would understand his place here.

Cottonmouth stepped out of the car, shut the door behind him. *Maybe I should put one of those sticks of dynamite in my pocket now,* he thought. *Could be a good bargaining chip. Of course, driving around the county these days with a few sticks of dynamite in your car is likely asking for trouble.* All the more reason to not get shot at, he figured.

"Careful now, careful," a man said, coming from the woods by the car, past Cottonmouth and to the center of the road. The man carried timber, small logs under each arm. Maybe a felled pine tree. Cottonmouth couldn't tell. He walked toward the camp, closing the distance to the man with the trees under his arms.

"What you got going on there?" Cottonmouth asked.

The man set down the trees along the road, forming planks of a sort with others that had been recently laid. Cottonmouth took a look at the road, the stretch between himself and the camp. The old cars, broken remnants of his uncle's security, gone now, the space cleared. He counted a half dozen men, plus the one nearest him, cutting back the edges of the piney woods, clearing the road, laying down planks, trees, to give a foundation to the road.

"Man said get the road passable; that's all," the man nearest Cottonmouth explained. "What's it to you?"

Cottonmouth asked which man was that.

"Mr. Martello."

Cottonmouth walked back to his car, drove toward the camp, along the planks that had already been laid, past the men clearing up ahead.

When he got to the camp, Cottonmouth saw two other cars already parked. A Lincoln roadster, convertible. He didn't know much about cars, but he knew those didn't come cheap. The other car was a Ford V8, which, in his experience, were more pilfered than purchased.

He settled his Dodge alongside the other cars, walked to the main cabin, found Martello and Othel Walker in conversation.

Othel nodded, walked back to the kitchen.

A few other men were there, but Cottonmouth didn't recognize any of them. While he was looking at them, trying to remember whether he knew them, four more men he didn't recognize walked in, sat down, and waited for Othel to bring them beers. He looked for Everett, Beans, Jimmy, or any of the men who'd been around the past couple of weeks but didn't see any of them.

"Make yourself at home," Cottonmouth said to Martello. "Like my uncle always said, if you're not at home, you oughta be."

Martello turned to him, spread wide an arm, said, "What do you think of the place?"

Cottonmouth looked around, noticed the lighting was a little better. "Saw the road. How long was I gone?"

Martello laughed. "Sit, sit," he said, taking a chair on the other side of a table near Cottonmouth, who sat, then wondered whether he should have been standing. He looked around the room, tried to gauge the threat.

He tried again. "You've been busy."

"The road?"

"There's more?"

"Here and there," Martello said. "Correcting your problem with the road took less time than I thought it would."

Cottonmouth nodded. "It's just that, well, the road. That was some protection. My uncle had a pretty good barricade set up there."

"He did. He did. But these men have done this work before. Wasn't much of a problem once they got started."

"But now," Cottonmouth said, "with this change, anyone can just pull up. There's no safety here."

"We discussed this," Martello said.

"Discussed, sure. I just didn't know we'd *decided* this."

"The clear road is necessary. This camp needs to be connected to the world out there," Martello said. "That's where the money is."

"That's fine, but what's to stop Johnny Law from coming in here, shotguns blasting?"

Martello shook his head, grinned. "We'll have an understanding with the law, of course. Besides, each man here is armed. And there's already one sentry along the road, and I'm considering having more once business picks up."

"I didn't see anyone along the road other than the work crew."

"That's rather the point, isn't it?" Martello waved his hand, and a man at a table along the wall stood, walked back to the kitchen.

Cottonmouth needed a moment to take it all in. The new men. The road. The sentry or whatever Martello considered it. "Hold on," he said. "What do you mean more once business picks up? We haven't talked about any of this."

"No," Martello said, "we haven't." He reached into his inside coat pocket as the man he'd signaled earlier returned from the kitchen and set two tumblers of gin on the table. Cottonmouth ignored the glasses, watched Martello's hands pull out a sheet of paper, a pen. He wrote down a number, signed the paper, slid it across the table to Cottonmouth.

Without reaching for the paper, Cottonmouth asked what was going on.

"Circumstances have changed," Martello said. "First, an associate of mine was shot dead while visiting your county seat."

"Shot dead?"

"Man by the name of Malone. He and some other agents were looking into an opportunity at the bank. I just received word that there was some misunderstanding and he was shot down in broad daylight by one of the townsfolk. A deputy from the county found him, but I've yet to determine whether the deputy shot him. Apparently there were no witnesses. My understanding from you was that this county was safe, that it was under a sort of truce."

"Truce?" Cottonmouth asked. "I don't think the truce holds when people are trying to stuff a banker into a Plymouth."

Martello shook his head. "I don't know how these rumors get started. I come to Arkansas to discuss business, and suddenly there are wild allegations and a murder to deal with."

"You're saying you didn't have anything to do with the kidnapping?" Cottonmouth asked.

"Who was kidnapped?"

"Well, the almost kidnapping, I suppose."

Martello shook his head. "Of the two of us, I believe you would know more about kidnappings in this county than I would."

Cottonmouth didn't know what to say for a moment. "And the second thing? You'd said *first* a moment ago."

"Oh, yes. The matter at hand. Fair market value for your stake in this place. The sliver remaining to you."

Something seems to be misfiring, Cottonmouth thought. The world, maybe. That moment when you first wake, not knowing dream from reality, specter from substance. Thinking about a night in Honduras, then stepping out of Moon's store into the Columbia County night, a quick moment of your mind losing its footing. "My *stake* in this camp? You mean my camp."

"You misunderstand," Martello said. "I'm offering to purchase the small portion of the camp that still belongs to you. I think you'll find the offer more than fair."

"That still belongs to me? What are you talking about?"

Martello attempted, and failed, to hide his slight grin. "According to an associate of mine just recently returned from your courthouse in town, your uncle, Beauregard Tomlin, had taken out loans against the camp."

"I know that," Cottonmouth said. "I plan on repaying those back myself."

"It's a nice change that someone can, I suppose, as your uncle never did."

"What?"

"Oh, you didn't know? I've seen the paperwork. It would appear that your uncle was unable to pay back the loan on time, so he had to sell off bits and pieces along the way to the women who held the loans, a pair of sisters named Rudd, whom I've had the pleasure of meeting, after a fashion." From his coat pocket, Martello pulled some pages, laid them on the table in front of Cottonmouth. "It's all there," Martello said, pointing to a list of transactions from the past two years. "If any of those words are confusing, I can walk you through them. I know your family doesn't really have a head for business."

Cottonmouth wasn't listening. He was reading through the entries—the Rudds getting a little more of the camp every couple of months, acreage drifting away, one set of pencil-scrawled numbers after another.

Martello said he needed Cottonmouth to sign over any claim he might have to the camp, in perpetuity. "Can't hand over a payment to you for what slice you still hold, then have you coming back later crying foul. Consider this a settling up. You came home, closed up your uncle's affairs, collected what was owed, and moved on. Get back to the business you were doing before you returned here. Perhaps we can do business down the road, once you're down the road, of course. My understanding is that the old ladies claiming to run this county are in need of cash, what with the locals being so broke they're paying off their debts in gold coins, certificates, and jewelry. But not much cash. I suppose they're lucky not to have to accept livestock as payment." Martello laughed, shook his head. "Good timing, I'd say."

"Timing?"

"They have an asset I'd like to acquire, and I have the cash they require," Martello said. "You agree to the terms for your piece; I'll settle up with the old prunes in town and be on my way."

Cottonmouth said he hadn't agreed to anything.

"I'm offering you fair market value. In cash."

"Please stop saying *fair*."

Martello chuckled, then stopped. "There is no 'next' offer."

"Take it or leave it?"

Martello looked around the room, made a slight motion that brought three men to standing. "I'd suggest you take it."

"Yeah," Cottonmouth said, looking at each of the men standing by. "I got the feeling that's what you were suggesting."

Martello looked to the sheet of paper on the table. "Don't you even want to look at the price?"

"I understand the price."

"This offer is good until this time tomorrow," Martello said.

"You have a funny idea of what's good."

40

When he got to town, Cottonmouth first tried J. William Smith's place on Calhoun, then Miss Lucy's boardinghouse on Madison, but there were no vacancies. *Off to the Culver Hotel it is,* he thought. Hoping all the bad luck he'd had recently could be evened out by not seeing Henrietta Rudd there.

Run out of his own place. Could he get it back? Did he want it back?

He walked into the lobby of the Culver, saw a Pribble he recognized but couldn't place having a drink with a couple of men who were strangers to Cottonmouth, though he nodded to all three anyway. *You never know who you'll need when,* he thought.

"Evening, Mr. Tomlin," Earl said from behind the bar. "What brings you to town? Afraid the Miss Rudds aren't receiving at the moment."

Cottonmouth said that was fine by him, said he just needed a room.

"Full house back at the camp?" Earl asked.

"Something like that."

Earl pulled a notebook from behind the counter, set it between him and Cottonmouth. "We've got two open up on the fourth floor, if that's fine with you."

"Fourth floor? Since when have you had a fourth floor?"

"Oh, expanded last year. Turned all that storage into a couple rooms. Right nice rooms, if I do say so myself. Drove over to El Dorado to bring back some furniture last summer. Fixed the rooms up. Used to be storage, sure, but you wouldn't know it to look at them. One of those do for you?"

Cottonmouth said it sounded fine. "Sounds like business has been good."

"The Miss Rudds have been doing all right, if that's what you're asking."

Cottonmouth said they sure seemed to be.

Earl made a note in the book, slid a key over to Cottonmouth. "You hear about the Stoneciphers over in El Dorado?"

Cottonmouth asked had something happened.

"Got one of them for hoarding gold. Can't remember which one. One of the good ones, I think," Earl said, then sighed. "Goddamn Roosevelt won't be happy till the government has control of everything. Used to be a man could rely on himself. Guess the government ain't too keen on that."

"I try to stay out of that kind of politics," Cottonmouth said. "Got enough to worry about locally, what with your boss upstairs."

Earl started to say something, then leaned in to whisper. "Speak of the devil, and her sister shall appear." He winked, turned back to the bottles, the glasses behind him.

Abigail Rudd had arrived at the bar, stood looking Cottonmouth Tomlin up and down. "As I live and breathe. If it isn't the Tomlin boy," she said, setting her emptied tumbler on the bar. "You're quite the popular boy these days."

Cottonmouth asked her what she meant by that, looked past her to see was her sister coming behind her, but he didn't see Henrietta anywhere.

Before Abigail could answer what she'd meant, Earl was at the bar asking could he help her with something.

"Gin," she said. "We're out of gin again. Gin again. Again with the gin. Begin again with gin." She seemed unsteady but pleased with herself.

"I'll have some sent up immediately," Earl said, asked was there anything else.

"Was there anything else?" Abigail asked. "Anything?" She looked around the room until she'd made it back to her emptied glass. "A drink. We're out of gin upstairs, and I need another drink."

"Like you need a hole in the head," Cottonmouth said under his breath.

"A what where?" Abigail asked.

Earl got her attention, asked what kind of drink. "Gin rickey?" he offered. "Tom Collins?"

"The one with the rabbit," she said.

Earl looked to Cottonmouth, each of them puzzled. "Rabbit?" Earl asked.

She nodded, then remembered, her eyebrows raising and mouth popping open. "Bunny Hug," she said. "The drink we talked about the other night."

"A Bunny Hug?" Cottonmouth asked.

"It's alcohol mixed with alcohol, mixed with more alcohol. Isn't that right, Earl?"

He said it was.

"Heard about it recently from, well"—she looked uncertainly at the ceiling, her drinkless hand waving away a cloud no one else saw—"well, I can't for the life of me remember where. Gin and whiskey and liquid licorice." She stopped, lost the word. Adjusted her tongue. Tried to get the word back. "Liquidish. Licorid. Liquid liquor. Ish."

"Absinthe," Earl offered as Abigail steadied herself on the back of a chair.

"And it's called a Bunny Hug?" Cottonmouth asked again, nodding.

"Absotootly correct," she said. "Gin and scotch and absence. Takes all the pain away. A warm absence where the pain used to be. What a drink. What a name. Bunny Hug. Ever heard of it?"

Cottonmouth said he had.

41

The next day, Jimmy the Hook parked along Washington Street in front of an empty storefront that had sold general merchandise a few years back, then clothes, then general merchandise again, before closing up.

"That pie shop Cottonmouth is always going on about," Beans said. "I think we passed it on the last section."

Everett said he had been there the other day, when he had come into town for supplies, met Cottonmouth there to give him a ride back. Said the pie was good.

Beans asked was there chocolate pie. "That's my favorite. Grandma used to make it, the white fluffy stuff on top, little gold sugar drops on top. Whatever that was. Be nice to have a piece of chocolate pie."

Jimmy laughed. "Dream big, Beans. Dream big."

As the three men stepped from the car toward the building, Jarvis Dolson, the new sheriff, pistol drawn, stepped out of the shadows, two other men with shotguns at his side.

"Good day to you, fellows," Dolson said. "You got Tomlin with you?"

Beans and Jimmy looked around. Everett decided if these men wanted to harass them, fine. He'd play along. He said to the deputy they hadn't seen Cottonmouth in a while. Said they'd heard he'd skipped town. Said good luck finding him. Probably back in Honduras by now.

"Need you boys to step over here, empty your pockets on the hood of that car, nice and slow."

Beans took a step behind Everett as Jimmy asked what was this about.

"Wanted to ask Tomlin about a shooting," Dolson said. "And we've been having some crimes reported in the county of late. About the time you fellows showed up."

Jimmy asked was that so.

Dolson said it was so. "You fellows seen Tomlin around?"

Jimmy said they hadn't.

"Let him know we're looking for him, and he should come by and see us," Dolson said.

Jimmy said they would. Asked if there was anything else.

Dolson said there was. "Like I said, seems someone broke into Old Man Crump's place on the edge of town, took some of his valuables."

Jimmy nodded. "I understand. You need us to ask around, help you bunglers find some clues?"

The two men flanked the trio by the car. "Maybe," Dolson said, "it would be easier if we could just all go down to the jail and take care of this there?" J. O. Bardsley and his wife walked by, said "Evening" to Dolson, who touched his hat in reply.

Everett took a step, closer now to the back seat, a couple of Brownings on the floorboard. So much for the chocolate pie.

"Not interested in performing in front of an audience?" Jimmy asked, nodding toward the passing family. Everett and Beans, still silent, looked back and forth to the men with the shotguns, to Dolson.

"So it's to the jail, then?" Dolson asked. "We don't want any trouble."

Jimmy looked at the men with the shotguns on them, looked at Beans and Everett, the latter staying uncharacteristically quiet, Jimmy noticed.

"I can say I've made some bad decisions in my life," Jimmy said. "Put a small fortune on Ladysman to win the derby last month, for one. Never bet on the favorite. That's what I learned there. Have to think of the odds. Sometimes you play the long shot, and sometimes you just try not to get shot. Seems like I know what kind of day today is, at least." He pulled a blue-cornered handkerchief, a small knife, and a wad of paper money and coins from his pockets, laid them on the hood of the car, most of the coins sliding off to the ground. "But far as I can reckon, I've never set foot in a house owned by someone named Old Man Grump, and I certainly am not walking around with some old man's valuables."

"Crump," Dolson corrected. "Now you two," he said, nodding to Everett and Beans.

Jimmy put his things back into his pockets, stepped aside, said, "Fine, your turn." He looked at Beans and Everett as Beans looked to Everett for a hint of what to do.

"What was taken?" Everett asked, remembering his chat with that man, Charles, back at camp. Wanting Everett to hold a ring until he came back. It seemed strange, seemed too good to be true.

"Looking for a money clip," Dolson said, and Everett nodded.

"And what else?"

"And a gold ring."

Everett nodded. *Charles,* he thought.

"It was expensive," Dolson said.

Everett chuckled, said, "I thought that looked like one of Martello's boys."

"Who what?" Jimmy asked.

Everett nodded as he thought, as he replayed the moment. "Must have heard me telling Cottonmouth what I'd heard about Martello."

"All right, all right," Dolson said, waving his gun. "That's enough. Empty those pockets." He stepped around, closer to Everett. "Empty them," he said, and when Dolson shifted, a small pistol that had been wedged behind his belt fell to the ground.

One of the deputized men, the one called Winters O'Brien, looked around the edge of the car to Dolson's boots, to the gun lying in the street between the cars.

O'Brien reached down for the pistol, picked it up. "Say, this looks like the kind of gun the Tomlin boy used to shoot the sheriff. Wasn't that a little Vest Pocket gun like this one here?"

Dolson looked at Everett, who was looking at the pistol. Everett looked up to Dolson for a second, for maybe a year. Dolson raised his gun to Everett's face, said, "Grab them."

At that point, it was a cloud of elbows and shoulders, guns used as hammers, arms swung wildly. Jimmy put a knee into one of the deputized; then they were all on Jimmy at once, even townspeople running for them, not wanting a repeat of the attempted kidnapping of Ambrose McLeach. Everett grabbed Beans from the pile, wove between parked cars to the edge of a building, cut through an alley without looking back, confident only that they were nearing the end of whatever this was.

42

Cottonmouth took a card from Bill Moon, who slid two cards to Monkey Pribble, then skipped Exrah Morris, who was waving him off.

"So you didn't tell me what you think of the new shelving," Moon said to Cottonmouth, leaning back in his chair and looking about the store.

"Shelving?" Cottonmouth asked.

"Right, got to thinking about promoting some of the inventory, all the men you got coming through. Keep them all happy, filled up on Baby Ruths, Mary Janes. Keep the cooler stocked with Coca-Colas up front. Even got new magazines coming in twice a week now," Moon said. "Keep your visitors happy around here; keep them coming back. Not even charging you a fee to keep your men happy."

"You fellas playing cards or talking shop?" Exrah asked, then tossed a few coins into the middle of the table. "Bill, it's to you."

Moon counted the money in the pot, added to it.

Cottonmouth looked at the hand he'd been dealt, knew he'd been beaten before the game had started, folded. Got up from the table and walked to the front of the store. "Back in a second. Need to stretch my legs."

Moon asked was his mind somewhere else, but Cottonmouth didn't hear him.

From the other side of the courthouse square came a commotion—men shouting, men running.

Pribble stood, walked to the front of the store to look out the windows with Cottonmouth, asked what was all the noise? Moon and Exrah Morris came along, all standing at the window, looking for a show.

Cottonmouth said he couldn't tell what the commotion was, probably just that stray dog getting chased around again. Someday that dog was going to get himself into some trouble he couldn't get himself out of, he thought and shrugged. He picked up an apple, set it down, picked up some stick candy, set it down. Outside, closer to the store, people in town were walking up and down the street, down and up, looking over to see what was happening on the other side of the square, wondering was it another attempted kidnapping. They were going to have a late meal, going to have a drink. A couple of women with purses too big for them. A man taking off his hat, scratching his head.

Martello making an offer on the camp was supposed to solve everything, wasn't it? And yet here he was, hiding out at Moon's.

Moon said it was a good time to take a break from the card game, came over right next to Cottonmouth. "Got true-crime and detective magazines now. One of your fellas down there had come in asking, so I figured must be a popular item. Got 'em coming in regular now. Business must be really picking up down there."

Cottonmouth said sure, must. *Maybe,* he thought. Maybe somehow Moon could help him. Maybe Moon could loan him money to get out of this trouble. Hadn't Moon said he'd been collecting gold coins and certificates? Maybe they could bribe Martello with that. Or pay the Rudds. He started to ask but couldn't find the words.

"Here, look at this one." Moon reached to a shelf behind him for a magazine. "This one's got cops with gas masks on the cover. Ever heard of such a thing?"

Cottonmouth said yeah, that was sure something.

"Your boys eat this up," Moon said. "One of these—last week, maybe—swear it had a drawing of one of your fellows what came through. Said 'Have You Seen This Man?' If I can find it, I'll set it behind the register so's he can autograph it for me next time he comes through. Be a nice thing to have hanging on the wall."

Cottonmouth kept his eyes focused out the window, said sure. "Would really class this place up."

"Well," Moon said, "cotton prices go up, we all do well. Lumber, same way. I figure this is just the same again. Things going well down at your place, things go well in town. Just let me know what you need and when you need. Detective magazines." Moon pulled up a recent copy of *Astounding Stories of Super-Science*. "Read this one? Fantastic stories."

I need money, Bill, he wanted to say. *I need my uncle here so he can help me figure a way out of this. I need the Banana Man. I need the time machine from the book that English fellow wrote. Or the ghost from that Christmas story. Harry Houdini couldn't get me out of this.*

"You look deep in thought," Moon said. "I'll leave you to it, then." He patted him on the shoulder. "When you're ready, we can go over updating any grocery list you need, things like that. Want apples, we'll get apples. Want a case of White Owls? I know you got a couple fellows smoke those up. I'll get you those."

"Seems like you know these men better than I do." Moon was a businessman, after all. He'd sell you what you asked for, but wasn't much point asking him for help, was there?

Moon grinned. "Well, that's the job, ain't it? Anyway, just let me know, and I'll take care of it. Until then, I'm going to go back there and let those two morons win a couple bucks off me so they'll have something to spend in here tomorrow."

Cottonmouth nodded as Moon walked to the back of the store for the card game. Tomorrow. What was the point of tomorrow, anyway? He knew he'd taken everything straight into the ditch since he'd been back. Why did he think this was any different? His mother had gone off with that salesman, and his father had gone off after them, and he'd gone off, running away. His uncle gone. Everyone gone.

Since he'd come back, he'd been reaching, he knew. Everett Logan was going to school to learn about business. Martello had been at it for years. The Rudd sisters had a handle on the county. Even Moon had been running this very store for as long as he could remember. Lorena taking over the garage from her family. The Banana Man had built an empire. And here he was, thinking he could make a go of the camp that his uncle had struggled with for years. His uncle. His uncle, who had given up everything for him, who had taken him in as best he could when his parents had gone and had tried his best to keep the camp running, Cottonmouth off in Honduras fighting someone else's war when he'd been needed right here. If he had come back last year. If he had never left. And now? Now there was nothing.

And he knew he didn't have the business sense to run the camp. All he'd picked up in New Orleans, in Honduras, was being able to force a peace with the locals for the Banana Man, identify weaknesses, and shore up the defenses. Mostly he followed orders. He recognized that. But he wasn't up for taking orders from the Rudds or from Martello.

He'd been searching for who he was, been reaching to do more than he could. He took a breath, seeing his own reflection in the window, Moon's name reversed on the glass.

He reached back for an apple in the bin, pulled out a banana instead. Maybe he could talk his way back into the banana job in Honduras. He could take Martello's offer, take the money, buy his way back down there. Leave everything behind. Was he really any worse off than he had been when he'd come back to the county? Let Martello and the Rudds fight it out. The Banana Man had talked about identifying a weakness and preparing for an opportunity to exploit that weakness. Identify and prepare. Let Martello and the Rudds exploit whatever weaknesses they could find. His opportunity might just be leaving again. Who did he owe anything to now? His uncle was dead and buried. Cottonmouth could pick up where he'd left off in Honduras. They'd still need weapons, muscle. You couldn't run a machine like that without quality cogs. And there wasn't a thing wrong with being a cog. Plenty of people were. Something nice to be said about finding your place in the world. He couldn't think of the nice thing to be said right then, but he was sure there had to be one.

Could he talk Lorena into going with him? Why would she? She'd be better off without him. Safer.

He walked to the back of the store to reclaim his place in the card game, watched the three men finish the hand they were playing.

"You know," Pribble said, "I got a guy over in Smackover can get you a good deal on some, well, on some tools for the work your guests are doing."

"Tools?" Cottonmouth asked.

"Selma—that's my Marie's sister—Selma has been seeing this fellow what works for Johnny Law over there, and they pulled in a mess of gu—er, tools few weeks back. Still have them. Group out of Mississippi had come over to, uh, do some banking at the same time. Three, now I think about it. Anyway, one of the groups got nabbed right away, and when one of the other groups came to help out the first group, well, they all ended up in jail or in coffins, and you can't really use a gun in either of those places, can you?"

"Tool," Exrah helped.

"Sorry, yeah. Tool. So turns out, after all that, I can get you a good deal on right many of them." Pribble nodded, grinned, as proud of himself as he'd been since he'd bested Punch Stonecipher last August in a drinking contest. Then he added, smirking, "If a good deal on those automatic tools is something you'd be interested in."

Cottonmouth wasn't sure it was, wasn't sure that would work out, even in Honduras. What would his uncle have done now? Or, maybe, what would Martello do in his boots? Or the Rudd sisters? Would they worry with guns? Buying and selling rifles. Making a little money. Very little money. Maybe it was time to think like them, like the Banana Man. Look at his resources. Instead of getting his hands dirty, he thought, why not be smart about it?

~

After a few hands, his mind lost, clouded, Cottonmouth stood, motioned for Moon to follow him.

Near the front of the store, Cottonmouth asked about the lawyer Moon used.

"Gus? Sure. He's a good guy. What do you need with Gus?"

"Got some business to see about."

"Oh, sure," Moon said. "He can help with that. He worked with me and Stanley over at the bank on some paperwork. And I used him for the deed to this place, too, while back. I've used him for all sorts of things. Gus. Good guy. Pretty much the only one around who can do that sort of thing. I'm sure you've met him, right? I think he was at your uncle's funeral."

Cottonmouth said he wouldn't have recognized the man. "Never had much use for a lawyer."

Moon told him where the office was.

Cottonmouth thanked him, took his hat off the rack by the door. "Be seeing you, Bill."

43

"Lorena, so nice to see you," Henrietta Rudd said. "Earl tells us you were in the middle of that scare yesterday."

For a moment, Lorena wasn't sure how to play this, whether to make something up from scratch, separate herself from the chaos, pretend that she didn't have anything to do with any of it. Henrietta Rudd had always seemed, at least to Lorena, the scolding but comforting Sunday school teacher, always one move away from making you apologize for something, from making you feel guilty about something.

"Wouldn't call it a scare," Lorena said. "Just caught out on the street when the shooting started."

Henrietta smiled. *Score one for the mechanic,* she thought. *Very well.* "And to what do we owe the pleasure of your company today, my dear?"

Lorena pulled from behind her an envelope of cash, set it on the coffee table. "Final payment for the shop," she said, then stepped back to take in the moment, the vision she'd fancied for years, when the shop would be hers completely, not a debt to anyone.

Henrietta scrunched her face, reached behind herself for a ledger Abigail was already handing her, spread open to a middle page.

"But you have months left," Henrietta said before she glanced down at the ledger. "A year, certainly."

"It's all there," Lorena said, looking down to the envelope. "Everything that was owed. To the penny."

Henrietta dragged a finger along the page, looked again at the envelope on the table in front of her.

"It's all there," Lorena said again, not to convince Henrietta but just because she liked the sound of it, the idea of it.

"I'm sure it is," Henrietta said, then shook her head. "I'm beginning to suspect I'm in the wrong line of work."

Lorena could have just left it at that, could have just enjoyed the moment, the kind you practice for a long time and then reflect on, savor for years to come, the sort of moment you carry with you like a charm to ward off the bad times, those moments you can pull out and dust off and think, "Remember when?"

She could have left it at that.

She didn't.

"Well, Miss Rudd, I can always use an extra set of hands down at the garage."

Abigail coughed on her gin, the light from the windows hovering, as Henrietta smiled, kept smiling, her unwavering smile set as she leveled her gaze to Lorena. "Yes, my dear. I suppose you could. There was word you and the Tomlin boy were spending time together. I'd thought perhaps you'd taken him on as a . . . What did you call it? An extra set of hands? Though I suspect you'll need someone else, now that he's planning to sell his uncle's camp and leave our county once again."

Her face gave her away.

"Oh, didn't you know?" Henrietta asked, her raised coffee cup hiding her silent delight.

In the Rudds' suite of the Culver Hotel, cars rolling along the street below, Lorena Whaley stood there, clouded in a moment she'd spend her life trying to forget.

44

"You think we lost them?" Beans asked Everett, crossing a small creek behind the town, woods beginning to loosen now into an opening.

"Don't see how they could have followed us all this way. Sure enough would have given up by now it was me."

"So maybe we just lean against some of these trees for a minute, catch a breath?"

"Let's keep moving a little longer. No telling what happened to Jimmy."

"You think they caught him?" Beans asked.

"No telling. But he'd been saying it was getting on time to move along. Maybe he took this as a hint. Sister about to have that baby and all, you know."

"Maybe so," Beans said, slowing.

Everett waved at him. "Come on. There's a barn right up here. We can hide there until night." Beans followed a few steps behind, said a little rest would be fine. "Thought they were going to get us for that ring Charles put on me—then they think we killed the sheriff? Where'd that pistol come from?"

"It just dropped," Beans said. "I heard it drop, and there it was."

"Why were they trying to hang that on us?" Everett mumbled, mostly to himself.

Beans said he was hungry, and Everett started laughing. "You're hungry?"

"I can't help it," Beans said. "Ain't had any food all day." As if to prove the point, his guts started rumbling, which brought both men to laughter.

Everett kept the lead as the men stepped from the tree line into the clearing near the barn, which turned out to be just a small shed. Everett took off his hat, scratched his scalp with his right hand. He put his hat back on, reached into his coat pocket, pulled out a mostly melted Baby Ruth from Moon's store that he'd been saving. "Beans, your prayers are answered," he said as the bark of the tree next to him ripped, and he spun, falling. In the tree line to the right of the shed, pops flew, leaves and trees next to the two men exploding.

"Christ," Everett said, reaching back for Beans, then throwing him to the ground.

Beans pulled himself up against a tree. "What happened? Are we OK? What happened?"

Everett leaned around a tree to see where the shots had come from, then looked to the shed. "We've got to run for it."

"They'll kill us," Beans said. "They shot at us. They'll kill us."

"They'll kill us if we stay here," Everett said.

"Should we go talk to them?" Beans asked. "Tell them we don't know about the sheriff?"

Everett said he didn't know. "Sounds like the talking's done."

"What if they're on our side?" Beans asked. "What if they're really looking for those new people who came to camp? The ones who did that thing in town? Reckon one of them killed the sheriff and they're pinning it on us?"

"There's no 'our side' anymore," Everett said, shifting his weight to move quickly. "It's just us now."

"The two of us," Beans said, looking around as if everyone else had just left a party and the two men were standing in the empty ballroom wondering what had happened.

Everett checked his pistol. He had three shots left. "You got your gun?" Everett asked.

Beans said he'd left it in the car.

"Why'd you do that?"

"Didn't know I'd need it, and then we were running, and . . ." Beans was nearly crying now, so much he was having trouble catching his breath.

Everett said it didn't matter, said not to worry about it. "Let's just get to that shed; that sound good? We just stay low," he said, nodding to the twenty feet of open space between the edge of the woods and the shed.

The two men dove through the open doorway as automatic fire followed them, hitting the outside of the shed's wall.

Everett grabbed him by the shoulders. "Beans, Beans. Look at me."

Beans looked down at his side, torn apart in ribbons of shirt and flesh, blood spilling through his fingers, his hand now unseeable in the gurgle of blood.

"Beans," Everett said again, his hand behind the other man's head, pulling them together, forehead to forehead. "Beans."

The men slumped behind the counter as shots flew over them, splinters erupting from walls behind them.

"I don't want to die," Beans said, tears and snot mixing down his face as his chin shook. "I don't want to die."

"You're not going to die," Everett said. "I just need you to be brave for five minutes."

Beans shook his head, sweat and tears dripping from his chin.

Outside, the patter of gunfire, automatic, tink-tink-tinking into everything metal, thunking into everything wooden, shards of glass flying over them.

"Beans. Just five minutes."

"But I'm scared."

"So am I."

"I never been this scared. You ever been this scared?"

"Look, we can be scared tomorrow, OK? We can be scared for the rest of our lives, OK? We can sit in our rooms and draw the curtains and be scared when we're eighty, OK?"

"But I'm scared *now*."

Everett slumped down, back to a chest of drawers someone had stored in the shed. "You know where Jimmy went?"

"I don't know. To his sister's?"

"No. I remember now. Before they came after us. This morning he was talking. Said he was heading over to El Dorado soon. Probably shopping for a new hat. Probably took off the other way, found a car, and made it to El Dorado."

"I guess. Maybe. Wish I was in El Dorado shopping for a hat."

"No, you don't. Don't say that. What's he going to think about his dumb hat when we tell him this story?"

Beans held his hand against his hip, blood dripping from his side onto the floor.

"That hole in your side. Next year, we'll be in Chicago or New York, and we'll go see that looker you like."

"Louise Brooks?"

"No. The other one."

"Una Merkel."

"That's her. We'll go see her in a picture show, then take her out on the town."

"You think she'd go?"

"Sure, why not? She has to go with somebody. Why not us?"

"Why not us."

"Handsome devils like us, with money and scars. Dames love scars. And we've got those in spades. So why not us?"

"Why not us."

"And we'll be out at a club, we'll be drinking brandy and smoking cigars, and when the band finishes playing their first set and Una Merkel and her lady friends look to us, we'll tell them all about tonight."

"At the club?"

"Sure. Why not?"

"Sure. Why not."

"And we'll tell them how there were two dozen men out there, all with tommy guns and Brownings firing into this very building right here, and still we made it out and took half of them with us, and no one will believe us, and they'll say 'You're a bunch of liars, you are,' and you'll lift your shirt and show them the scars, and you'll never pay for another drink the rest of your life. And you know what Jimmy will be doing?"

"No."

"He'll be fetching us the drinks and sorry he went hat shopping instead of shooting his way out of trouble."

Beans laughed himself to coughing.

"They'll say from across the room, 'That's Beans.' Uh, Beans, I don't think I ever knew your family name."

"Talbot."

"Talbot? Are you sure?"

"Pretty sure. It's what my mother and father told me."

"That's fine. That's fine. They'll say, 'There goes Beans Talbot. The man who fought off half the highway patrol and two-thirds of the FBI and only slowed down to wipe someone else's blood off his face. Hip hip hoorah.' And they'll want to throw you a parade, but you say, 'Fellas, it'll have to wait,' because you and I have a fishing trip planned."

Beans said, "Hang on. Hang on."

"Yeah?"

"When we were coming here, when you and me and Jimmy were in that cottage up north on the way here, you said we'd go fishing."

"I did say that."

"And you still ain't took me fishing," Beans said.

"Would you like to go tomorrow?"

Beans said yeah, he'd like that.

"OK. Una Merkel and her lot will have to wait. You and I are going fishing first, just you and me, and then we'll go meet them in Chicago. Just—"

"I know," Beans said, shuffling himself against a stack of crates so that he could stand. "Just be brave for five minutes. I can do that. Just five minutes. Then we go fishing." Beans took a breath. "So are we going to do this or not?"

Everett pulled himself up, readied.

As Beans stepped toward a shattered window, they heard the snap, saw the wood in the wall of the barn splinter as the bullet lit fire in his shoulder.

Everett dove across the room, caught Beans as he was falling.

The bullets continued for another ten seconds. Ten hours. Everett couldn't tell. He set down his gun, lifted Beans to him, saw the wound in his chest, his shoulder. He looked down to his face, Beans waiting to catch his look.

"Can I tell you a secret?" Beans asked.

Everett could hear the men getting closer, shuffle steps—quick, then nothing—likely finding cover, then moving. Everett reached for his pistol, fired off a shot toward the sound, knowing he'd hit nothing but wall, ceiling. Just trying to slow them. He held Beans in his lap, pressed his palm to the man's gushing shoulder, his chest. "Tell me tomorrow, Beans. You can tell me tomorrow. When we're fishing."

"I cheated."

"You what?"

"I cheated. The jelly beans in the jar."

Everett tried to look around the corner, to find the men coming toward them, but he heard only a low rumbling of movement. "Jelly beans in what jar?"

"When I was a boy. What they call me Beans for. I cheated."

"What are you talking about?"

Beans coughed, his body shaking, the blood coming out in waves now, Everett losing sight of his hand in the redness. "Paid a boy who worked there, at the drugstore. Paid him five dollars to tell me how many."

Everett laughed. "That's not cheating, Beans. That's being resourceful. You've got a great future in finance."

Everett emptied what was left from his pistol, then tossed it out the front window, yelled their surrender.

He heard the door to the room fall open, the shattered wood falling to the ground, the footsteps nearly on them now.

Beans smiled. "Finance. A great future. That's good to hear. I always wanted a great future," he said as his eyes glazed over and Everett held him as tightly as he could. Even tighter.

45

Cottonmouth shut the door to Moon's behind him, walked down Jefferson, past the Coggins' harness store, past Sullivan's Drugstore, past a few more he didn't pay much attention to as he went.

A boy came running around an alley corner, slammed into him, and careened, sprawling, into the front of a parked car.

"Sorry, Mister," the boy said, standing up, then seeing Cottonmouth. "Mr. Tomlin," he said. "Sorry, Mr. Tomlin," he said again, then turtled his head down, his shoulders coming up, him seeming to shrink right there. "I didn't mean nothing."

Cottonmouth reached for the boy, who shook, and dusted off the boy's arm, his shoulder.

"You all right?" Cottonmouth asked. "Ain't you one of the Thurman twins?"

"Yes, sir," the boy said, standing a little taller now. "I am."

"Jack or John?"

"I'm John," the boy said, easily enough Cottonmouth knew he was trying to pull one over.

"Well, that's a shame. I had a nickel I was going to give to Jack when I saw him."

"I can give it to him," the boy said quickly, taking a half step forward.

"Sorry, John. Have to give it to Jack directly."

"Mr. Tomlin. I got to say a confession to you, sir."

"That a fact?"

"I'm Jack," the boy said, grabbing the nickel and taking off.

Cottonmouth laughed, turned to watch him dart down another alley. Two more storefronts, and Cottonmouth turned in to Augustus Webster's law office.

A small man in a white dress shirt and mostly buttoned vest greeted Cottonmouth, whose eyes were adjusting to the windowless office, each wall a welter of preavalanche books. Floor to ceiling, some with spines out, some flayed open, yellowing underbellies of pages exposed to the dim lamplight. "Can I help you, sir? Are you lost?"

Cottonmouth shook his head, then stopped, worried to make any sudden movement that might bring the walls tumbling in on the pair of them. "Here to see Mr. Webster. Bill Moon sent me."

The small man's face seemed to brighten, and he took on a slight accent Cottonmouth thought was probably British, somehow. "Very good, sir. Right this way."

Cottonmouth turned to look at the door behind him, then chose to follow the man toward the back of the office, where there were two chairs in front of an uncluttered desk, the only open space save for a slight path cut through the middle of books and folders and papers, likely carved out by Lewis and Clark themselves, Cottonmouth thought.

The small man sat on the other side of the desk, pulled a bottle of rye and two glasses from a drawer. Poured a half inch in one glass, threw it back, then filled that one and the other glass about halfway.

"So how is Mr. Moon?" the small man asked.

"Fine a few minutes ago. I'm Cottonmouth Tomlin. You Webster?"

"Quite so, old chap. How can I help you? I don't recall seeing you in town."

"Came home a while back," Cottonmouth said. "My family has a piece of land down along Dorcheat." Cottonmouth picked up his glass, spun the whiskey around in it.

"Tomlin, you say. Yes, yes. I met with your uncle concerning that very land, I daresay."

Cottonmouth drained the glass, made a clicking sound with his tongue. "That so?"

"Question of ownership now. You're next of kin, I presume. My condolences, of course. I should have come to you sooner about this, but"—he waved his arms around toward the stacks of books, papers—"life intervenes, I'm afraid."

Cottonmouth said, "So it does, so it does. And so does death."

Augustus Webster coughed a little, slipped his fingers into the armholes of his vest, drummed them along his chest. "Seems your uncle Beauregard and his brother had owned the camp. The brother was your father, I presume."

Cottonmouth nodded.

"And your uncle updated the deed. Give me a moment." Webster stood, walked to a heap of papers and books along the far wall. "Let's see. Moulton. Brister. Emerson." He mumbled a few more words Cottonmouth couldn't make out, but he wouldn't have been surprised had the mountains parted and Boris Karloff himself walked through, arms outstretched. "Here it is. Here it is." Webster pulled a handful of papers from between two books, the stack wobbling into the next stack, which wobbled into the next, until each stack retreated, as if they'd each decided now was not the time for collapse. Webster sat back down at the desk, licking his fingers as he thumbed through each sheet.

"I was wondering about the process for reversing what my uncle did," Cottonmouth said. "Want to know if he had the right, you know, legally, to do that. Did my father's share pass to my uncle or to me, I guess is what I'm asking. If my uncle got a loan on a share of the camp that wasn't his, are there options to reverse that? Contest it? Or if I want to sell my share to somebody, say, or if maybe I can get whatever my uncle did taking out a loan reversed somehow. I'm just trying to understand the standing here, where things are in terms of who has the rights to what." *Christ,* Cottonmouth thought. He should stop this, head back, and bring Everett in here. Maybe there'd been a class on land law, whatever it was called.

"I must admit," Webster said, "that, while I readily acknowledge your status as next of kin, I'm rather unclear on what action you are presently contemplating."

"So am I," Cottonmouth said. "I'm not a businessman. I'm just trying to figure out whether all of this, this taking a loan and selling part of the camp to pay the loan—I mean, it sounds settled, but, well, I guess with me not being a businessman, I guess I'm just trying to see if there's a businessman's solution I'm not seeing or whether this takes a nonbusinessman's answer."

"Yes, your uncle was here—let's see," he said, looking at the papers, "two years back now. Came in, had your father declared dead, his being missing for so long. That's what he came in here about, to change the ownership, have your father declared dead. If you will just sit down, Mr. Tomlin."

Cottonmouth slid the other chair behind him, sat. "Go on."

"Your uncle asked for my help in declaring your father dead. It took him some time with the courthouse, but he managed it. Obtained ownership, your father being dead and your being ruled *in absentia*."

"Absent?"

"Yes. There was a letter sent to you in Mexico."

"I was in Honduras."

The lawyer nodded. "I suppose that explains the lack of response. Because you were unreachable by the courts, you know, yes, your uncle held the title. Perhaps we can clear all that up, now that you're here."

Cottonmouth said, yes, he'd like to clear that up. "Undo the loan my uncle took out. My father owned half. My uncle owned half. If they're both gone, I should own all of it."

"But your uncle brokered a deal with Henrietta and Abigail Rudd."

"I'm back now."

"We can settle what we can as soon as we can. Though your uncle was quite adamant about his not owning all, that he wanted ownership somewhat complicated."

"Why?"

"Ah, yes. I recall the what but not the why. Just a moment," he said, thumbing through the papers as Cottonmouth watched the leaning piles of books for any movement. "According to my notes of our meeting, he was being pressured to sell."

"The Rudds pressured him to sell the camp."

"No, no. Seems there was another camp like it, a Mr. Clapton?"

"Campbell?"

"Yes," the lawyer said, squinting at his own handwriting. "Campbell. Seems one of Mr. Campbell's partners had approached your uncle. I have the word *scared* written here, though I don't know what this is in reference to, I'm afraid."

"Campbell," Cottonmouth said. "He's the man owns a camp like ours down north of Shreveport, in the Vivian area. And he had ties or still has ties to Victor Martello. My uncle was worried because Martello was already reaching out, already had a plan in place, I guess. Get one camp, get the other. Or get one and close down the competition? I don't know."

"I'm sorry?" Webster asked.

"Sorry. Just thinking out loud. I thought we were doing something. Thought *I* was doing something. But maybe I was just a part of someone else's plans. A cog."

"I don't see anything about that here." The lawyer dragged his index finger along the page, thumbed to the next page.

"And my uncle was able to work out his own solution, to keep the camp here, keep outsiders from pressuring him to sell out. And that's why he was so ready to deal with the Rudds. To get the loan. To sell to them to make the loan payments. Just trying to hold off Martello. Keep the outsiders from taking over."

"Outsiders?"

"Martello. Campbell. The Rudds never would have wanted that. And neither would my uncle. And here I just let Martello right back, gave him everything he wanted on a platter." Cottonmouth moved to leave.

"Glad I could help," the lawyer said, moving the now-emptied rye bottle to a wooden crate next to the desk, where it rattled against a half dozen similar bottles. The lawyer stood, watching Cottonmouth walk away. "Don't you want to know what your uncle's plan was?" As soon as he asked, he regretted that he'd said anything. He could have just let Cottonmouth Tomlin walk out of the office, locked the door behind him, and counted himself lucky.

Cottonmouth stopped. "My uncle's plan? What does it matter now?"

The lawyer, rattled and exhausted now, had given up what was passing for his British accent. "I just thought you'd want to know."

"Tell me."

"He was trying to sign it all over to your name. Hand you the camp in a couple years."

"What?"

"Borrowing the money, wanting to get back on his feet and set things up for you. As I recall, and I could be wrong, but I recall he said all this was short term to get through. That when you returned, it would be yours. Free and clear. He knew he didn't have long left. Didn't want that news spread around, of course. Look weak and so forth. He'd had to take out loans—that was the problem. Loans to get by, to just hold on until you came back. But the loans weren't enough. Guess it didn't work out the way he'd intended."

"Guess not," Cottonmouth said, turning back to the door.

"Man plans; God laughs—as my mum would say," Webster said.

46

As Cottonmouth walked into the street from Augustus Webster's office, he saw a couple of Martello's men, Charles and a larger man he didn't know by name, arguing with Silas and Roy Lee Kitchens, two men Cottonmouth had gone to school with but hadn't much thought of since. He and Roy Lee had gotten in trouble once in school for taking all of Miss Jernigan's chalk, hiding it under a floorboard. Roy Lee had taken his whipping for it first, Cottonmouth watching as he didn't cry, didn't squeal. Just took it. Cottonmouth had tried to do the same, tried to follow Roy Lee's example. Hadn't worked out as well as he'd hoped.

Now Cottonmouth stepped through the muck and mud of Washington Street toward the courthouse well, said "Come on now, come on," as he got closer.

The man he didn't know by name looked up, saw it was Cottonmouth, and went back to what he was doing, which was shoving his fingers into Roy Lee's shoulder.

Cottonmouth asked what was going on.

The man shook his head. "Don't concern you, Tomlin. Move along now."

Cottonmouth asked again.

Roy Lee looked to Cottonmouth. “These fellows just took my wristwatch and Silas’s money clip.”

“Don’t know what these church bells are clanging on about. I already have a money clip and a watch.” He held out his hand, palm up, showing Cottonmouth a money clip, a little money folded into it, bearing the initials SJK. He put the money clip into his pants pocket. “Now, if you’ll excuse us, we’ll be going.” As he turned to leave, Silas James Kitchens looked to Cottonmouth, who hadn’t taken his eye from the man he didn’t know by name.

“I think you’re forgetting something,” Cottonmouth said.

Charles, who was just behind the larger man walking away, turned and said, “Oh, right. Have a nice day.” He tipped his hat, winked a smile to them, turned away again, and started walking.

Cottonmouth reached for Charles’s shoulder, and the man said, “Hey now, hey now,” turning back to Cottonmouth.

“Soon as you return the watch and the money clip,” Cottonmouth said.

Charles spun, popping Cottonmouth in the jaw. The man whose name Cottonmouth didn’t know stepped back to the group, punched Cottonmouth in the gut, doubling him over. As Cottonmouth dropped to a knee, one of the Thurman boys came flashing by, knocking the larger man over Cottonmouth, both men falling to the ground. Charles reached for the larger man, helped him to his feet. “Come on, Lou,” he said, the pair turning away as the Kitchens brothers watched, a few steps removed.

Cottonmouth stood. A small crowd had now gathered in the street, watching from a distance. “Not until you give back what you took.”

Charles took a step toward Cottonmouth. “Whose side are you on here?”

“Just give these men back what you took,” Cottonmouth said, wiping blood from his lip.

"Look," Charles said, "it doesn't have to be like this."

"Not if you give back what you took."

Charles cursed, turned to the man called Lou, who grabbed Cottonmouth as Charles punched him in the gut, the jaw. Cottonmouth crumpled into Lou as Charles drove a fist into Cottonmouth's temple.

After starting to walk away, Charles stopped to look back at Cottonmouth. "You got any idea what you're doing?"

The Kitchens men and a couple of women from the crowd came to help Cottonmouth up.

"They could have killed you," Silas said, helping dust Cottonmouth's jacket. A woman handed him a handkerchief, and he wiped blood and rocks from his opened temple.

Cottonmouth looked at the bloody handkerchief, sighed. He held out the money clip for Silas. "Managed to pilfer this back for you, but I couldn't get the watch."

"You what?" Silas asked, blinking.

"Don't know what happened to the watch," Cottonmouth said, losing his balance for a moment before straightening, "but it'll turn up."

Little Jack Thurman stepped from the crowd. "Found this in that man's pocket," he said, handing Cottonmouth the watch. "What'll you give me for it?"

Cottonmouth grinned through a split lip, asked, "How about that nickel?"

Roy Lee Kitchens thanked Cottonmouth and the Thurman boy, waited for the Thurman boy to move on. When he did, Roy leaned toward Cottonmouth. "Might want to hightail it on out of here. Hear they got your friends."

"Who got my friends?"

"Sheriff."

Cottonmouth turned to look toward the sheriff's office. "For what?"

"Don't know," Kitchens said, "but it didn't look good. Right many of them. Sheriff, deputies. Got one earlier, just brought another in, I think they were saying."

Cottonmouth turned to go, lost his balance again, sat down against a parked car. He watched the sheriff's office for a few minutes before he could stand up again, starting to regain his balance.

47

On the way to the sheriff's office, Cottonmouth saw Lorena walking out of Miss Phoebe's.

"Oh, Lord," she said. "What happened to your face?" She pulled him against the front of the restaurant, away from the people walking by, some looking at the part of his face that was blossoming crimson, some looking at the little flap of skin that was trying to peel away from the top of his cheek. Lorena dabbed at both with the handkerchief she'd pulled from his hand.

Cottonmouth winced, looked at her with one eye open. "Good to see you again. Been meaning to come over after yesterday's nonsense, but . . ."

"But you've been slammed with work?" she said, only partly making a joke, as she continued to hold the handkerchief against his cheek, slowing the bleeding being all she could do for him at the moment.

He pulled back the corner of his mouth in what could have been a smile.

"You should go have Doc Sessions take a look at this," she said, pulling away the handkerchief to get a better look, gasping, then putting the handkerchief back against his face. "What did you fall into?"

"A bad dream," he said, reaching up to the hand she'd pressed against his face, holding her wrist. "I have to get to the sheriff's office, but is it all right if I come by later?" He took the handkerchief from her hand, held it against one of his wounds, the other more swelling than draining at the moment.

"I'm not sure that would be such a good idea," she said as a man walked past them, tipped his hat, and said "Miss Whaley" to her.

He asked was she busy later, and she said, "Something like that."

He asked was tomorrow any better.

She said she understood from Miss Rudd that he had places to be.

"I'm not sure I need to clear my dance card with her, but sure, I got a list of things need to get done."

She asked was that so, asked was he done with all this. She raised her eyebrows toward the street, the town, the whole county.

Blood throbbing his temple, he figured she meant the fighting in the streets. "Figure so. Been too much too crazy lately."

She asked was he sure about moving on.

He nodded, grimacing from the blood moving around in his face, the throbbing pain starting to show in new places. He pressed the inside of his elbow against his ribs, trying to hold them tight so they hurt less when he breathed. "Time to make a change. Time to move on."

"That's what you're good at, is it? The moving on?"

He said it had gotten too easy, getting stuck in a rut.

"That some sort of car joke?" she asked.

"Car joke?" He blinked, wiped away some fresh blood from his face.

"Doesn't matter," she said. "Thought it did, but I guess it doesn't."

He asked what didn't matter.

"Any of it. Doesn't any of it matter?"

He said he knew the past few days had been rough. He could tell she was upset, but he wasn't sure at what.

"Past few days? Are you serious right now? It's been, well, since you came back. Everything's been . . ."

"Exciting?"

"Terrifying," she said, starting to walk down the street, away from the sheriff's office and back toward her garage.

"I thought you liked exciting," he said, taking a few steps to follow her. "I thought you liked—"

"I don't like men coming in with guns. I don't like threats. I don't like any of this."

He asked where all this was coming from.

She stopped, turned. "A man came into my garage, threatened me, pulled a gun on me. You should remember. It was yesterday, and he was a friend of yours."

"I remember you handled it just fine," he said, stupidly proud of her.

"I shouldn't have to handle it." She turned, started walking away again. "And now you're running off."

He followed her. "You're running off," he called after her.

Lorena waved him off. "I should be working on cars, not working on my last will and testament."

He called after her again.

She stopped, and he quickly moved to cover the distance between them.

"Let me ask you this," she said. "What is next on your dance card? What is it that you have to do right now?"

He said he had to go to the sheriff's office to get his friends.

"Those friends of yours at the sheriff's office. Which side of the bars will they be on?"

She walked away, but this time he let her go as Othel Walker waved him down from across the street.

48

Othel waved from across the street, the courthouse square emptied of any commotion now, late afternoon.

Cottonmouth stopped, waited as Othel crossed the street. Cottonmouth asked what was going on.

Othel got half a word out before stopping and squinting at Cottonmouth's face, asked what had happened.

Cottonmouth said there'd been a disagreement, and Othel asked was he all right.

"No," Cottonmouth said, scratching away some dried blood at the corner of his eye. "Now what's going on? Something happened at camp?" While Othel hesitated, Cottonmouth ran through everything he could think of. Highway patrol, G-men, deputies all deciding today was the day. Or Martello was there. Maybe he'd brought Campbell. Expanding the reach. Another camp along the road between Little Rock and Shreveport. Maybe they'd add more. Maybe they'd take Doc Gramm's camp next. Maybe they already had. *It's what the Banana Man would do,* he realized. All this time, he'd been thinking what he should do, ignoring what he'd do if he were dealt someone else's hand. Or maybe Martello had decided to burn the camp to the ground. Could be anything. Could be everything. He asked Othel again what was going on.

Othel said he had to tell him but didn't want him to get mad about it, to just let him say the whole thing before he decided.

"Christ, what is it?"

"The whole idea was to keep the peace. That's what I want you to understand. When your uncle passed and you came back, I didn't think—look, a lot of us, wasn't just me, a lot of us didn't think you'd come back here, much less stay here. Thought they'd send word about your uncle, and that would be the end of it. You'd stay down there doing whatever it was you were doing, and we'd just keep doing what we were doing."

Cottonmouth said if he was going anywhere with this, he'd best get going.

"The plan was when you didn't show, the plan was to just keep going along, follow your uncle's path, keep things the way they were, long as we could. Settled. That was the plan we had, anyway."

"Who was *we*? Whose plan?" Cottonmouth asked, then answered his own question. "The Rudds?"

Othel stopped, took half a step back. "You knew? The Rudds? You knew?"

Cottonmouth shook his head. "Figured something like that. Just thought you were giving the sheriff too much information, that he was passing it along to the Rudds. Didn't expect you to be working with the Rudds all this time, behind my back like this. Then when Abigail offered me this new drink she'd heard of called a Bunny Hug—the one from Havird's in Shreveport that night, the one Jimmy couldn't shut up about when we got back—wondered why all of a sudden she knew about it. Well, I didn't reckon she and Jimmy had started dating."

"Wasn't supposed to be behind your back. Nobody thought you'd come home. Your back was supposed to be in Honduras."

Cottonmouth said well, he was home. Standing in the city square at the moment. "And I'm going to guess there's a reason you're telling me all this now, some kind of reason that makes sense and keeps me from severing our relationship?"

"I see how I was wrong."

"Wrong?"

"I was wrong about how when you got here, about how you were doing this for you. I mean, I figure maybe you were, but then I saw how you were trying to do good for your uncle, how you do belong here, and how I was wrong to be working behind your back like that."

"No, Othel. I mean how come you're telling me this now. Right here, in this minute?"

"I think the Rudds might be working on a new plan."

Cottonmouth asked how was that.

"I just went over to the hotel and asked Earl could I see Miss Rudd, and it turns out she ain't in because she's driven off with Victor Martello."

"That so? Been thinking of a new plan myself," Cottonmouth said. "Think Miss Rudd may have gotten too used to being in charge, may have overplayed her hand."

Othel raised his eyebrows, relieved, ready to hear the plan.

"You know how you've maybe had more contact with the Rudd sisters than I have, maybe been around them while they're working with folks?"

Othel said he guessed so, said he wasn't sure what Cottonmouth was getting at.

"My understanding is that pair doesn't trust banks any more than I do."

Othel said that was right. "I mean, they have some money in the bank."

"But mostly?"

"Mostly at the hotel, near as I can figure."

"Hiding it under their mattresses?"

"Believe it's a Mosler safe, as I recall."

Cottonmouth asked had he seen the safe.

Othel said he had, said he'd seen Miss Rudd open it, put in payments they'd gotten.

"You get a look inside the safe?"

"Little cash. Little bit of gold. Little bit of alcohol."

Cottonmouth asked could either of the Miss Rudds open the safe.

"If they've a mind to, I reckon. Wouldn't want to test their will against mine," Othel said. "Or theirs against yours, either, now I'm being all honest about everything."

Cottonmouth said he hoped it wouldn't come to a test of wills, asked was there much gold in there.

"A little, but not too much. You planning on making a withdrawal?"

Cottonmouth said he wasn't. "Planning to make a deposit."

49

Cottonmouth walked into the sheriff's office, the little bell above jingling. He shut the door behind him, saw Dolson sitting at the sheriff's desk.

"Deputy Dolson, the sheriff in?" Cottonmouth asked.

"You're looking at him."

"I mean Sheriff McCollum," Cottonmouth said, wondering if the boy here was old enough to get drunk this early in the day.

"Mr. McCollum has been, uh, relieved of his duties. I'm the new sheriff," he said, showing the badge pinned to his jacket, which was hanging on the chairback behind him.

"When did that . . . ," Cottonmouth started, then said, "I mean, well, what?"

"Yes, well, about that," the deputy said, eyes bright as if he'd suddenly remembered an errand he was supposed to be in the middle of doing. "You're just the man I wanted to talk to about that."

As Dolson stood, he reached for the Vest Pocket pistol that had been sitting on his desk. Cottonmouth crossed the distance between them in three swift steps, pulled the snub nose from his own pocket, lifted it toward Dolson's chest as he set his free hand on Dolson's gun.

"Easy now, new sheriff," Cottonmouth said. "I don't know what's going on here."

Dolson swallowed a loud reverberating gulp and said, "No. No, you don't. But I'd suggest you don't go around pointing guns at the sheriff."

Cottonmouth took the Vest Pocket pistol, reached to the desk for the handcuffs with the other, told Dolson to sit back down.

Dolson said he didn't take orders from Cottonmouth, so Cottonmouth shook the gun at him.

When he was done securing Dolson to the chair, he locked the front door and pulled the curtains together. Then he took the cell keys from the wall, walked to the back of the room to the two cells, opened the one with Everett. "Feel like leaving?" he asked, looked around. "Where's Jimmy and Beans?"

"They grabbed Jimmy," he said. "Brought him in, already sent him to Hope or Little Rock, I figure. Beans and I made a run for it. They made up something to bring us in on, hoping we got ourselves killed so they could take credit. Didn't even give us a chance to explain ourselves."

Cottonmouth looked around. "Us? Beans?"

Everett shook his head.

"Christ," Cottonmouth said.

Dolson, from the front of the office, yelled back, "You can't just escape a prisoner on my watch, Tomlin."

Cottonmouth walked back to Dolson, said, "Don't worry about all that. Where's the sheriff? Need to take all this up with him. He'll know what's going on."

"I'm the sheriff," Dolson said.

"You keep saying that. Why is that?"

"It's true."

"How are you the sheriff? Where's Monroe McCollum?"

Dolson shook his head, started crying.

Cottonmouth turned to Everett, hoping for some explanation, but Everett was still in the back of the office looking for something.

"Shot dead," Dolson said through heaving sobs.

"Shot?" Cottonmouth said, sitting against the desk, stunned. "Dead?"

Dolson nodded. "And they wanted me to arrest you for it."

"Well, why didn't you?"

"I don't know," Dolson said. "I meant to, but," he said, the crying taking over.

"Christ," Cottonmouth said. "When? Who? How?"

Dolson nodded to the gun Cottonmouth was holding.

Cottonmouth set the gun down on the desk, said "Christ" again.

Everett finally found his boots under a bench, came walking to the front of the office, started pulling his belongings from a desk drawer near Dolson. He took a breath, shook his head to clear it.

Cottonmouth started to ask Dolson again who'd killed Sheriff McCollum, but Everett interrupted, asked, "What happened with Martello?"

Cottonmouth said, "Yeah, don't worry about that," then slipped the pistol from the desk to his pocket.

"He's gone?" Everett asked.

"Martello?" Dolson asked.

"Don't worry about it," Cottonmouth said to Dolson. "We can take care of it," he said to Everett.

"Take care of what?" Everett asked.

Dolson asked, "Yeah, what?"

"Martello," Cottonmouth said.

"Take care of him?" Dolson asked. "But they said you—"

"Don't worry about it," Cottonmouth said; then he turned to Everett. "Doesn't matter who said what. Just matters what we do now."

Everett stopped, looked at Cottonmouth. "So I was right?" Everett asked. "About not being able to trust him?"

Cottonmouth said yeah, he had been right.

The front door shook, rattled. Then someone started knocking. "Hey, in there," the voice said.

Cottonmouth and Everett ignored the knocking. "And now you need my help? After what they did to Beans?"

"Which one's Beans?" Dolson asked, looking back and forth at the pair, then the door. "What happened with Martello?"

Cottonmouth and Everett looked at each other, together picked up Dolson's chair, carried him to the back, and locked him in a cell.

When they'd closed the cell door, Dolson asked what Martello had done, said, "That's what you get, bringing him here."

"What are you talking about?" Cottonmouth asked Dolson, the knocking up front getting louder, coupled with an "Open up, open up."

"The Rudds. Henrietta. She said you'd brought him here. Said the sheriff had let it happen. That's why they . . . ," he said, trailing off.

"Yeah," Cottonmouth said. "I did. But it wasn't supposed to happen this way."

Everett shook his head. "It was always going to happen this way."

The door rattled louder, more voices out front.

"You two better run if you gonna run," Dolson said.

The door in the front burst open as two lawmen Cottonmouth didn't recognize came through, looking around the front of the office.

Cottonmouth walked to the back hall while Everett reached through the bars of the cell, shoved a piece of cloth into Dolson's mouth.

In the back, they stopped at the never-locked safe, pulled out a couple of shotguns for good measure and boxes of shells they emptied into their pockets, walked out the back into the sunlight.

50

Walking along the backs of the buildings down Lone Alley, Cottonmouth said again he was sorry about Beans, said there wasn't anything Everett could have done differently.

"Could have zigged instead of zagged. Could have gone right past your camp a few days back. Beans and Jimmy and I could have hopped a boat to wherever you went when you took off. Where was that, Honduras?"

Cottonmouth said that was right.

"Plenty I could have done differently."

Cottonmouth just nodded as they walked, thinking of a few different things he could say, none of them seeming helpful enough to say out loud.

"Could zig now instead of zagging," Everett said. "Could still take off. Bust Jimmy out."

Cottonmouth said sure, he could take off. Cottonmouth stopped walking, behind the back door to K. G. McMahen's notions shop. Cottonmouth reached into his pants pocket. "Here," he said, holding his hand out for Everett. "This here is twenty-seven dollars. It's what I've got. Should get you down the road a bit. Not to Honduras but sure enough down the road. You get to New Orleans, find a guy called

Joey Grasso. He's got a place on Tchoupitoulas around Napoleon. He's always got work."

Everett asked what Cottonmouth thought he was doing.

"You want to take off, go ahead," Cottonmouth said. "I've done that. Left here and headed down that way. Took off from New Orleans when there was trouble there. Took off farther south to Honduras. Left trouble there. Run around like that and ended up back here, like I had one shoe nailed to the floor and I been running in circles all this time. East of here is Mississippi and Alabama, and I never much cared for the people I knew from there. And the other way ain't nothing but Lubbock, Texas, I hear, and I ain't that desperate yet. This here," he said, waving his hand about, "this here is home. Was, is, and will be. And if I'm being honest, maybe this whole place would have been better off without me. Othel thinks he and the Rudds could have been running the camp, and maybe so. I figured I could do it, figured wrong. Thought I was doing the right thing, coming in and making changes."

Everett said grabbing men and stashing them at the camp was his idea, said if they hadn't started on that, said maybe. "And we all thought going to Martello's to get his attention was a good plan."

"No," Cottonmouth said. "This is on me. But I can't fix it myself. I need your help to get Martello and those men out of here."

"Put that money away, and tell me what you need. Your uncle was always good to me and my friends. Owe it to him. Owe it to Beans."

"Othel tells me the Rudds and Martello are going into a partnership."

"Makes a certain kind of sense, I suppose."

"I've always known them to be wary of outsiders. Henrietta has said as much to me."

"I don't know them," Everett said. "Know the type. Sometimes you have to adjust. Adapt. Speaking of, you met with that lawyer?"

"He said I've got a big payment due to the Rudds end of the year."

"And that's news to you?"

"Didn't know a thing. Just that my uncle had to keep making payments. Everything was so rushed when I got back. Didn't know about the big one coming up."

Everett asked how big, and Cottonmouth told him.

Everett took a sharp breath through his teeth. "So how many oilmen and bankers do you know we can grab?"

"Not enough."

"Is the plan to talk to Martello now? If you need it, I have some of that money from grabbing the oilman still in the bank," Everett said, patting his pocket where he kept his new bankbook.

"You put it in the bank?" Cottonmouth asked.

"Sometimes you have to adjust. Adapt."

Cottonmouth said that was a good idea.

"Speaking of good ideas," Everett said, "I'm hoping you have one."

"I have an idea. Was playing cards the other night, fellow kept overplaying his hand. I think I'm starting to see this all a little clearer."

"Just let me know. I've got some scores to settle."

Cottonmouth nodded. "We'll get it all settled. I asked Othel to head over to the Rudds' place, make sure Henrietta was out closing the deal with Martello."

"You want them to close the deal?"

"Just need her there at the camp and need Othel to be at the hotel with the other Miss Rudd."

Everett said he didn't need to know all that. "Where do you need me?"

"Need you to go see Othel at the Rudds' hotel. But first, you have to make a pass through town. Use that cash you have. Anyone carrying around a gold coin. Don't reckon they would be, but if they are, that's mostly what would help. We need gold. Jewelry. See how many watches and necklaces and what have you that you can collect. Need to make this look good. After you see Othel, meet me at Moon's store."

"You and Moon opening a jewelry shop?" Everett asked.

"Even better."

51

Cottonmouth knocked on Lorena's door, asked did she mind if he came in.

"I'm open for business," she said, "if that's what you're here for."

"Was hoping to finish our conversation from earlier."

She said she thought they'd finished it.

He nodded. "It's just that you caught me by surprise is all. Wasn't expecting that."

She said that seemed to be happening to him lately.

"So it seems. I just . . . I just wanted to say I haven't been honest with you. Up front."

She stopped whatever it was she was doing, asked about what.

"I just wanted you to know, whatever happens, that I never meant for any of this to have anything to do with you. And I'm sorry that man came in here and caused all that trouble, scared you and all."

She closed her eyes, pressed her hand against her head, dragged her fingers through her hair. "I don't give a damn about scared."

He said he knew that. Said that wasn't what he'd meant.

"What did you mean?"

He sat down on a wooden chair near the front door to her shop, leaned forward, hands together. "I was down in New Orleans, down in Honduras. I wanted to leave all that behind when I came back here."

"The way you left all this behind when you went down there? You're all about the leaving, aren't you?"

He leaned back. "I don't know. Maybe. I guess. I don't know."

"It's like I don't even know who you are," she said. "This man who does whatever you did down there—none of it good, from what you say. And the man sitting here with me, thinking he's apologizing but not knowing what for."

"I don't even know about the apologizing. That's if you step on someone's foot or start talking before they're done talking. Apologizing ain't going to help. I've gone past that. I've come back, made everything worse, and I'm just trying to make it right is all."

"On your way out of town?" she asked.

He said he wanted to make it right with her.

"Don't see why. I already know you plan to skip town again. Where is it this time? Kansas City? Chicago?"

He asked her what she was talking about.

"Miss Rudd told me you were leaving again," she said. "Heard it from the grapevine, somehow."

"I never said anything to any Rudd about leaving," he said. "I'm working on a way to fix all this so I can stay. And I'm working on a way to fix it with the Rudds. Come to find out I didn't understand any of it. I can fix it, but I need help, if you're willing."

"You're not leaving?"

"Not unless you tell me to leave. Look, I didn't mean for you to get caught up in any of this, to so much as put a drop of mud on your shoes. I came back here, and you're one of the best things to ever happen to me, the being with you, and I just wanted you to know, and sure, maybe I did want to say I'm sorry."

"One of the best things? One? How long is the list?"

He said it wasn't a long list.

"With all that's going on out there," she said, nodding toward the window of her shop, "you decided you'd come in here and talk to me and apologize and set things straight between me and you?"

"That and ask for your help."

"Long as you're staying, just tell me what you need."

"If I can," he said, then started over. "If we can figure out a way to keep you safe—hell, keep us all safe. I mean a way that's not dangerous, where you won't have lunatics with guns barging in—well, how would you feel about more business being sent your way? Paint jobs. Lead in the trunks. Cow traps?"

"Caltrops," she correct. "And tell me more."

52

Cottonmouth saw Everett in front of Moon's store, waiting.

"So how'd you do?" Cottonmouth asked.

"Ran out of cash before I ran out of jewelry to buy," Everett said. "Folks in town seem to have sold off most of their gold already, else paid the Rudds with it. Picked up some gold coins from a few of them, though. Guess it adds up."

"Any bargains?"

"Might have overpaid for a couple items, but I was in a hurry."

"Othel seem all right at the hotel?"

"He did. Was sharing a drink with one Miss Rudd. Said the other was at the camp, as you'd said she'd likely be."

"At least I got that right," Cottonmouth said, opening the door to Moon's store before they walked in to see Bill Moon helping one of the Talley women pick the right tooth powder. When she was done and was on her way, Cottonmouth asked Everett to flip the sign to **CLOSED**.

"Now hold up, fellows," Moon said, hands raised, elbows bent. "This ain't about to go down that way. Think about what you're doing. Couple men from Little Rock were just in here flashing badges. Don't reckon they got far."

Cottonmouth said, "Calm down, Bill. Calm down. For Christ's sake."

Moon sat in a chair Everett had pulled from the back of the store. Everett stood next to Moon and paced while Cottonmouth found another chair.

"Just need a minute, Bill," Cottonmouth said. "I think you'll be interested."

Moon said he wasn't interested in any of the crazy nonsense that had been going on in town. "Starting to doubt who I been trusting, if I'm being honest with you. Nothing makes sense. Those men from Little Rock said the sheriff's been shot, and they're looking for you and your men."

"Barking up the wrong tree on that one. We need . . . ," Cottonmouth said, looked at Everett, back at Moon. "I need your help."

Moon asked with what.

"Bill, remember a few days back we were in here playing cards, and you were asking me about investors in your store? Wanting to expand?"

Moon said sure he did. "If you've come to invest, you've got an odd way about it."

"Was thinking of the other way around, in a sense."

"How's that?"

"What do you think about maybe having a permanent corner down at the camp?"

"Permanent corner?"

"We had something like that down in Honduras, with the Banana Man. He had a corner set up, goods and prices up on a chalkboard. They told the boy there what they wanted in the morning; in the evening he'd be back from town with whatever he could carry back."

Moon whistled. "So every day or so, you'd send me an order."

Cottonmouth asked was that simple enough to work or did they need to complicate it a little.

"No, no. That should work. That means I'm exclusive to your clientele. You're not setting up other little shops there, are you?"

"Thought about training someone up to give shaves and haircuts."

"You expecting more men to start showing up there?"

"Hoping to get control back, letting you know what I was thinking for down the road, how things are going to be set up. Everett here is in school for economics. Relying on him. And you, too, if you've a mind to join us. Camp needs more than just me."

"Suppose we could work on something like that. Maybe even have a few things there men might need."

"You carrying guns now?"

"I was thinking more of Colgate's shaving cream," Moon said. "Shave and haircuts, as you say."

"Figure a man needs that too," Cottonmouth said, rubbing his jaw.

"Got some new Schick razors, you're interested."

"Have to work it into my schedule," Cottonmouth said. "Few things left to get done today."

"Speaking of our talks," Moon said, "weren't you the one who was complaining about being a cog in the machine? And now you're asking me to be a cog in your machine?"

"And what of it?"

"It's just odd; that's all."

"Nothing odd about it," Cottonmouth said. "We're all cogs."

"You had a handshake deal with this Martello fellow?" Moon asked.

"Not sure what we had, but that was before I realized what I was dealing with, inviting the devil into the house. That was before he tried to kidnap folks in town here and before I found out my uncle had not only taken loans from the Rudds but had sold off part of the camp to make loan payments. Not sure a handshake deal means much to Martello anyway. He'd wanted it signed in blood, but he'd be bleeding you dry in the meantime."

"So you have something figured out?" Moon asked.

"Something Victor Martello said to me."

"Looking to buy out the Rudds?"

"You said you had some gold coins and certificates from folks," Cottonmouth said. "Was hoping to borrow some of that off you tonight."

"Wouldn't figure I have enough gold to buy your camp."

"Don't need to buy the camp," Cottonmouth said. "Just some time."

53

As Moon and Cottonmouth were talking, Everett kept an eye out the front window until he saw the new sheriff walking down the sidewalk. "Our friend Dolson is just outside."

Cottonmouth asked was there anyone with him, and Everett said there wasn't.

"If Othel has taken care of his part, we're still going to need Dolson and them," Cottonmouth said.

Moon asked, "Dolson and who?" but Cottonmouth was drawing his pistol, and Moon stopped asking questions.

"Bill, I need you to wave Dolson over this way while Everett and I duck out of sight for a second."

"Wave him over?" Moon asked. "You mean get him inside?"

Cottonmouth said that was what he meant.

"What do I say? Just wave?"

"Think of something," Cottonmouth said. "Tell him you need his help. Tell him you've got that new foot powder he likes. I don't care."

As Cottonmouth and Everett hid behind some shelving, Moon stepped out into the street, waved Dolson over.

Dolson walked over, saying he didn't have time for anything, saying he was on his way to meet up with the rangers.

Moon backed into the store, nodding for Dolson to follow. "There's a problem with the cigars you ordered."

Dolson said he hadn't ordered any cigars.

"I guess that's part of the problem," Moon said as Dolson stepped into the store, Everett coming behind him to close the door, Cottonmouth raising a gun to Dolson's temple.

"What in the sam hill?" Moon said while Dolson stopped, turned his eyes to see Cottonmouth.

"Didn't expect to see you again so soon," Dolson said, as calm as he could, seeing as how his chest was throbbing.

Everett took Dolson's pistol, pushed him forward to the back of the store, back to the card-playing table.

Cottonmouth nodded for Moon to lock the door, and then the two of them followed Everett and Dolson to the back, where Everett helped Dolson find a chair.

Everett looked to Cottonmouth.

"Hands on the table," Cottonmouth said to Dolson, who did as he was told.

Dolson asked what they wanted, said the cops from Little Rock were expecting him, said they weren't far.

"Not interested in killing a lawman," Cottonmouth said. "Interested in finding out who already killed one. Miss Rudd have you do it? This part of the plan? Sheriff wouldn't go along with what y'all had planned? Or did you do it on your own?"

"Me?"

Cottonmouth held out the Vest Pocket pistol for Dolson to see. "I know the Rudds carry pistols like this one, the one that seems to have shot Sheriff McCollum. I just want to know if it was you on your own, or were you doing it on Henrietta's orders?"

Everett was looking at Dolson. "What the hell?"

Moon, too, couldn't stop looking at Dolson. "You're the one who killed the sheriff?"

The shaking that had rattled Dolson's chest at the front of the store had spread to his jaw, his cheeks, now that he was sitting in the back of the store. "Never," he said. "I would never. He was like a, he was," he started and may have blubbered "father to me," but Cottonmouth couldn't tell.

Cottonmouth handed Everett the pistol, sat down in a chair next to Dolson, put his hand on the lawman's arm. "If it wasn't you, it was Henrietta?"

Dolson said it wasn't Henrietta.

Cottonmouth looked back at Everett and Moon, who were just as surprised as he was.

"Abigail," Dolson said. "It was Abigail."

"Abigail?" all three men said, looking at each other, then back at Dolson.

Everett and Moon raised their palms, confounded. How? Why? What?

"Did Henrietta tell her to?" Cottonmouth asked, trying to work it out. "Drunk? Was it an accident?"

In the street, a few cars went by in the same direction, voices yelling as one had gotten too close to the sidewalk, but no one inside had any interest in what was outside the store.

Dolson wiped his face on his sleeve. "You," he said to Cottonmouth. "Miss Rudd, Henrietta, said the sheriff couldn't keep you under her thumb. And you'd brought Martello here. And he—the sheriff, I mean," Dolson said, finding a dry spot on his other sleeve, then wiping his eyes. "The sheriff said he was working on it, and she, Miss Abigail, she just walked up behind him; I didn't even see her—nobody did. She just walked up behind him and . . . ," Dolson said, taking three quick breaths, then a long one. "She shot him. Just shot him."

Cottonmouth sat back in his chair, tried starting a sentence with "I" a few times but couldn't make it further. *My fault?* he thought. And in a split second, he saw the county as if he'd never come back. Othel running the camp, working with the Rudds and Sheriff McCollum. Victor Martello confined to Louisiana, to running things there. Everett and Jimmy and Beans, off pulling a heist in Oklahoma City. Lorena working on cars. Moon selling toothpaste, maybe buying up some fields.

Moon put a hand on Cottonmouth's shoulder. "I know what you're thinking."

"You don't," Cottonmouth said.

"It's not your fault," Moon said.

Everett slapped the table. "That's all done," he said. "Doesn't matter whose fault it was."

"No," Cottonmouth said. "It matters."

"The Rudds pulled the trigger," Everett said.

"And this Martello," Moon said. "He crossed the line. Burned the bridges. Whatever you want to call it."

"Cottonmouth has a plan," Everett said to Dolson. "It's going to work out. He has a plan."

"We have a plan for Martello and for Henrietta Rudd," Cottonmouth said. "They've overplayed their hand. And it's going to take all of us to call them on it. And we need your help, Sheriff Dolson."

54

The Buick slowed, then stopped as it came to the turn to camp. Everett Logan stepped out, three sticks of dynamite in a burlap sack in hand, then walked into the woods toward the camp. Cottonmouth had told him the best route to keep to the high ground through the bayou, but he knew he'd get his boots wet—no matter. Only real worry were the dogs, snakes, and whatever Cottonmouth hadn't warned him about.

As Cottonmouth made his way along the newly laid planks, he had to admit that Victor Martello certainly knew how to clear a road.

He pulled to a stop where Martello had stationed a guard behind a stack of stones on the edge of the road, near a patch of woods where, a couple of decades earlier, young Cottonmouth himself had fought pirates and Morlocks and Yankee soldiers and whatever other monsters threatened his imagination.

Martello's man leaned down to Cottonmouth, asked could he help.

"Here to see your boss," Cottonmouth said.

"Boss is already occupied. You'll have to come back."

"Need to take care of this now, then be on my way. You know who I am?"

"Used to own this place," the man said. "So I guess I know who you used to be."

Cottonmouth laughed. “You and me both, buddy. Look, I need to sign those papers your boss has and catch a train out of here. So I’ll wait here, and you can just go get the papers, tell your boss to add another ten percent, and be quick about it, and I’ll be gone when we’re done.”

Now it was the man’s turn to laugh. He stepped away from the car. “Oh, no. You go ahead. Tell that to Mr. Martello yourself. Just one thing.”

“What’s that?” Cottonmouth asked, ready to pull away.

“After he kills you, can I have your car? I hear there’s a lady in town runs a garage, has a soft spot for old junk.”

55

Pulling off to the edge of a clearing, away from the other cars, Cottonmouth saw a car he knew to be Henrietta Rudd's and a Duesenberg he'd never seen before. There was a Buick on the other side of that and a couple of Ford V8s. Cottonmouth stepped from his sedan.

Two men, one Martello's man Charles and one Cottonmouth didn't recognize, came up to meet him at the car, escort Cottonmouth to the main cabin.

"What's with parking over here by yourself?" the man asked.

Cottonmouth said he didn't want to chance scratching any of the nice cars, and the man laughed.

"Sorry about that dustup in town," Charles said. "But it's good for a man to know his place, know which side he's on. Glad you're coming around."

"What makes you think I'm coming around?" Cottonmouth asked, pausing steps from the cabin's front porch.

Charles looked to the other man, then to Cottonmouth. "Well, you're here, ain't you?"

When Cottonmouth stepped inside, he saw Martello seated at one of the tables, suit and tie, hat on the table in front of him. Cottonmouth assumed there was a gun underneath. Seated on the side of the table was Henrietta Rudd, a darkened tumbler in front of her. She raised the glass to Cottonmouth as he entered.

"Mr. Martello had some coffee made for me, but it seems the previous owners never bothered with anything other than liquor glasses."

"Good of you to join us," Martello said. "It would appear we can settle all the pieces of ownership today."

"Expect we can," Cottonmouth said. "And I love what you've done with the place." He looked around at the men standing along the walls. Five. Six. Seven. "I see you decided to go early-American jackass."

"Please," Martello said. "There is a lady present."

"A lady who was just about to leave," Henrietta said, straightening her skirts as she sat up, moving her feet to stand.

"Now, now," Martello said, putting three men in motion, men stepping away from the walls, men unbuttoning their jackets. "There's no need to hurry off. The Tomlin boy is here now. Let's get all this settled, and everyone can move on with their lives." Martello snapped his fingers, and the three men moved back to stand along the wall while another man came forward to hand him paperwork. "You see," Martello said to Cottonmouth, "Miss Rudd and I were negotiating the terms. She seems to be confused about, let's call it *bargaining power*. So let's you and I finish what we'd begun discussing the other day, finalize everything between us, you know, for legal reasons."

Cottonmouth shifted. "You think I'm just going to hand over my camp to you?"

"That's nearly word for word what this lady said to me not five minutes ago," Martello said, shaking his head. "Look around. This is my camp now. My men. Possession is nine-tenths of the law. Just a matter of making it legal, as I said. So that there's no confusion. This would guarantee your safety."

"Nine-tenths? Nine-tenths? My family has owned this land for nearly a hundred years," Cottonmouth said.

"This isn't about the history of the place," Martello said. "It's about the future of the place. What you'll learn, or would have learned if you'd lived long enough, is that the only person you can help is yourself. The world is at war."

"The world can be at war," Cottonmouth said. "You can go fight it. Just leave our community."

"You think this is a game?" Martello asked. "That what happens doesn't matter? Government taking away our gold. People losing their houses to the banks, having to move into Hoovervilles. Your community? It's every man for himself, and you'd better believe that. Community? You still believe in a chicken in every pot? Concrete roads and knitted highways? That's what we were promised by the government. Look out the window. If you want a road, you have to build it yourself. You rely on yourself and provide for yourself. And if you want to fill your pot with chicken, you should be taking it for yourself—else you're damned to starve."

Cottonmouth nodded, stared at Henrietta Rudd until she looked at him. "Everybody's already damned," he said, repeating the words she'd said to him that he'd barely heard at the time. "That's the whole point of staying together. Bill Moon. Mr. McMahen. Pribble. Morris. Talley. Names I'd forgotten when I left but can't help remembering now I'm back. The families in this county. Helping each other. You say you had to build that plank road out there yourself because the government wouldn't do it. Well, you didn't do it yourself. You hired that done. That's relying on others but only as long as your money holds out."

"Wouldn't count on my money running out anytime soon," Martello said.

"Fair enough," Cottonmouth said. "But I'll take family and community over Hessian soldiers any day. You know, when my mother left, it wasn't anyone paid for helping, and it wasn't anyone from Shreveport or Little Rock or Washington come to help. Mrs. Hutcheson and Miss Hattie Thomas did. Brought me and my father suppers and socks, and the good Lord knows what all else that I've forgotten about but started remembering of late. It was a Beasley, I forget which, who came from Magnolia down to the house to help us after my father broke his arm that time. And whatever happens now, whatever you've got cooking up, I know that this county's got plenty more where that came from, and there's no way you'll manage whatever you think you're doing."

Martello laughed, asked was that so.

"It is. And one other thing."

"What's that?"

"This county's also got the best pie in the state, long as Miss Phoebe's in business. Next time you're in her restaurant, you'll do well to remember that."

Martello stood, took a step toward him, then another. "Speaking of business, why don't we get down to it?"

Henrietta had been watching Cottonmouth, but he'd kept his eyes on Martello, so Cottonmouth had no idea whether she'd understood what he was saying, that he had a handle on the notion of community now, whatever good it would do at the moment.

"It might be too early for business," Cottonmouth said. "What time is it?"

"Too early? What do you mean?" Martello asked.

"I was stalling until all my men could get into place. What time is it?"

Martello pulled a watch from his pocket. "One minute until the top of the hour. Why? What men?"

Cottonmouth pulled Henrietta Rudd's Vest Pocket pistol, pointed it at Martello. "I'm leaving with Miss Rudd."

Martello laughed as three shotguns, two rifles, and two pistols were pointed at Cottonmouth from around the room. "Again, I ask you, Where's your community?"

Cottonmouth said to give it a second.

"Take the poor fellow's little pistol," Martello said, and someone did, handed it to Martello, who turned it over, slid it into his coat pocket. "Be a shame to have you buried with this cute little thing," he said, just before two explosions reverberated around the camp.

The men with the guns lowered them, ran to the door, asking, "What was that? What was that?"

"If I had to guess?" Cottonmouth said. "That'd be the Duesenberg."

"What have you done?" Martello demanded.

"That's the community you were speaking of," Cottonmouth said. "They gave us a few minutes to talk sense into you, and now they're going to blow the place to hell."

Martello said he couldn't be serious.

Cottonmouth smiled, nodded. "I said to start with the expensive cars first." Martello walked to the front window to see the Duesenberg and a Buick in flaming shards, three of his men running about.

"What have you done?" Martello asked.

"They've placed dynamite along all the buildings, the cars." Cottonmouth grinned. "It should be spectacular."

Martello screamed to his men to stop it. "Go stop it!"

The men scrambled from the cabin, running to check the other cabins, check the burning cars.

When they'd left, Cottonmouth looked to Martello. "Seems you're outnumbered."

Martello held up the revolver he'd had under his hat. "Perhaps you should count again."

"I don't need to count," Cottonmouth said. "Just needed to clear the room."

56

A federal agent named Phil Wareham and a couple of his men walked through the cabin's front door and into the big room, moved around some playing cards on the tables, used the tips of their boots to push emptied beer bottles along the floor.

Another of his men walked into the room from the kitchen, said there was enough beer back there to drown an army.

Martello slid his pistol back under his hat, hoping the law hadn't seen.

One of the agents knelt, picked up a bottle, set it on a table.

"Thank God you're here," Martello said. "This Tomlin fellow has just threatened to blow the whole camp up, kill us all, if I didn't do what they said."

"Blow the camp up?" Wareham asked.

"Didn't you hear the explosion? They said there was more coming. I think you'll find they set crates of dynamite outside the cabins," Martello said.

Wareham nodded for one of his men to check. "We heard explosions on our way in. And that would explain the burning cars, I suppose." He tipped his hat to Henrietta Rudd. "Miss Rudd."

"Agent Wareham," Henrietta said. "What a pleasure to see you. How's your father? I trust Little Rock is treating you all well?"

"Doing well, all things considered. He'll be glad to hear you asked after him."

Wareham's man came back, shaking his head. "No explosives around the cabins. Just those two burning cars."

Martello looked to Cottonmouth, who just shrugged.

Wareham asked which one was Martello, and Henrietta Rudd pointed him out.

"We're not here to look for dynamite, Mr. Martello," Wareham said. "Sorry to barge in on you all. But we got a tip, and we're looking for . . . What was it?"

One of Wareham's agents stepped forward. "Witnesses said they heard a small pop at the hotel. With that and the sheriff's wound, we're looking for a small pistol, probably the kind a lady would carry in her purse."

"Miss Rudd, you mind opening your purse for us?" Wareham asked.

Henrietta Rudd looked confused. "Why would I ever need a purse?"

Under his breath, Martello mumbled, "Son of a bitch. You son of a bitch."

An agent patted Cottonmouth down, pulled a knife from his boot, said "This is all he had on him," then tossed the knife to a side table.

Wareham patted Martello's ribs, checked his pockets, patted his back, his thighs. "Got this," Wareham said, pulling the Vest Pocket pistol from Martello's coat pocket. He set the pistol on the table; then he and two other men took a closer look at the pistol. Wareham turned to the front door, asked was the new sheriff out there yet.

Someone outside the cabin said he wasn't, so Wareham went on. "Likely as not that's the gun that killed the sheriff."

"Now wait a minute," Martello said. "That's not my gun. That's this boy's gun. I took it off him when he came in here threatening to shoot me unless I gave him what he wanted."

Wareham scowled. “The same way he was going to blow up them cabins with all that dynamite that didn’t exist?”

“They’ve been running a string of kidnappings,” Martello said. “Ask around. Bankers. Oilmen.”

“And they were going to kidnap you?” Wareham asked. “Dumbest thing I ever heard.”

Henrietta Rudd saw her chance. “Kidnapping. That must be what this Martello fellow was arguing with the sheriff about the other day.”

“What?” Martello said.

“That right?” Wareham asked. “Where and when was this argument?”

“In town,” Henrietta said. “You don’t think the sheriff asked this man about the kidnapping and then this man killed him? Or had him killed? If that’s what you’re suggesting, that would make sense.” She was laying it on now, Cottonmouth thought as she kept going. “Agent Wareham, you think that’s why he killed our sheriff? I mean, I’ve heard about men like this in magazine stories, but to have one so close, in our town . . .” She shivered.

“Lady, what are you going on about?” Martello asked as Wareham nodded for a couple of agents to take him away.

“Possession of the murder weapon. At least one witness,” Wareham said. “Guess you’re done.”

Martello shook himself free of the man holding him, straightened himself, his tie. “But it’s not my gun,” he said again.

“We found it on you, pal,” one of the other agents said.

Cottonmouth looked to Martello, then back to Agent Wareham. “I’m no expert, but from what I hear, possession is nine-tenths of the law.”

57

As Martello was being led away, Agent Wareham turned to follow.

Cottonmouth exhaled, and Henrietta Rudd said for Wareham to let her know if she could be of any further help. He thanked her, continued walking away.

Quietly, Henrietta Rudd told Cottonmouth he was the luckiest man alive.

"We'll see," Cottonmouth said, watching movement through the doorway.

Sheriff Dolson walked through the front door of the cabin with Agent Wareham and two other agents, only one of whom had been there a moment ago.

Wareham said he had some questions.

"I'll leave you all to it, then," Henrietta Rudd said as she moved to leave.

"Questions for you, Miss Rudd," Wareham said.

"For me?"

Cottonmouth asked did anyone mind if he took a seat. No one did.

"Yes, ma'am," Wareham said. "Now, the sheriff here and one of my men went to your hotel, as the sheriff said he thought you might be in danger from this Martello man he suspected of shooting Sheriff Monroe McCollum."

When Cottonmouth had asked Othel to deliver some liquor to Abigail at the top of the hour and encourage her to keep it safe, he'd worried about the timing of his plan, about Sheriff Dolson being able to show up at just the right time, especially considering how everything had been going wrong. But there'd seemed nothing to do but to go ahead, hope his luck had changed. Had to eventually, he'd figured.

As Agent Wareham got to the part about his agent and the sheriff walking into the Rudds' suite, Cottonmouth watched Henrietta's face and was reminded of a word he'd heard used once at a poker game when the dealer had ended up with every ace in the deck. He thought she looked consternated.

"So," she said, head tilted and an eyebrow raised, "you went to the hotel to check on my well-being?"

Wareham said that was the case. "And your sister. You never know with these men like Martello. And we've had dealings with him before. My office has. So he was known to us."

"I see," she said, and she was beginning to.

"And when they arrived," Wareham said, "we found"—he looked at the notebook his agent had given him a moment before—"we found a young man in your employ, a man named Othel Walker, with your sister, Abigail."

"And?" Henrietta asked. "Was he hurting her?"

"He was watching," Wareham said, "as she rearranged bottles of gin in a safe."

"I hardly think the government is interested in prosecuting her for bottles of gin, as that law is being repealed. May I go now? I presume my sister needs me after all this nonsense."

Wareham shook his head. "Not quite, Miss Rudd. It's the law that's the concern here. Are you aware of what else was in the safe?"

She was. She glared at Cottonmouth, and to Wareham she said, "I haven't the slightest idea what you're referring to, Agent Wareham."

"Are you familiar with an executive order, from President Roosevelt?" he asked, not waiting for a response. "About the hoarding of gold. As it happens, you had, well, you had a good number of gold coins and a stack of gold certificates and various bags of gold jewelry."

"Is it illegal to have gold jewelry now?" she asked. "Has it come to that?"

"The jewelry is only a problem as it relates to the gold coins and the certificates," Wareham said. "I believe a prosecutor would argue it exhibits a pattern."

"Prosecutor?" Henrietta asked. "Surely this is some misunderstanding."

"I'm sure everything can be sorted out," Wareham said, "but I'll need you to come with me to Little Rock."

"Gracious," Cottonmouth said. "All that gold, right in our little town. I hope you're locking it back in the safe. Would hate for any miscreants to cause any trouble."

"You can tell any miscreants you run across that they're out of luck. As we speak, everything is being cataloged and ready to get loaded onto an armored Brink's truck as soon as one can get here." He turned, yelled to one of his men. "Someone see about getting that armored truck over here."

One of his men yelled back that he'd already made the call, that the truck had been to Texarkana and El Dorado and could make a detour on the way back to Little Rock or Saint Louis or wherever it was headed with all that gold.

"Glad to hear it," Cottonmouth said, and he was.

As Henrietta Rudd walked past Cottonmouth, she turned to him. "This isn't over," she said.

"No," he said. "I'm just getting started."

58

A few days after all the commotion down at the Tomlin camp, Bill Moon leaned his head into Lorena's garage, said morning to her and Cottonmouth.

Cottonmouth asked what was the news of the world.

"Local boy does good," Moon said.

"That right?"

"You better believe it," Moon answered. "Travis Jackson got two doubles, and the Giants won by three." When he was done laughing, he told Lorena and Cottonmouth to stay out of trouble.

"See you later today," Cottonmouth said.

When Moon had gone, Lorena asked was he going over to Moon's to join in on a card game.

He said he was in the middle of one right now.

She nodded, said she'd noticed that. "I hear your friend, Everett, is partnering up with Moon."

Cottonmouth asked was that so.

"Way I hear," she said, "your friend is going to be the financial brains to turn that place around."

"Guess I'll have to check on that when I stop by."

"Might ought to," she said. "Made some changes. Cantaloupes up front, a stack of novels on the shelf for those of us who like to read, and even has one of those 'guess how many jelly beans' jars on the counter now."

He said that sounded mighty nice. "How'd you hear all this? You and Everett pals now?"

"I was by there yesterday, after he came by here needing something for his car, said he had to head up to Hazelton, pay a man for a goat."

"We got goats here," Cottonmouth said. "No reason to go to Hazelton."

"Couldn't think of one myself, but I didn't ask. By the by, you going to Monroe's memorial service tomorrow?"

"Likely as not." He moved cards around in his hand. "You?"

She said she was, said maybe they could go together, strength in numbers and all that.

"I'd like that," he said. "We should do something in memory of him. He was a good sheriff, as lawmen go."

Lorena handed Cottonmouth an orange soda, asked what he was going to do after the service.

"Stop by Miss Phoebe's place, I figure. Othel's there learning to cook. And it turns out Miss Phoebe and the sheriff had a thing between them most folks don't know about."

She laughed, shook her head. "Everybody knew about it 'cept the two of them," Lorena said. "And now . . . ," she started but let it fade.

"Let's stop by there after, then, see can she use some help, one way or another. Folks take some looking after, you know, after something like that."

She said that sounded like a good plan. "But I meant, you know, when that's done. I mean, down the road. I'm just asking what your plans are is all. Stay or go. It's fine you don't want to say or you ain't figured it out just yet. It's fine," she said, waving it off. "Don't matter."

"I have to stay," he said. "Something important keeping me here."

She said, "Oh, is that so?"

"Othel's taking cooking lessons from Miss Phoebe, as I say, so I'll have to go spell him at the camp two nights a week. And I have some other plans too."

"So if you're not going to run the camp, not going to cook at Miss Phoebe's, not going to clerk at Moon's, what will you do?"

As if on cue, Earl Withers Jr. knocked on the garage door. "Sorry to interrupt. Hello, Miss Whaley. Cottonmouth, Othel said to come tell you those men from the Brink's truck were leaving the restaurant."

"Brink's truck?" Lorena asked.

"Yes, ma'am," Earl said. "They're taking the—"

"I got the message," Cottonmouth interrupted. "Tell Othel to tell the boys we'll give the truck a little head start. Let it get out of the county first."

"Got it," Earl said, heading back to the restaurant to deliver the message.

Lorena stared at Cottonmouth, who wouldn't look up from his cards.

Finally he looked up to see she'd raised an eyebrow in his direction. "This wouldn't have anything to do with all that gold I was hearing about, would it? This is the 'other plans' you were talking about?"

"Well," he said, "there was some discussion in certain circles about whether Roosevelt really needed all the necklaces and rings and what have you that rightfully belong to the fine people of our county."

"So you're just going to return some jewelry to the rightful owners?" she asked, trying not very hard to hide a grin.

"First things first," he said, looking at his cards. "Got any sevens?"

She smiled. "Go fish."

ACKNOWLEDGMENTS

The only reason you're reading this is because my agent, Josh Getzler, found this book the perfect home. There are few things in the world as wonderful as having an agent who gets what you're doing, so many thanks to Josh and to Jon Cobb and everyone at HG Literary for their faith.

Thanks to Alison Dasho and Lake Union Publishing for being that perfect home for this book of scofflaws. The passionate dedication to this story shown by the entire team at Lake Union has been an absolute wonder to watch. I can't begin to count the number of ways Alison and the Lake Union team have made this book better.

Thanks to David Downing, whose close reading and insights were invaluable during the editing stages of this book.

Thanks go to Chris Holm, Nick Kolakowski, and Lein Shory, three talented writers who read this book at various stages and are always available when I think I've written a good paragraph and need encouragement, criticism, or a little of both.

Thanks also to Jeff Macfee, Holly West, Jerry Bloomfield, and Chad Williamson who read drafts of this book and offered needed insight.

You could do worse than the group of readers and writers in the 'Cord, though I don't think you could do much better. So thanks to that group of raconteurs for their unwavering support.

Thanks to the #5amwritersclub, the candlelit writers who are there with me each morning.

Thanks to Ben LeRoy and Jay Stringer, who have always been there.

While many books and articles were consulted, I want to mention here some that were essential.

For local history, I couldn't have done without Nettie Killgore's *History of Columbia County* or Godspeed Publishing's *History of Columbia County*. I was especially grateful to have Dwight D. Taylor's book *The Elisha Talley Family* for histories of my own Talley and Tomlin blood, as well as that of Pribbles, Rudds, Stoneciphers, and others.

For the outlaw camp and kidnapping in the book, I owe a debt to Peter D. Tattersall's *Conviction*, Ace Atkins's *Infamous*, Jeff Guinn's *Go Down Together*, Blanche Caldwell Barrow's *My Life with Bonnie & Clyde*, John Neal Phillips's *Running with Bonnie and Clyde*, Joe Urschel's *The Year of Fear*, and Tim Mahoney's *Secret Partners: Big Tom Brown and the Barker Gang*.

For a better understanding of Arkansas in 1933, I studied Carl H. Moneyhon's *Arkansas and the New South, 1874–1929*; Ben F. Johnson III's *Arkansas in Modern America, 1930–1999*; *The WPA Guide to 1930s Arkansas*; and Timothy Egan's *The Worst Hard Time*.

Rich Cohen's *The Fish That Ate the Whale: The Life and Times of America's Banana King* and Peter Chapman's *Bananas: How the United Fruit Company Shaped the World* provided great lessons on Sam "the Banana Man" Zemurray.

I should also mention the Columbia County Historical Society's excellent online group, which is consistently filled with family photographs and newspaper articles, each of which deserves its own novel.

And thank you to Helen, who read this book and laughed and cried in all the right places. Love you, babe.

ABOUT THE AUTHOR

Steve Weddle is an American author, best known for his book *Country Hardball*, which the *New York Times* called "downright dazzling." He is the cofounder of the crime fiction collection Do Some Damage, he is the cocreator of the noir magazine *Needle*, and he was an instructor at LitReactor.

Weddle grew up in Louisiana. He received his undergraduate degree from Centenary College of Louisiana, his master of arts from Pittsburg State University, and his master of fine arts in poetry from Louisiana State University.

He lives in Virginia with his family.